Praise for Marco Missiroli and *Fidelity*

'*Fidelity* thrilled me (I read it in one sitting), made me think, and moved me deeply. It manages to be as deep as any literature, and as irresistible as any gossip. It is a brilliant work by a brilliant writer'
Jonathan Safran Foer

'A gripping novel exploring the tensions in an apparently idyllic marriage, where a couple in their thirties is tested by their attraction to others, and by their own accumulation of desires and disappointments'
Financial Times

'A writer of pure excellence'
Emmanuel Carrère

'Missiroli cuts right through to the darkness of our inner lives. I admire his strength in showcasing the attitudes and feelings of our time'
Roberto Saviano

'Powerful, delicate and exquisite'
Claudio Magris

'You'll feel like taking refuge in the pages of this book and never leaving its confines'
La Stampa

'With all-encompassing writing, Missiroli opens the rooms and the streets, the thoughts and the concealed desires, makes dialogue and silences reverberate with the spontaneity of great narrators'
Il Foglio

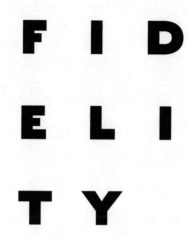

FID
ELI
TY

FIDELITY

MARCO MISSIROLI

Translated by Alex Valente

WEIDENFELD & NICOLSON

First published in Great Britain in 2021 by Weidenfeld & Nicolson
an imprint of The Orion Publishing Group Ltd
Carmelite House, 50 Victoria Embankment
London EC4Y 0DZ

An Hachette UK Company

1 3 5 7 9 10 8 6 4 2

Copyright © Marco Missiroli 2021
This edition published in agreement with the Proprietor
through MalaTesta Literary Agency, Milan
English translation © Alex Valente 2021

Quote on p.45 from *Suite Française* (2004) by Irène Némirovsky

A CIP catalogue record for this book is
available from the British Library.

ISBN (Hardback) 978 1 4746 1334 7
ISBN (Export Trade Paperback) 978 1 4746 1335 4
ISBN (eBook) 978 1 4746 1337 8

Typeset by Input Data Services Ltd, Somerset

Printed in the United States of America by LSC Communications

www.weidenfeldandnicolson.co.uk
www.orionbooks.co.uk

To Maddalena, again
To Silvia Missiroli

That's how we know we're alive: we're wrong.

Philip Roth, *American Pastoral* (1997)

'Your wife followed me.'

'My wife?'

'Yes. Here.' Sofia stared at him. 'Professor?'

He was watching the classroom door.

'I think she's in the courtyard.'

Carlo Pentecoste moved towards the window and recognised Margherita by her crimson coat, worn since the second day of spring. She was sitting on the low wall reading a book – still the Némirowsky – one leg crossed over the other, guarding her bag with one hand. It was the end of March, yet an unexpected light fog was passing through Milan.

Carlo turned towards his students. Sofia was taking her place in the second row and had pulled out her notebook and her almonds as usual. She looked younger than her twenty-two years, with her small face and the gentle movements that softened the unexpected curve of her hips. She looked at him with the same worry as when the Dean had called them into his office: they had been caught by a first-year in the ground-floor bathroom, his body covering hers, hands stroking neck. Something like that, anyway, because the fresher's version of the story had been one thing, then another, then several – all lending strength to the rumour that Professor Pentecoste and one of his students

I

had had 'a close encounter of questionable nature'.

He didn't start the lesson. Instead, he put on his coat and left the classroom, took the stairs to the hall, stopped, and turned towards the bathroom. He'd come back there to clear things up, first with one of his colleagues, then again with the Dean. Both times he'd performed a re-enactment of what he referred to as 'the misunderstanding': entering the men's bathroom, pissing, stepping out into the shared area, the washing of the hands, of the face, the drying, hearing a thud from the women's toilet, noticing the door slightly ajar and finding his student, Sofia Casadei, almost unconscious. What did he mean by 'almost'? Well, he'd leaned over her and called her name several times, helping her to sit up and to her feet – he'd shown the Dean how – propping her up against the wall for a second. It had all been no more than a couple of minutes, then the girl had felt better and he'd helped her to the sinks: he'd never even noticed the first-year student.

He stopped just before heading towards his wife and checked his phone: no, Margherita had not warned him she'd be coming. He continued into the courtyard; she was still sitting there, reading.

'How did you know I was here?'

'Your coat is unmistakable.' He pointed to the classroom's window.

'I'm giving my tendons a rest. I was about to come up.' She closed the book and stood up. 'You forgot this.' She handed him a small bottle.

'You're here for my antihistamines?'

'Seeing you in that state last week was enough.'

'I don't like you tiring out your leg.'

'I took the metro.' She straightened his collar. 'If I were you I'd hold your class outside – the fog has its charm.'

'They get distracted.' He moved his hand to the lower part of her back just as he'd done when they'd first met, at his sister's dinner party. The curve there teased her athletic body. 'Do you want to come up? I have to get started.'

Margherita loved his hands; they were not the hands of a teacher. She let him help her with her bag, then walked with him to the entrance.

'Did you really come here for—'

She cut him off mid-sentence, pointing at the clock and gesturing him to hurry. He smiled at her and headed up.

As soon as she saw him disappear, Margherita let herself rest against the glass door and lowered her head. Why hadn't she had the courage to accompany him to his classroom? Why hadn't she had the guts, as her mother said, to cross the threshold and head towards *that* bathroom? And why was she shaking now? She left, slowly; she didn't want to go but forced herself to reach the main road. She passed the university gates and buttoned up her coat. She stopped in her tracks and closed her eyes, looking for something to anchor herself to, to contain the dejection; she brought herself to think about the fifty minutes awaiting her, the appointment that made her feel so different every time. Different and threatened. She'd write it down in her diary under *Physio* but really she meant 'adventure'. She clung to that feeling like an antidote to her insecurity as she left the university behind her and headed to the taxi stand. Her leg had been hurting since she'd woken up. The pain tortured her from pelvis to knee and had first appeared after a jog in the gym three months earlier. Since then, she'd been thinking about the many details that saddened her: gym shoes substituting her high heels, having to give up on visiting potential properties without lifts, not being able to run after a small child.

She pulled out her phone and saw a message from the owner of Corso Concordia: *I signed, dear Margherita. Now it's up to you*, and one from her colleague – the agency had received the keys to start the sale. There was a missed call from her mother. She ignored it and kept her phone in her hand, managing not to open Facebook. Every time she looked at Sofia Casadei's profile there her head swarmed with strange ideas – the café where she worked, the bar where she had breakfast in the morning, her neighbourhood, heading in that vague direction. She reached the taxi queue, gave a driver the FisioLab address, Via Cappuccini 6, and finally relaxed by leaning against the car seat and closing her eyes. The driver suggested taking a longer route – there were roadworks on the inner ring road; she said it was fine and then stopped thinking. She peered out of the window every now and then, at Milan and the people on the pavement and the porters in front of the buildings. Then she remembered her mother; she called her back and got a reply on the first ring. 'Mum.'

'I was about to call the plumber.'

'What happened?'

'That,' she took a deep breath, 'that *fucking* boiler.'

'Well, hello.'

'Oh, you know I've always liked swearing, but your father was of the opinion that a woman's mouth needs to be clean.' She went quiet. 'Anyway, I wanted to ask about the property in Via Concordia.'

'I just got a message.'

'And?'

'There's no lift but it's interesting. I'm sending Carlo to look at it before putting it up in the agency.'

'And your leg?'

'Mum, what would you do if you had a bad feeling?'

'It's hurting, I knew it.'

'What would you *do*?'

'What kind of "bad feeling"?'

'A suspicion.'

'A suspicion is a piece of evidence.'

'We're not on *Real Crime*, Mum.'

'It's life, sweetheart.' She hesitated, then, 'Do you want to tell me what this is all about?'

'I'm here, got to go.'

'Darling,' she cleared her throat, 'you can clear up all of your suspicions at the appointment tomorrow.'

'Oh God.'

Her mother snorted. 'You've been meaning to go for months and I went through a lot of trouble to arrange it for you: half past ten, Via Vigevano 18, ring the F bell.'

'Remind me again how you talked me into this?'

'Because Dino Buzzati used to go there. Write it on your hand.'

'And *you* write down my mother-in-law's birthday.'

'I'm not coming.'

'Oh yes you are.'

'Oh no I'm not. And you're coming by to see your mother sooner or later, but only if you want to.'

Her mother had stayed awake for three days after burying her husband, sitting in the armchair where he used to read the papers on Sunday mornings. Then she'd said, '*Who am I going to cook for now?*', and for a while she'd refused to talk about that man who had got them both used to routines – flea markets, Tex Willer comics, 'being proper'. He'd been a man of silences and the mother and daughter had replaced his quietness with constant chatter, bickering with each other, phone calls, a forced kind of liveliness.

She paid the driver and got out in front of FisioLab. She was uncomfortably warm but knew it was due to her impatience. She opened up her bag and checked her swimming costume, body wash, towel, comb. She gave her name at the reception and headed to the changing rooms, put on her swimming costume – she'd bought a new one after realising what type of therapy she'd have to go through – slipped back into her gym shorts, tied up her hair, picked up her phone and earphones and headed out again, worried that the beautician had rushed the job. She picked up the water bottle that the centre gifted its customers and stepped into the gym area of the clinic.

Andrea was always on time and that day was no different. He shook her hand and asked her how the pain had been. She always replied with 'Ups and downs', and let herself go to the sound of the privacy screen snapping shut. She'd got used to sharing that space with a serious-looking twenty-six-year-old whose job it was to soothe her chronic inflammation. He asked her to lie down; she touched the band of her shorts and looked at him, he nodded and she removed them. Andrea took the medical equipment and placed it on the inside of her thigh, running it up towards the crotch, applying the appropriate pressure on her pubic region. When this happened, Margherita focused on one corner of the screen, forcing herself to breathe slowly. The warm-up – as he called it – lasted the ten minutes it took her to overcome the embarrassment. Then she'd let go.

The firm touch of Andrea released her every time, the wisdom in his fingers, the low gaze. She averted hers too, except for when – like now – he went to move her costume a little further: it was the instant in which Margherita expected to find some form of forbidden arousal, beyond what would be considered professional. She'd try feeling his tentative fingers as they pressed down on her pubis, looking for the tendon. He'd press with his thumb, his middle finger, sometimes his index, almost digging into the skin. During the first session he'd explained what would happen throughout the therapy: the anti-inflammatory machines, the thinning effect of the hand massages, the exercises she would be expected to do in the gym. She would need twenty-five sessions, on top of check-ups and ultrasounds, for a total of two thousand eight hundred and twenty euros. She could barely afford that; she'd tried with the public health services but felt lost in the unending waits, eventually conceding to the choice that her father would've called *easy*. Easy was paying three thousand euros for a physiotherapist; easy was receiving an Interrail pass as a teenager despite not being among the top students in her class; easy was settling for an estate agent's job with an architect's degree. Easy, probably, was mixing up physiotherapy sessions with lust.

And now that she was being touched by her physio with the right intensity in a liminal space, waiting to tell him exactly where the painful spot was, Margherita went back to that place: her husband, the bathroom door, university building 5, ground-floor ladies' bathroom. That had been the *painful spot* for the past two months. She avoided the full force of the thought, as she'd learned to do in the past couple of weeks, turning the tables completely. Had she been an affectionate, caring daughter, willing to listen? She *could* have been infinitely less than she was. Was she a proper estate agent, someone who didn't abuse her time between visits? She *could* have easily abused that time. Was she a patient who would never fall for the expertise of three fingers? She *could* have let go. Every time the thought of that bathroom appeared, she *could* subvert her own instinct and move away from suspicions.

Andrea asked her if the pain stopped in the exact spot he was massaging. All she had to say was 'A little more to the right' to realise her fantasy. Andrea would've slipped a little to the right and the effect would've been immediate: pleasure, for God's sake.

'A little more to the left,' she said.

He moved. 'Does the pain get worse at night?'

'Depends on the day.'

'Are you doing your exercises?'

'Depends on the day.' She shifted her weight on the bed. 'I'm usually a very committed woman.'

'All women say that.'

'All women?'

'Then they back down.'

'How so?'

'They don't actually face the issue.' He pushed a little harder. 'It's got thicker in this spot – can you feel it?'

She fell quiet. She was *all* the women that crowded that place: the outfit bought for the occasion, the pearls on her ears and the flat in the city centre, a questionable husband, the lure of temptation.

'I can feel you love your job, Andrea.'

He lessened the pressure.

'I mean, you're very good. Do they all tell you you're very good?'

'It happens.' He moved away and around the bed, massaged the lower part of her leg with his fingers and made his way back up, slowly.

Margherita felt him move closer to her groin, harpooning the tendon inch by inch. She allowed herself to think about his skills in bed. Brutal, maybe; definitely inexperienced. For a moment she thought of the two empty properties she could've taken him to: Viale Sabotino 3, the flat they couldn't rent because of the excessive property fees, and Via Bazzini 18, the three-roomer with a small hot tub.

'More to the right,' she suddenly gasped, surprising herself.

He slowed down. 'To the right?'

'Just a little.'

He knew that it was the wrong direction. He was already pinching the tendon between his fingertips, holding the precise painful spot. More to the right was risky, except for a subtle move: lowering his little finger to feel the warmth, the moistness, the difference to the touch, then raising it again, without ever interrupting his work. He'd never done it, but his colleagues had shown him the exact execution needed to maintain the professional façade. Every time a new case of adductor tendonitis showed up and the patient was *interesting*, they'd squabble over who'd get her.

Margherita was his patient because of her seeming invisibility. A pretty woman, almost muted. Yet she'd revealed a body full of surprises: and not for the muscular harmony, or sensual strong legs, or smooth hips; the revelation was in how she offered her tendon and joints and all of herself for those fifty minutes of therapeutic tension. He loved the silences of that woman, which allowed him to focus on his work: Margherita gave the impression of not having any thoughts until she suddenly had several. So he never looked at her, almost scared of surprising her during one of those flashes of her mind. He preferred taking in her scent: she had a smell of something he'd never encountered – almost milky – and it stuck to him until he got into the shower.

He checked his watch, five minutes left. He helped her flex her leg and asked her where the pain got worse when she did so, realised he needed to loosen a small hamstring contracture. He rested her ankle on his shoulder and pressed on the underside of her thigh, pinching the muscle group, digging in once he felt the knot. He heard her moan as she'd done during their first sessions: it was definitely a moan and not a yelp. Be patient, he told her, and dug in once more to hear that moan which suggested something else entirely. Was he just like his colleagues? He moved, light and fast, until his arm started going numb. He rested her leg back onto the bed. 'Go use the elliptical machine for a while, then Alice will help you with your exercises.'

'Alice?'

'I need to leave early today. But you need to come in again

9

tomorrow, there's an inflammation here I don't like.'

'So soon?'

'If you can make it, yes.'

She thought about it. 'I can do nine.' She lifted her back and let her legs dangle. 'Where are you off to this afternoon?'

He started opening the screen.

'I'm sorry, you're right, it's none of my business.' She slipped her shorts back on. 'It's just that a free afternoon in Milan is unheard of.'

'Not that free.'

'Really?' Margherita grimaced with embarrassment. 'I'm sorry, I can't help myself.' She slid past him, setting herself on the elliptical in the machine area of the gym.

Andrea looked at her for a while longer, then headed to the changing room. He got dressed quickly, no longer thinking about her or any of his patients as he left FisioLab. He used to carry the bodies with him: how to fix them, how long it would take him, how to optimise each session. Then he'd learned to let them go, walking through the residential streets of Milan around Via Cappuccini, the sudden bustling of Corso Buenos Aires, the angry traffic of the ring road, *Milano la complicata*. *Difficult* was the adjective his teachers and everyone else had used to describe him since he was very young. Difficult: doesn't talk much. Difficult: doesn't listen. Difficult: he hit a classmate. Difficult: he abandoned his dog out of the blue. Difficult: never had a girlfriend, then too many, and the wrong kind. Difficult: Andrea Manfredi. And when his mother had said that her son was as difficult as Milan – difficult only when first glimpsed – he knew what it meant to be seen.

Now he needed this 'belonging', brushing past Villa Invernizzi and the improbable flamingos in its fountain, under the display of smog-blackened art nouveau buildings, walking back along the streets that ended up in Porta Venezia, with the queers and the blacks and the bourgeois all muddled together, following the tracks on Viale Piave, covered in fresh grass. He followed them for a mile – he had this habit of wandering with his hands in his pockets and his shoulders hunched, almost elegantly – reached Piazza Tricolore and took the number 9 to Porta Romana, a working-class neighbourhood before it became cool. He'd grown up there. For twenty-three years his parents had run the newsagent's in front of the church of Sant'Andrea. He'd studied for his physiotherapy degree in the newsagent's, working from dawn for six summers in a row and two full winters. He'd learned to carefully check the returns and carried out his personal aesthetic on the shelves: he'd slip in an intruder between the magazines, a Marvel comic or an animal special or a Panini album. His father let him do so, then tidied it up. His father was always tidying up, and today was no different: he was bent over a crate, stacking the Urania sci-fi books with care, to be sold for two euros apiece.

'I'm not coming,' he said, as he saw Andrea arrive.

'He's stubborn.' His mother stepped out of the newsagent's and gestured to him. Andrea took his father by the arm and helped him up. His eyes were watery and Andrea held him there as his mother handed over the folder with the medical documents.

'Let me know.'

They crossed the road and brushed past the church, huddled to each other as if cold, then the old man said, again, 'I'm not coming.'

'It took us two months to book this.'

'You sound like your mother.'

'It's just a check-up.'

'Don't insist.'

'Do it your way, then.'

He'd been doing it is his way since the customers of Bar

Rock had found him on the ground in front of the shop, holding his left arm and moaning about the pain in his chest; he'd left the hospital with three bypasses, blaming the Vatican – not the Pope, but the bishops – and Inter – not Moratti, but the players – for his heart failure. Then he'd said 'The newsagent's.' And the doctors had agreed with him: only sleeping four hours per night most of his life had undermined the myocardium. So he'd started sleeping an extra hour, stopped ranting at the Sunday football on TV, stopped overdoing it, only taking four drags of his wife's Marlboro. He'd stopped being the breadwinner way before the change in priorities. Andrea would be fine. Maria would be fine. He had that single order: listen to no one but himself.

'Dad, give it a rest and go get checked.'

'Get another dog and leave me alone.'

Andrea followed him to the bench by the swings, half a step behind. They sat down. The sun was weakened by the fog and his father buttoned his polo shirt all the way up, drowning in his jeans, his legs swinging like pendulums.

'A nice German shepherd, and you'll be fine.'

On the bench opposite them, a girl was holding a leather backpack. She fished something out of the bag and took a bite. Andrea was watching her; she seemed sad.

'Or maybe a Maremmano.' His father straightened his back, grabbed his shoulder.

'Why don't you get one?'

'So you'll stop looking after me.' His father kept holding his shoulder.

'Is something wrong?'

'The stool in the shop stiffens my joints.'

Andrea stared at his own hands. They were large and smooth, his ring finger longer than his index. He rubbed them together; he always did when he was unsure about something. He looked at his father, still clutching his shoulder, out of the corner of his eye. He tried ignoring him, looked towards the sad girl and realised she was looking at him too; in the background, South American nannies were chatting over by the swings. He brought his hands to his face. They still smelled of Margherita. He lowered them. 'Where is this stiffness, then?'

'Mrs Venuti doesn't buy the *Corriere della Sera* any more, her husband reads it online.'

'Your shoulder?'

'You need to sell the newsagent's as soon as I'm gone.'

'Just the shoulder?'

'The neck a little, too.'

'Lean back and keep your arms by your sides.'

'You sell the shop, you hear me?'

'Do as I tell you.'

His father didn't move and Andrea moved behind the bench, helped him lie against its back and, as he started massaging him, he felt how light he was and was scared of hurting him. They had the same nose, but it was the eyes – the same evasive expression – that gave away the fact they were father and son.

Sofia looked away from them and finished eating her almonds, picked up her backpack and slid it over her shoulders. She'd left halfway through Pentecoste's lesson, had taken the 91 and got off as soon as she'd spotted the Ravizza park from the tram's window. She'd been longing for open spaces ever since she'd left Rimini. Six months earlier she'd arrived at Milano Centrale station, tortured by a yearning and knowing that her life would change. But here she was, still at square one: a twenty-two-year-old bound to the suburbs, making regretful choices.

She set off over the grass, reached the road with a last glance back at the old man and the young man massaging him, the fog blotting them out. She continued slowly. Porta Romana was a neighbourhood that made her feel at ease, with its low-roofed houses and its small shops. When she passed the church she stopped, admitted to herself that she would've liked to apologise to Pentecoste. Walking up to his desk in front of her classmates had exposed him even further. She would've liked to confess that his wife hadn't followed her and that they'd shared part of the route by coincidence. But what would she have said if he'd asked her why she'd lied to him? She didn't know herself.

When she'd noticed Pentecoste's wife on the metro, Sofia had blended in with the other passengers and kept an eye on her, keeping her distance until they'd reached the university. She'd seen her sit in the yard and had gone to the classroom, telling the professor that little lie. And as she did, she'd felt a sense of retribution. After the bathroom misunderstanding he'd kept her at a distance, hadn't even given her the chance to have a proper conversation after their meeting with the Dean, not even about the second short story she'd handed in almost two months earlier. He'd left her only with the feedback about her first – insubstantial, he thought.

'Insubstantial?'

'Insubstantial.'

That's why she had given him the second story, seven pages, handwritten, in which she told what had happened with her mother in the Fiat Punto. She'd called it 'How Things Are'. When she'd handed it to the professor, he'd said that he didn't accept unsolicited submissions. She stood there, papers in hand, left them on his desk, keeping watch for the entire lesson until he'd picked them up with his books and laptop, stuffing them into his bag, avoiding her gaze, just like when they'd been called to the Dean's office. He'd never deigned to give her a hint of complicity, even though he knew everything depended on what she'd say. She'd stuck to her script: the sudden illness, him helping her to her feet. The Dean had repeated that there would be no consequences, he wouldn't even have gone this far if not for Pentecoste's insistence.

In order to agree on that shared lie, she'd met up with the professor two days earlier in a café in the Chinese quarter. They'd fine-tuned the details of the events, with natural sequences and gestures and timings. They'd planned it, rehearsed it, and spent the rest of the time making small talk. When they'd left – he paid for both of them – she'd walked along the road leading to the Cimitero Monumentale, had taken out her phone and stopped the recorder. She wore her earphones and listened to it once, twice, three times. Having decided to record the meeting meant one thing: the apple hadn't fallen far from the tree. Protection, prevention, defence against a reality that hosted constant persecutions. It was her family's obsession. Numbers will get you ahead in life, not books: three-year degree in Tourism & Economics. Keep up ballet, a famous company might hire you. Stay away from older boys. Milan will be a waste of your time. Holding on to the fifty-one minutes and thirty-seven seconds of the recording were proof that she was also *this*. There was one detail, however, that kept bringing her back to herself: the timbre of Pentecoste's voice. The sweet cadence, his barely open Os, his timid laugh turning into a hearty one – they excited her. Maybe she was *this* instead, finding pleasure in lingering over the twenty-one-minute mark.

'Can you bring us half a litre of still water, too, please? You want anything else Sofia? OK, only half a litre, thanks. As I was saying, my parents gave me a chick as a present after the tonsil operation; I was maybe four and I called the chick Alfredo and we kept him at my grandparents', downstairs, in a box. He was well-behaved and peeped very little and whenever I was alone I'd let him loose in the kitchen and I'd see him trying to jump, to sprint – and what fascinated me the most was putting him back in his box and immediately granting him freedom again. After thirty or so years, I realise that was my interest – the transition between box and kitchen, the precise moment when his tiny feet took up the most timid, but also unstoppable, propulsion, and still not feeling bad about seeing him caged up in his box. I was drawn to his transformation. I'm fascinated by the change rushing through someone that has found an opportunity – do you know what I mean?'

She'd listen to the monologue and stop it at Pentecoste's *propulsion*, rewind and listen again. The plosive *p* and the shy *s*. Propulsion, peep, Milan, the Master's she was enrolled in, her job in the café where she was headed now, slipping into the nook between the San Nazaro basilica and the Cederna gardens. During her shifts she blended her lessons on narrative techniques with her pragmatic instincts, sometimes noting ideas on the pad for the customers' orders. The place was cosy, with its stripped-wood flooring and vegan options on the menu – couscous was their most popular dish – and it paid nine euros an hour, after tax. She'd found the job listing on the university notice board and she'd got it after a two-day trial; they'd asked her to perfect the technique of drawing a heart on the cappuccinos. If she worked six shifts a week, with a few extras, minus rent, she'd be able to pay back part of the seven thousand euros that her dad had paid for her course. She'd earn forty-five euros that day too, tidy up the sesame bars at the till while chatting to Khalil about his family back in Jordan, decorate the specials blackboard with coloured frames, be nice to the customers: this way she'd be able not to imagine her future in a place like that.

When she arrived there were five customers sitting at the small tables; she quickly ate a salmon and avocado toast, then got changed in the closet, tying her apron so it wouldn't be too tight on her hips, removing her watch and pocketing a small handful of sea salt – her aunt always said that a couple of crystals were enough to ward off bad energies. She walked over to Khalil and tidied his rolled-up shirt sleeves. 'I still miss Rimini,' she said, stroking his shoulder.

'You haven't been here long.'

'Six months is long enough.'

'For Milan?'

'Can I take the till today?'

They stood next to each other, her on receipts, him at the counter. When no one needed them they'd remain silent, or Khalil would ask her to note down a list of tasks, as he did today. She picked up a Post-it and started writing: *Clean window*, he replied *Put out rubbish*, her *Arrange breakfast goods*, him *Revise rota*, her *Cut fruit*, him *Pray five times*.

'I thought you were a Christian from Jordan?'

'You try growing up in a 94 per cent Muslim population and see if you don't get a little competitive.'

She smiled.

'Now, Rimini girl, write something of yours and finish that list.'

'I already wrote something of mine.'

'Cut the fruit? Very deep of you.'

They heard the door open and she looked up and saw Pentecoste's wife. She came in, gently closing the door behind her. Sofia went to the coffee machine and asked Khalil if he could take over from her, turned her back to the room, picked up the sponge and started cleaning the counter. The wife moved towards the wall, checking the menu, and ordered a green smoothie.

Khalil asked her small, medium, or large.

'Small will be fine, thank you.'

'We'll bring it over for you.'

Sofia threw the sponge aside and moved the chopping board onto the counter. She took out of the fridge the required apple, fennel, basil, lime, ginger. As she was chopping, she looked round; the wife was sitting down at one of the window seats. She threw the ingredients into the blender and whirred it seven times. She filled the cup, put on its lid and straw, handed it to Khalil and ran to the closet. She leaned against the wall and held her hands together, lifting them to her eyes. She stayed still until she realised she had to go back. When she did, Khalil was changing radio stations. 'You OK, Sofi?'

But she was staring at the wife who was sipping her smoothie and leafing through one of the magazines, red coat now on the chair. She looked lost in her own thoughts, the tip of the straw grazing her lips.

Khalil waved his hand at her. 'You OK?'

She nodded and threw out the waste. That was the second time in the same day that she'd seen the professor's wife, the third in total, if you counted the Master's opening ceremony. She thought her a handsome woman, still did, with her men's shirt and pumps coordinated to her careful walk. She gave off that same charm now, her brown fringe covering one eye and her legs coiled one around the other; she reminded her of Virna Lisi. She really liked old films starring Virna Lisi, used to watch them with her mother. She stopped staring at her and picked up the register, integrating it with the returns Khalil had filled in after the breakfast rush. She focused on the orders of semi-skimmed milk – they'd have to order one fewer carton a week – then heard the stool scrape against the wooden floor. She looked up and saw the wife walking towards her. 'Can I talk to you?'

Sofia put the pen down. 'Me?'

The wife nodded.

Khalil was watching. 'You can go.'

Sofia grabbed at her apron, then slid past the till and headed towards the door. The wife thanked Khalil and followed her.

They were now on the cobbled yard, a hundred yards from the walls separating them from the university.

'You're Sofia, and you're in Professor Pentecoste's class.'

She nodded.

'I wanted to meet you.' The wife put down her backpack and handbag, moved her hair away from her eyes. Sofia realised it was the eyes that made her look like Virna Lisi, they were laughing even when she wasn't. 'I wanted to ask you for your version.'

Two customers brushed against Sofia on their way into the café. 'My version of what?'

'Please.'

'Oh,' she mumbled, and smoothed out her apron. 'The professor already said that—'

'You,' the wife cut her short. 'I want to hear you say it.'

'I felt faint and he helped me.'

'Really?'

'Really.'

'And before, before that, what happened?'

The fog had lifted, but looked like it might move back in. 'Before when?'

'Before the day in that bathroom.'

'The usual.'

'What does the usual mean?'

'Lessons, sometimes he took us out to give us feedback on our stories.' A border collie and its owner walked past her. 'It's his method.'

'The Pentecoste method.'

Sofia looked at the border collie, it was sniffing a couple of dogs by the flowerbed. 'The professor takes us to a place of particular importance and—'

'He teaches a lesson there.'

'Yes.'

'Where did he take you?'

'The sandwich place.'

'The Bianciardi one in Brera?'

Sofia nodded.

'Where else?'

'Once to the Chinese quarter.' She let her hands fall along her sides. 'This feels like an interrogation.'

'Oh please.' Pentecoste's wife tried smiling. 'Why did he take you there?'

Rimini. Her father and the blue overalls of the hardware store. The base of the yellow lighthouse at the eastern point. Going back. 'There was a group of us students and the professor wanted us to,' she cleared her throat, 'he wanted us to set a story in the area.'

'So you weren't alone?'

'That's right.' The lie made her lower her head, she looked at her feet.

'You're right, it does feel like an interrogation.'

'It's OK.'

'By the way, I'm Margherita.' She leaned in to shake her hand.

Sofia took it; the wife's hand was soft.

'I needed to have this chat, I hope you understand. Do you understand?'

She nodded, and she wasn't lying this time. She felt a strange closeness to this woman, who also hadn't been able to hold back, whose slim figure and hip curve jarred in the most attractive way.

'Goodbye, then.' Sofia made to go back inside.

'Hey . . .' The wife had slipped her bag back onto her shoulder.

Sofia looked back at her.

'Hey, I'm – sorry for being so intrusive.'

Margherita set off, wondering how she'd ended up saying *sorry*, then confusion took over. She'd messed up her final line. And what did she mean, anyway? The important part was not to have come across as desperate, one of those trembling women, those weak women, she repeated to herself in front of an Indian takeaway – but why had she done it? Maybe because she had been Sofia a dozen years ago and maybe because now she was *all the women*, as the physio had said. She stopped in her tracks, certain that in the same situation she would've done exactly the same as Sofia Casadei: undermine the limits of an underminable male. She looked at her right hand. Had her grip been strong enough? It was drenched with sweat; she tucked it into her pocket and started walking with the conviction of someone who has just accomplished something. Maybe now she'd stop playing the bathroom scene in her mind, him over the girl that welcomed his insisting tongue, or her on her knees and Carlo standing in front of her with his trousers undone. She'd avoided pinning the blame entirely on her husband, except for the fact that he'd been the one to make all the noise about it, expecting the Dean to know his side of the story, his wife to know his side, the whole world to know his fucking side. Carlo had spilled his rhetoric all over them – this is what enraged her. She sped up and her tendon twitched; she was exhausted by the time she reached Piazza Duomo.

She sent a message to the office to warn them she wouldn't make it back, swayed a little near the Galleria, then headed down to the metro and towards the only place she wanted to be right now. She bought a ticket at the self-service machines and waited on the northbound platform. She pulled out the Némirowsky and clutched the book. *Suite Française* was a novel teeming with vitality; there was, however, an omen in its pages, a swansong to life, before Auschwitz interrupted the dreams of its author. She stepped onto the train, silently reciting the telegram that Némirowsky's husband wrote to her editor when she was taken by the police: '*Irène suddenly taken today destination Pithiviers (Loiret) – hope you can intercede urgently – trying to telephone no success.*'

She wielded the book until she reached Pasteur, resurfaced and walked through the neighbourhood where she grew up. It used to be only white *milanesi*, now it held together twenty-seven ethnicities, students, a bustling that never failed to lift her spirits. She slowed down as she took Via delle Leghe, with its Chinese restaurants and Moroccan corner shops. Here she had been herself before her troubles. The building of her youth was on a corner, on the ground floor the dairy was now a café run by a Tunisian family, they had illy coffee and free Wi-Fi. She took out her keys but decided to ring the doorbell, twice. The intercom croaked and she said, 'It's me.'

'Me?'

'Your daughter.'

She pushed the front door and walked up the first flight of stairs; her mother was waiting for her on the landing.

'Something's happened.'

'Did the boiler guy come over?'

'Don't change the subject.'

'Can't I just want to come see my mum? Tell me about the boiler.'

Her mother pursed her lips. 'It was a de-com-pres-sion,' she enunciated. 'The expansion vessel was empty.'

She kissed her on her cheek, her mum smelled of Olay. She was small and always looked at you from below. 'You hungry, darling?'

Margherita stepped into the tiny lounge. Her father's armchair had been moved away from the bookcase, the TV showed the first channel, muted.

'Darling, tell me what's going on.'

'I just wanted to spend an hour here with you.'

'Like Churchill taking a holiday during the Second World War.' She sat down next to her. She'd quieten down whenever she felt her daughter's heart was bruised. Sometimes, when Margherita was still a girl, in the more troubled moments, she'd kiss her head. After she married, though, she sought a more careful proximity, side by side, straightening her shirt collar, brushing the coat she was wearing with the back of her hand.

She pulled the Némirowsky out of her clutch. 'Darling, you know, I have to confess – I don't read as much as before.' She pointed to the bookcases. 'I realised I was only reading out of marital duties.'

'Dad bored you that much?'

'Quite the opposite! Reading was like an amplifier.' She moved her hair from her eyes. 'If you don't want to tell me what's going on, I'll tell you.'

'Nothing is going on, I told you.'

'I dreamt of Pannella, something's off.'

'Mum!' She couldn't hold back a smile. 'Why is it always about politics with you?'

'I lived with a man who voted for Berlusconi. You know what he told me when I asked him why?'

'What?'

'I'm voting for Silvio because of that TV show of his, *Drive In*.'

'Tits and ass.'

'The ease of it, my darling.' She relaxed onto the sofa. 'And you'll know how "tits and ass" can be good entertainment.'

'Can we change the subject now?'

Her mother looked up. 'So it *is* about your husband.'

'I don't want to talk about it,' she said, staring at the glass door. The balcony was on the same level as the lounge; when she was a child her father used to keep the doors open so she could cycle in and out, back and forth, with her stabilisers. Her mother would sew, perched on a stool. She sewed like she read, surgical and fast, bringing home the same money as her husband, a railway worker.

'If you don't want to talk about it that's fine,' her mother kissed her shoulder, 'but you should know that your husband drops in, every now and then.'

'My husband, here?'

'Don't tell him I told you.' She went into the kitchen and came back with two slices of quiche. 'Spinach. Do you want me to heat it up?'

Margherita took a bite. 'And what does my husband do here, when he drops in "every now and then"?'

'I make him something to eat, he rummages through the bookcases, picks out a couple of books. Usually it's a Thursday, if you're suspicious about Thursdays.'

'I'm suspicious about every day of the week, Mum.'

'That's OK, my darling.'

'Why does he come here?'

'I'm not a bad cook. And I think it's because of your father.'

'That's too predictable.'

'Don't be thankless.' She rested her hands on the armchair. 'Are you forgetting what he did for him?'

'I'm not,' Margherita interrupted her, 'but this seems too much.'

'You underestimate Carlo.'

She laughed, nervously. 'I really don't think so.'

They ate in silence, they'd always eaten in silence, chewing slowly, carefully, every now and then covering their mouths out of modesty. Her mother's food, the good, simple ingredients and the way of holding them together in a light sauce. They didn't rush, chatting about the fading wallpaper in one of the corners, then her mother took her plate away from her, rested it on the table, made her stand up, and hugged her.

'She's a twenty-two-year-old student, Mum, and she's not a suspicion.'

'What is she, then?'

'*Una paturnia*.'

Her mother leaned back to look at her. 'A strop, huh? So, as Maigret would say, you got nothing.'

'But I don't want to have anything.'

'A good choice, darling. And if you're looking for the truth,' she tapped her index finger on her daughter's chest, 'your husband wouldn't be able to deal with those kind of girls.'

'You think?'

'Same as your father.'

Her father, when he'd left for three days for a training course in Turin. It was the first time he'd slept away from home and her mother had confessed she'd stayed up all night sewing until he got back – with a present for each of them: a winter hat and an Iridella jigsaw. He'd come back happy, bearing those gifts and a new scarf. Margherita had gone to her room and had listened to her parents talk for hours from the lounge. And what had emerged, years later, had been something that her mother dismissed as a *misunderstanding*.

Maybe hers, now, was also a *misunderstanding*. She rested her chin on her mum's head and hugged her shoulders. She told her she had to leave, but didn't let her go and they walked down the corridor with the Milan prints and the red wooden coat rack and the ticking wall clock, the polished floor of marble *graniglia*. She envied her mother's furniture and how she'd foreseen its wear and the repairs. She stopped at the door and kissed her, smelling her hairspray.

'And do you think I can't handle the *Drive In* boys?'

'I don't remember any men on *Drive In*.' Her mother had

gone serious. 'But in any case, of course we would.' She smiled. 'Tomorrow, at your appointment with Buzzati, you'll clear up the suspicion or strop or whatever it is.'

'You think so?'

'I know so. And let me know about that flat in Concordia.' She tidied up her coat. 'Remember that your father had put aside some spare change for you.'

'You should've bought this house.'

'We've always been the renting types.' She blew her a kiss from the landing.

Margherita blew one back as she walked down the stairs, the feeling of missing her father coming over her as she left the building. She rushed out of Via delle Leghe and the block, turned onto Viale Monza and walked up to Piazzale Loreto. Her father and his bushy eyebrows and his dangling cigarette, the small clippers he used to fix everything, or how he used to watch her do her Latin homework, pretending he was sorting out the kitchen. His colleagues used to say he'd fix train stations while smoking, sometimes dropping a line about Milan AC or Scirea – even if he played with Juventus – Margherita's good marks in high school, then his son-in-law, who was *un bel fioeu*, a good man. He'd told Carlo, 'Give the women a hand, where you can.' It was the day that the doctors had told him about the shadow on his lung.

'What kind of shadow?' this imposing man had asked, swallowing his words and refusing to sit down as they gave him his results.

'We're looking into it now,' they'd said, and he'd come home and started organising the documents he kept in the folder in the lounge.

Every time she'd feel like an orphan, Margherita went to her husband. She saw the time and called the agency, she'd be dropping by to pick up the keys for the property in Corso

26

Concordia. Then she called Carlo, 'We have the flat, I want you to come see it with me. Now.'

She had become insistent since the moment she had come to appreciate priorities. She was a frugal woman; she left no loose ends, she pushed people into choosing only the essential without that feeling of missing out. Her husband had learned to indulge those urgencies. Renting a seventy-square-metre flat with a two-square-metre bathroom, a sacrifice worth a three hundred euros a month discount. Booking holidays one year in advance and checking flights to intercept the direct ones at a fair price. Cooking with leftovers from the fridge.

She walked along Corso Buenos Aires and through the Milan she hated, the sequence of shops, turned into Via Spontini. Her agency was halfway down; she'd opened it three years earlier and had taken on Gabriele and Isabella. After the American crash of the previous year, things were still going OK. She stepped in and saw Isabella was out for some on-site visits; Gabriele was on the phone and when he handed her the keys she smiled at him and stepped back out. She headed towards Viale Monte Nero, it would take her twenty minutes at a good pace, if her leg could keep up.

The Corso Concordia flat was on the top floor, no lift; she'd got it after a long courting of its owner. They'd spent eight months in the same Pilates class, and the possibility of a sale had come up in the changing rooms – provided the owner actually decided to move to Majorca with her partner. When Margherita had seen the place – she'd been invited for an informal appraisal and a cup of tea – what struck her most had been the light. The two wide bedrooms, the lounge, the large kitchen and the two balconies were just details. The owner had confessed that she was looking for five hundred and fifty thousand euros for one hundred and seventeen metres, given the location. She'd poured her some tea – actually a red-fruits infusion – and accompanied it with some Norwegian butter biscuits, and added that all women, around fifty, should allow themselves a big change in their life – in her case, moving in with a lover that had soothed her divorce.

Margherita had nodded, sipped her infusion, and pointed out the lift situation: four floors and a hundred steps to climb could be a serious hindrance. Then she'd told her about the two-square-metre bathroom where *she* showered every day, had had fun trying to mime the difficulties of coordinating shower head and shampoo bottle. She'd smiled, almost laughed, aware of having declared a paradox: being the owner of a real estate agency without any proper real estate to her own name. However, the revelation had worked at the resistance, starting a series of small intimacies: the owner had told her that the Spanish lover was in choppy waters, and she wasn't talking about tight showers. With this Concordia sale, they would both be able to live comfortably in Majorca. After Margherita's tendon injury, they'd lost sight of each other, but kept exchanging formal messages until the owner had told her that she wanted her to lead the sale, that she'd felt a connection that was more than skin-deep.

Now she was ready to show Concordia to Carlo, even if he'd insisted that it was impossible to make the five hundred and fifty thousand euros work. She'd replied that there was wiggle room to negotiate, they just needed a strategy. They'd talked about it almost with joy, then the mishap had sidetracked them, even though she'd never stopped dreaming about it. She'd imagined the light of the lounge, finally wide bookshelves, the opportunity of inviting over more than a couple of friends at a time, sipping wine on the balcony, taking baths. As soon as she arrived at the door of number 8 she was taken over by nerves. She ventured into the courtyard and introduced herself to the porter, she sat down on one of the steps of staircase A. She massaged her leg and felt the thought of Andrea invade her mind, took out the Némirowsky and placed it on her knees. She rested her forehead on its cover. Dear Irène, you would not be this patient. She smiled; whispering to Irène made her feel better.

'That book drains you.'

She lifted her head from the book and, seeing her husband coming towards her, she got to her feet. 'I was waiting for you.'

'I came as soon as I could.' He kissed her. 'So we're here.' Carlo untucked his jacket collar, which had folded in on itself.

'The owner handed over the keys sooner than planned.'

'And if I like it?'

'I don't want to think about that.' She gestured him to follow her.

'So we should keep renting.'

'So you should go back to work, then.'

'I'm joking, come on.' He grabbed her hand. 'Where's the entrance?'

It was the building in front of them, nestled in the courtyard. She messed with the keys, let his hand go and opened the iron door. They found themselves at the foot of the stairs. There was a heavy smell of plaster as they walked up, one behind the other, stopping at each landing.

'It's hard without a lift.' She grabbed the handrail, her leg in pain by the time they reached the fourth floor. 'I'll go in first and open the blinds.'

'Let me help.'

'Stay here.'

She came back swiftly. 'Now you can come in.'

Carlo stepped forward, careful in his height, his way of inspecting almost by scent, grazing furniture without actually touching it, then touching it – the frame of a mirror in the bedroom, the notched wood headboard, his touch a little heavier on the lacquer of a lamp – still wandering at a pace that suggested both obsessive attention and sudden distraction. They moved to the lounge, with its table and eight wicker chairs, a sofa and a throw with stylised elephants. He stared at her. 'We have a problem.'

'Wait until you're finished.'

'We have a problem.'

'You think so?'

'A *big* problem.' He leaned against one of the windows and she admired her husband in that light. She was taken by how natural he was in appropriating his wife's instincts. Like Michel, Némirowsky's husband, who'd taken her to the Parisian countryside, almost by force, after one morning she'd whispered to him, 'I dreamt of a field of blue and lilac flowers and there was no war.'

Margherita went to join him, stopped, he stayed by the window. She overcame her hesitation and as soon as she was close to him she hugged him from behind. His was a body she had claimed since that dinner when they'd first met; imposing and shy, it had allowed her to overcome the word modesty. They'd ended up in bed one week later – she'd been the one to invite him upstairs, after an afternoon ice cream – and it had been a little strange to witness in herself the breaking of a seal, listening to her own voice moaning, governing her muscles with ease, navigating these new anatomies. The swelling, her mouth straining to hold it, opening her legs, throbbing, waiting for pleasure. She'd realised it would be *him* from the way in which she'd given herself to him. She'd told herself so immediately. As of that afternoon, they'd been able to maintain the fire of that passion, making the most of strange places, inappropriate moments, teasing a collaborative chemistry. She wanted it to happen again, now, in the shimmer of a too expensive flat in Corso Concordia. Sheer force could still repair misunderstandings: let herself be fucked with her elbows on the table, waiting for the spasm sparked by a physiotherapist to become *her husband*. She wanted it, to be taken, she really did . . . but he might've taken Sofia Casadei, too. It was an infraction that humiliated her, even now, as she held her hands upon Carlo's ribs. She did not let them move lower because that girl might have done the same. She pulled herself away and told him that this would not be their house.

He turned to her. 'Where else are we going to find this much light?'

'Where are we going to find five hundred and fifty thousand euros?'

'You said there's wiggle room.'

'A wiggle of maybe fifty thousand.'

'It's 2009, and we're all going through the same recession.'

'It's not enough.'

'There's no lift.'

'It's not enough.'

'We have a plan, right?'

She tucked her hair behind her ears. 'That plan is evil.'

'Evil can be interesting.'

'I'm not one of your students.'

His wife could sniff him out. *Evil can be interesting* might've been the dramatic start to one of his lessons. Every time she unveiled him, he'd look for an exit strategy, the imperceptible twitch of the eyelids, suggesting a topic that could throw her off, a wry comeback, a change of physical location, and so he crossed the lounge into the kitchen. There was a sealed bottle of water in the fridge; he wanted to take a sip, but closed the fridge and headed to the bedrooms, standing in the doorway of the first one as he figured out what was happening, what he was doing.

He popped his head into the corridor. 'The owner needs money, right?'

Margherita gestured him to lower his voice. 'Her partner's in rough waters.'

'So we have the solution.'

'Your family's money is not the solution.'

'Don't deflect. Your evil plan is the solution.'

She'd been the one to explain to him that their only chance was to slowly chip away at the owner: trick her about the visits, inflating the difficulty of the sale. She could've made her reconsider the demand, and at that point they would've slipped into the negotiation. They would need three to six months. The risk was that they might lose the flat as agents, in which case they'd change tactics. She'd told him before going to sleep – the moments before sleep in their marriage gave life to exciting schemes.

'I'm not sure I'm up to it, Carlo.'

I'm not sure about opening my own real estate agency. I'm not sure about becoming my father's carer. I'm not sure about getting married. *I'm not sure* – four words to say that she was, in fact, sure. In those years, he'd come to know how *not sure* for his wife meant being afraid of appearing shameless. Until the misunderstanding. Since then, she really had become *unsure*. Just like a couple of hours earlier, when she hadn't wanted to come up to his classroom – a relief – after his invitation, staying instead in the courtyard, eyes to the ground. Or in the weeks before that, when she'd stopped asking him if he still held lessons outside of the classroom, who with, how many. Or when she'd put aside minor light-hearted idiosyncrasies, like her mascara, or the naked dancing on Sunday mornings. They were timid stages of mutiny, even at night, with her looking for the side of the bed rather than arranging herself despotically in the middle. And as the mattress kept drooping along its sides, before falling asleep, his wife would tell him about this property with its magnificent light. Was a deed for a new flat really their big hope? He'd tried not to answer that question, just as he'd tried not to face the claims that kept piling up in his mind, day after day: you're hostage to a novel you'll never write. You're a professor six hours a week and your real job is writing tourist brochures, with a monthly family allowance you try to hide. You are a male stereotype incarnate.

He'd been able to hide those basic facts, but he was starting to flounder. He could feel it as he kept exploring the Concordia lounge and looking at this wife from the corner of his eye. 'This home is the right one for us, Margherita.'

34

'Do you really think so?'

He nodded and invited her to the stylised elephant sofa, made her lie down, resting her head on his thighs. She seemed smaller; he stroked her face and she let go, eyes to the ceiling and one leg grazing the floor. Now his wife's body was his wife's body: earlier, when she'd hugged him from behind, it had escaped him. It happened every now and then and he wasn't sure whether this also depended on the misunderstanding. He held her there for a while, and somehow knew that Margherita had not, that same morning, followed Sofia Casadei to class.

She took his hand. 'Promise me you won't tell your parents about this.'

'Promise me you'll tell your mother.'

'Why don't you do that?' She took a deep breath. 'On Thursdays, maybe, isn't that when you tiptoe over to her to confess your sins?'

Carlo looked at her and felt the same pain as when he'd joined her in their living room, one Tuesday evening in January. Margherita was watching *Back to the Future* and he'd said, 'Something's happened at the university.'

'What sort of thing?'

'A thing with a student.' He didn't feel it necessary to point out her gender.

'And you're telling me this why?'

He'd paused for a second. 'Because I have nothing to hide.'

'What are you talking about?'

He'd told her his version of the events.

She'd crossed her arms. 'It's like in that novel.'

'Which one?'

'The South African one, the Nobel Prize.'

'You're accusing me.'

'Or the other one. The Nabokov.' She'd looked at him.

'What's the opening line again? "Light of my life, fire of my loins"?'

He'd sat down on the sofa. 'I was trusting in your intelligence.'

'And I in yours.'

He'd watched his wife turning back towards the TV. The scientist from *Back to the Future* was explaining how the time machine worked on plutonium; the characters were in a car park in the middle of the night and Marty was about to start his first trip, destination 1955. Suddenly Margherita had said, 'But I trust you', and she'd gone to bed, leaving him alone in the middle of the sofa.

He was back on a sofa right now, and he was angry at himself: she'd teased him about Thursdays at his mother-in-law's and he felt once again unable to camouflage, keep himself secretive, hiding a small part of intimacy. He'd learned in his teenage years to flee from his parents – how could he have left that apprenticeship behind?

He said he needed to get back to work – he had half a Thailand catalogue to finish off – but first he wanted to be sure she really wanted that flat.

'Oh,' Margherita perked up, 'I really want it.'

'You want it?'

'There's no lift and it's too expensive.'

'You want it?'

'I want it, but . . .'

'You want this place?'

'I would like it.'

'You want it?'

She smiled. 'I want it. God, I want it.'

They found each other, held each other tight. Carlo slowly pulled away and stared at her. She was beautiful when happy. Margherita straightened his shirt collar and told him to go back to work. Instead, they both remained there for a few minutes before he stood up and kissed her goodbye. As he left the flat, he was certain he was fleeing. From the home that would've buried him in debt, from the material attempt at reparations, from the official seal of adulthood.

He walked, almost ran, down the ninety-six steps holding on to the handrail, crossed the courtyard and, when he reached Corso Concordia, stopped. He leaned against the building's front wall, thinking about Daniele Bucchi, his childhood friend from primary school, middle school, high school, who now worked in his family's launderette outside Milan after bringing three kids into this world and hanging up his football boots. He lived in a terraced house in Cabiate, population seven thousand, and during their last phone call he'd told him he was actually happy. Happy. His children were healthy and his wife was healthy and the launderette gave him enough to live on without worrying. He'd lost touch with Daniele after his first child – lost touch: a phone call a week, then one a month – and every time they'd hear from each other their voices needed to warm up.

While he started walking again he kept Daniele with him, squeezed into his mind, his long sideburns as they'd been when he was younger; he decided he probably wouldn't go back to work, he needed to do nothing, he needed to clear his mind, to write to Sofia. He took out his phone, saw a missed phone call from his sister, ignored it, scrolled down his contacts to the letter S.

Write to Sofia, call her, they'd make small talk – about what, though? He'd ask her why that morning she had picked up her things from her desk and suddenly left the classroom; he could tell her what he thought of her second story, the one he'd ignored for so embarrassingly long – the pages about the last trip with her mother, in the Fiat Punto, that day in May on the road towards Santarcangelo, the Ornella Vanoni song, the moment before the car swerved off the road. He could tell her the truth: it was a moving story. After he'd finished reading it, he'd lingered on the title, 'How Things Are', brushed the papers on the desk, picked up the notebook he'd never been able to write anything sensible in, closed it again, annoyed. Now he could call her to tell her how much he'd liked the writing, he wouldn't ask her to explain why she'd said she'd been followed by Margherita.

He didn't call her. He headed towards the Duomo, phone in hand, and called his sister before reaching San Babila. He told her that, maybe, Margherita's mother would not be coming to the birthday party.

'You know Mum would really appreciate it,' his sister insisted, 'but in any case, for the present, I'd go with the juggling seal from Swarovski.'

'OK for the seal, Simo, and I'll insist a little more with her. How's everything else?'

She told him she was holding up, Mamadou had had a few job interviews, then she told him how nappies were an amazing technological discovery, almost like future knickers, thinner with each new model. 'They hold up to point ten litres of piss without leaking, can you believe?'

His sister always calmed him down; he listened to her tell him about how Nico climbed all over the furniture to then fall onto his bum, a muted thup from his nappy. 'Thup, it's just thupping all over the house. If you had a child this fat and adventurous you'd know what I mean, but how are you? And Margherita?' He could talk to his sister and walk in silence. He told her about the Corso Concordia visit, she told him that their father would be more than happy to help them out.

'Don't mention Dad's money.'

'I'm not mentioning Dad's money. I mentioned Dad to mean Mum to mean us – you're thirty-five and you still haven't come

38

to accept you were born in a middle-class family?'

'Simona, you've accepted it a little too much.'

'I was able to afford Nico without a father looking after us, nothing wrong with that. Come for dinner tonight so we can talk about your possible future abode?'

'Thank you, but I have assignments to go over.' He slipped past the church of San Babila and asked her if she ever thought about her childhood years.

'Why are you asking me that? We're not old yet.'

'Do you?'

She said, 'Sometimes. I liked the walk home from school when Valeria Pari and I stopped at the dairy to buy Haribos, the crocodiles and the liquorice ones. I was never hungry enough for lunch and Mum used to get furious, I guess you miss those days?'

He replied that he liked these days too. And it was true; after all, all he was asking for was to be able to hold the different compartments together. His sister and Margherita, Nico and his father, his parents and Valeria Pari, Daniele Bucchi, Sofia, all pieces of an endless jigsaw. He hung up and found himself in front of the rear round window of the Duomo; sometimes it looked just like a Bonelli comic book. He moved around the cathedral, crossed the square without looking back, then slowed down. He could actually stop by the Statale, dropping in on Sofia's café, taking the last table by the window and waiting for her to finish her shift or take a long break.

He placed a foot on one of the Duomo's steps, the Arengario building covered by scaffolding, two men operating a crane. How had he brought himself to place his hands on her, in that bathroom? He had done it, after all. He'd got up the morning of the misunderstanding with a foggy brain, had washed quickly, dressed quickly, had a quick coffee with Margherita without sitting down, left the house, stopped at the office and set up the

39

day's schedule with the graphic designer, all before heading to the university. He'd got the post because someone on the board knew his father – *we'd really need a young man like your son, with his passion for reading. Narrative techniques, six hours a week.* As soon as his father had passed on the news of that opportunity, he'd accepted, avoiding the long talk about it being who you know and not what you do.

When he'd reached the classroom the morning of the misunderstanding – half an hour early, as usual – he remembers he'd sat down on the desk and waited for the students without doing anything in particular. He wanted to ask Margherita to drop by for lunch, but hadn't, still taken over by a weird energy that he hadn't been able to shake since he woke up. Then the students had started filing in. He'd chatted with Gianluca, a kid from Lecce, big fan of Russian literature and *Topolino* comics whose birthday was that day: they'd be celebrating at Plastic, did he want to join them?

'I'm too old for Plastic, but did you finish your story?'

Sofia had come in with the last few, light jeans and boots. She'd picked the desk in the third row and switched on her computer, accidentally knocking over her pencil case and jumping with embarrassment at the sudden noise. He'd already met with her twice outside of university to go over feedback, once with the group, once alone to talk about her first story. There, as he was showing her why the writing was insubstantial, he'd noticed her freshly shampooed hair, a new scent to him; he'd inhaled it, almost embarrassed. He'd placed a hand on the middle of her back, as if to console her, letting it slowly move towards her neck.

'Sorry,' he'd said, pulling his hand away.

'What for?' she'd replied.

He'd masturbated later to that *What for?* in the office bathroom, and the following days, waiting to see what impact those two words would have on his marriage. *What for?* had taken on, in his mind, the shape of an echo towards which he'd been drawn every time Margherita took on the form he liked to call *subterranean*: whenever she'd lose sight of herself, becoming distracted, in need of being drawn out, like he needed drawing-out of his literary delusions – he was aware – the drawing out was the process at stake now. Since the *What for?* something had changed and he'd done nothing to set it back: he'd look at his right hand, where he'd felt the warmth of Sofia Casadei's back and neck, at the base of his fingers. He'd felt a warmer body temperature, he'd tried to take in its heat in the few seconds of contact, turning it into a memory to bring out during work stress: *What for?*; when Sofia listened to him during lessons – *What for?*; when he had to unearth a buried libido – *What for?* clawing chaotically at his senses. *What for? What for? What for?*

And he had been less scared as soon as he'd realised that his marriage wasn't actually being affected by those thoughts. His hand on Sofia's back wasn't an interference, it was a parallel universe, it was the aphorism haunting the collective image of adultery: 'It means nothing'. Or rather: 'It means nothing much.'

'It means nothing, Professor Pentecoste?' he'd ask himself, aware of his difficulty in being around this kind, quiet, composed twenty-two-year-old.

It was a girl's camouflage that had made him lose control. The first sign had come weeks before the bathroom incident, when he'd noticed that during his lectures he looked at his students' desks, lingering on each, except hers. This had sent up a flag, this change to his liturgy of teaching: it still means nothing, Professor Pentecoste? Did it still mean nothing going out to buy different shampoos to discover, on the third try, that her hair that day of the feedback, did not smell of Pantene or Garnier but Head & Shoulders? When he'd realised, he'd

41

frozen under the shower, dripping foam. This still means nothing, Professor Pentecoste?

Then, the morning of the misunderstanding, he'd set an exercise that would last forty minutes. He'd lingered at the desk for a short while, watching the class grappling with the unexpected test, feeling how much he wanted to be them, writing the beginning of something that would lead to a sentence and a paragraph and a page and another and a chapter and another and eventually a book. Instead, he had nothing. And, every time, he'd ask himself how it could've happened, how he'd become someone who'd always rummaged around literature without ever actually trying to write just one story, one sheet that might validate him, maybe a short story . . . nothing. He'd tried a couple of drafts, given up, gathering crumbs of self-esteem by listening to his own voice in class, convincing himself that the sound – his teaching – was the sound of his novel. But he knew it was that contradiction which bound him to his students. They, thanks to one of his random writing exercises, might find themselves in a story – they were plucking inspiration out of him. And the more he showed up at his desk, the more likely was the threat one of them might make it, publish something, become popular, maybe name him in an acceptance speech for an important prize. 'None of this would've been possible without Carlo Pentecoste, thank you, Professor!'

Each time a personal situation quarrelled with his profession, he felt a diffused headache, almost like a buzzing, like the morning of the misunderstanding, when he'd stepped out into the corridor after giving the assignment to the students. He'd sat down on the chair by the coffee machine, massaging his temples with his fingers to soothe the pain. Ten minutes later he'd seen Sofia leave the classroom. He'd got to his feet, spotting her at the top of the stairs, her gaze fixed on the entrance hall. He'd gone towards her, knowing he would place his hand on the middle of her back again. He did so, with gentle pressure, tethering himself again to the warmth he had never forgotten.

'Is something wrong?'

She hadn't moved. 'I'm not a writer.'

'You got that from one exercise?'

'I've always known.'

'Sofia . . .' He'd removed his hand from her back.

'I just need to accept it.'

He remembered what happened from that moment on from a bizarre point of view, almost above ground: a student calmly walking down the stairs, a professor watching her from the top, rubbing the hand he'd just touched her with. Him deciding to follow her, seeing her make for the bathrooms, his headache increasing, his pulse throbbing at the base of his neck, an anxious gag reflex. That man wasn't him, and yet it was, stepping into the bathroom, finding the student looking at him from the sinks.

'Sofia, I understand you,' he'd said.

She'd let the tap run and washed her face, knuckles against her eyes, dripping water until he'd offered her some paper towels from the dispenser. After she'd dried herself, he'd rested his hands on her shoulders. He'd tightened his grip a little, feeling her shirt crinkle between his fingers. He'd let his hand fall down her back, asking her if she was uncomfortable. She'd moved imperceptibly, letting him know everything was OK, he'd seen it in the reflection. So he'd moved further down, wrapping her small waist, clasping it with his thumbs and index fingers. He'd leaned against her, lightly, then more heavily, surprised in seeing on her face a pleasure he had only tried to imagine until then. From this point onwards, he was no longer able to tell clearly what had happened. Walking into the women's bathroom – did she move them there, or had it been him? – the awkward hug – was it really that awkward? – hardly contained heavy breathing, her saying, 'We can't' and pressing herself against him, and their mouths, always their mouths, then her body collapsing.

He'd suddenly had her at his feet, Sofia. He'd bent down to hold her up, her head hanging back. 'Sofia . . .' He'd shaken her, leant her against the wall stroking her cheek. 'Sofia, hey.'

She'd come back to her senses almost immediately, with a small jolt; he'd helped her to her feet. They'd remained in each other's arms, against the wall, trying to ease their breath, stalling. He'd helped her back outside and only then had he realised they hadn't actually closed the door. He'd looked around before helping her to the sink to wash her face. He was suddenly furious about not having been able to go through with it. Undress her, remove her knickers, undo his trousers and sit on the toilet, lowering her on top of him, feeling himself move inside her, maybe clasping her mouth shut to contain the moans. That had hurt him. It was a dull type of irritation, mixed with a feeling similar to worry. Sofia was feeling better; she'd hinted a smile in the mirror.

'I'm not sure what happened,' she'd said.

'Nothing happened,' he'd murmured and saw her nod, undo and redo her hair, stretching her back as if to compose herself, then whisper, 'Let's get back to class.'

He still tried remembering new details, even now, sitting in Piazza Duomo, watching the two men with the crane climbing up the Arengario. He realised he was alarmed. Not only for the fear of being found out by Margherita: it was the humiliation of having confirmed to himself he couldn't do it. He couldn't fuck a student, and the way he handled himself after the fact, pretending nothing had happened with the Dean, with his father, with his wife, with his sister – with anyone – justifying himself for something he hadn't even been able to do. And that he would never be able to. If she hadn't fainted, he would've come

44

up with something to self-sabotage, something that would've allowed him to say, 'I am not unfaithful.'

How did he know? He knew. Just like the two men with the Arengario crane knew that they had to roll the steel cable to prevent it from knotting up during the climb. They were hooking up the cement bucket, holding it gently, then following it for the first part of its climb, knowing that without doing so it would twist. He watched them intently; they could've easily been twenty or fifty, sun-baked skin and bandannas that ended in small knots on the backs of their necks. They worked the crane and waited, eyes to the sky, tired and having fun, like children in a game of lorries and diggers. He would think about them again before bed, their bandannas and red skin; he always thought about comforting details before sleep. Daniele Bucchi and his launderette, his delicate way of sorting out the laundry based on the wash cycles; his sister, how she held her baby as she cooked; his colleague at the publisher's, happy about landing the supermarket line of plates and crockery. Sofia Casadei, how she rubbed her hands during moments of worry, how she stayed in her place despite not really wanting to. Every time he looked for her before sleep, he also looked for Margherita: he'd look at her curled up in bed, her dark silhouette and calm breathing, and recognise her. He wanted to feel pleasure with Sofia and he felt pleasure with his wife – and he still pined for horizons he would never see. And this conflict would die down because *'In the heart of every man and every woman a kind of Garden of Eden endures, where there is no war, no death, where wild animals and deer live together in peace. All we have to do is to reclaim that paradise.'* His mother-in-law had given him the Némirowsky novel with a fabric bookmark on that page . . . the wild animals and the deer, all he had to do was to reclaim that paradise.

He got up from the steps of the Duomo and raised his head, the Madonnina was so small. Some form of awareness had come to him: the outside world — facts and reality and the changes of the era — everything had been taken over by a more personal, intimate measure of time — obsession, intimacy, visceral machinations — as if outside our personal ecosystem everything vanished. He headed towards the Statale; he needed to talk to her one last time.

He tucked his hands in his pockets and swiftly set off, head low. When he reached the café he peered through the window and spotted the guy at the till, Sofia's back among the queuing customers. He fiddled with his phone; he should've called his mother about her birthday lunch, updated his colleague on the leaflets. He put his phone away, showed himself at the window until she noticed him.

He waited for her there; there was a raised cobblestone, he tried adjusting it with his heel and kept doing so as she reached him. 'I can't leave Khalil alone in there.'

'Just for a minute.' He stared at her freckles. 'I wanted to talk to you.'

'About what?'

'Just talk.'

But she wasn't really listening, her hands twisting a pen.

He moved closer. 'I read your story.'

'Why did you come here? Why do you all keep coming here?'

'You all?'

'I don't care about the story, professor. But thank you for reading it.'

'Can we go back to being friends?'

'I need to get back to work.'

'Sofia,' he moved one step closer, 'I believed every line you wrote.'

'Believed?'

'The accident, your mother, what you felt. What I mean is,' he inhaled, 'you were real.'

'I wrote what I remembered.'

'But in literature, truth is what we remember.'

A woman in her sixties was looking for something in her bag; her purse fell to the ground. Sofia watched her pick it up and walk into the café. 'Your wife never followed me, professor.'

They stood in silence, the noise of the Statale surrounded them. 'Why did you tell me she did, then?'

'I don't know.'

He cleared his throat. 'What if I'd talked about it with my wife this morning?'

'You would've ended up talking about the same thing.'

'The same thing?'

'Professor, I need to go.'

He touched her arm. 'The same thing?'

'Yeah, the same thing.'

'Nothing happened in that bathroom.'

'You think so?'

'It's the truth.'

'And truth is what we remember, right?'

'So what do you remember, then?'

She looked at him. 'Did you know that the day of the accident my mother and I were headed to the church where she got married? It's a stone church in Santarcangelo di Romagna, it's called the Pieve. It's very bare; there's a wooden cross and the light makes it shimmer almost silver. My mother had told me that she thought about the Pieve every time she felt sad. "So you're sad today?" I asked her as she drove. She didn't answer. She hadn't been talking to my father for a while – he slept downstairs, in my grandmother's old flat, and the two of us had the upstairs to ourselves. We called it the women's flat. One night I'd gone to Mum's room because her light was on, and I found her reading something my dad had written for her a long time ago: it was a note on a Filon café serviette, the place where

47

they used to meet before work, in their twenties. She made me read it, it said *A te dég me che t ci béla!* It means *I'm telling you: you're beautiful!* And you know what struck me the most? The exclamation mark. My father and exclamation marks are two polar opposites. That's how I realised they were happy. And that afternoon, as we were headed towards the place where they got married, I was witnessing my mother's last attempt to remember that happiness. Reality is what we remember, and my mother was forgetting everything. She was tired, driving, yielding herself to the seat, half-singing an old Vanoni song, I then realised it was "Rossetto e cioccolato".

'That's the last memory I want to have of my mother. Vanoni in my mum's raspy voice. I don't remember the rest. I don't remember the moment when I thought I might become like her, the steering wheel, my arm jolting out and trying to swerve us back from her distraction. I don't remember if she had intentionally taken over the Punto, if she really had twisted her wrists with the intention of ending her sadness. It's not my story. Just like my story is not the hands of a teacher who groped me.'

He kept poking at the cobblestone; some other students were leaving the Statale and were headed their way. He wanted to sit down, he did so on the wall running along the pavement. He lowered his gaze to his loafers.

'I need to go back in, professor.'

He kept his head down, realised she'd left only by the sound of her footsteps and of the café door closing.

Andrea had stuck around the newsagent's with his father for the rest of the afternoon; his mother had taken the metro home early. Later in the evening he'd asked for the keys of the car which was parked next to the shop. As he started the engine, his father tapped at the car window. 'Be careful.'

'Tell Mum you'll book another appointment.'

'I told you to give it up.'

'Tell her.' He extended his arm to wave goodbye. 'I'll bring the car back tonight.'

As he left, his fingertips were still on his father's shoulder knots, which he'd successfully loosened. He rubbed them together, then kept a steady pace; it would take him twenty-five minutes to make the eight miles that separated him from the dog. He drove almost absent-mindedly, imagining crossing the southern Milan barrier or going on to Piacenza or Parma or Tuscany and beyond; he'd never been further than Florence.

He arrived with no delays; the fog was heavier and he could hardly see the farmstead. He left the car on the street and made it through the gate, knocked at the door three times. The girl let him in while still on the phone and gestured him to be quiet and take a seat. He found himself in the kitchen, adverts showing on the TV, a smell of cigarettes and nail polish. He walked down the corridor to a glass door looking on to the back. It was ajar already. He opened it and listened to the barking. The dog strained against the chain, pulling with his neck and standing on his back legs.

'César, hey, down boy!'

But he kept going.

'I said down.'

'He's been like this all day.' The girl had joined him and was smoking at the door, her nails a fresh red.

'It's this fog.'

'Let him know it's you.'

'No need.' He crouched down with his arms out and the dog calmed down and came to him. Andrea petted him.

'I think it got infected.' The girl went back inside.

Andrea looked at the Dogo Argentino's paw; the bite mark was still shiny. A bump on the animal's left side concerned him.

He grazed it, touched it, rested the palm of his hand on it and slowly applied some pressure.

'Good boy, César, good boy.'

The dog listened, and he was able to explore his muscles and bone. He'd learned that animals are better at hiding pain than humans so each time they went quiet he worried. He took a closer look at the paw as he told him about his day, his afternoon off and his dad who'd skipped the appointment to go to the park, just like him. 'Do you want to go to the park, César? Do you? Tomorrow. Now be a good boy and let me feel.' He stroked him down to the docked tail, a truncated comma, slipped down to his belly and César lurched forward. Andrea called him back and kept feeling him. He raised his injured paw, and when he placed it down again he noticed it wasn't holding up the weight properly. Maybe it was over and they would let him free. He checked again, but first he looked up, and realised the fog had swallowed them.

'Don't be afraid, come here.'

The dog circled once; the girl and the others were coming into the courtyard.

'How's he doing?' they asked as soon as they reached them.

Andrea wasn't looking at them. 'He's not ready, and he can't fight any more.'

'What do you mean he's not ready?'

'The tendon, it's inflamed.'

'And what do you mean he can't fight?'

'The leg's gone.'

'Everyone heard the doctor?'

'Shut up, Giulio.' The girl turned towards her brother. He was a baby-faced thirty-year-old, with tidied hair, wearing a chequered shirt highlighting his droopy shoulders.

Andrea hadn't stopped stroking the dog. 'You said you'd bring a new one tonight.'

'It's in the car. It's a wolf, but something isn't clicking.'

Something not clicking to them meant there was a hint of fear. He'd learned to notice the signs too: bad posture, pleading looks, whining on the first injury, going for the owners leading them to the arena. They were the animals compromised by a docile past.

'Let's see.' The girl's brother went back inside and came out with a wooden cane and lowered it towards the animal's back. The dog bit it and pulled it out of his grasp – the chain was choking him but he wouldn't let go. 'Hey, hey, down boy!'

'He looks ready,' said the others.

Andrea stood up, staring at the girl. He'd discovered illegal dog fights the year before, when she'd asked her brother permission to bring him along and he'd found himself at the first Chiaravalle match, one May night, Dogo against Dogo. One of the two owners had stopped the fight because a bite to the paw had compromised his animal. They'd separated the dogs, the man had lost his money and someone else's. Three streaks of blood were left on the ring. Andrea had felt a languor. The torn flesh, the domination . . . when he'd got home he'd lain down on his bed unable to sleep.

'The dog will not fight. He needs injections, so he can heal faster.' Andrea had spoken to her.

'After this fight,' said the others.

When he and the girl had first met – at the Magnolia, during an electro night with Prozac+ – she already had César. Her brother had brought him home. He was a really sweet pup, then suddenly he was not, and she hadn't been able to keep him at home or even take him to the park any longer. César had only attacked her once, because of a sudden movement of hers in front of his muzzle; he'd growled at her and the chain had stopped him. He often attacked her brother. They'd left César at the old farmstead, taking turns to bring him food;

Andrea would head over to look after him as soon as he could. He realised that he'd lurch at clubs over his head and sudden movements, would calm down if you talked to him. The girl claimed she loved César even like this, and she claimed she even loved Andrea like this. *Like this* was their complication.

Andrea moved closer to César, took one end of the club the dog was still holding in his teeth. 'César, leave!' He managed to take it away. 'He needs rest.'

'Let him try one more time,' she said. 'One last time, Andre.'

'What's this last time thing?' asked the brother.

'It's the last time,' she insisted. 'If he can't fight, you'll start complaining that he's making you lose money.'

'Fine,' said her brother, gesturing to remove the chains. 'He'll fight.'

Andrea let the club fall, moved to one side, and waited for the brother to leash the dog – he tried multiple times, with no result. The girl crouched down and tried to calm César.

'Andrea,' she said, 'you do it.'

But he moved a few steps away.

'Fucking do it,' said her brother. 'Please.'

Andrea went back inside, into the kitchen and sat down on the sofa. The worn-down cushions, the smell of old, the lumpy seat . . . this is where he'd told the girl that physical touch was enough, he couldn't give her – or any other woman – anything more. He abandoned his head to the corner of the sofa.

She found him staring at the ceiling. 'César is losing it. Can you come?'

He shook his head and she just stood there. She was a thin shape with long hair falling onto her shoulders. 'My brother is a dick but he loves you.'

'He beat him again – there's a bump that wasn't there last time.'

'It's an old one.'

'He beat him again.' He looked at her, then closed his eyes. He was tired.

The girl sat down and stroked his leg, pinched him, smiled. 'We can make the money for three days at the seaside. Me and you.'

'Why?'

'Because we love the seaside.'

'Why are we still doing this?' Andrea stood up from the sofa and walked through the corridor to the back. He found the others in a corner of the courtyard, smoking. He moved closer to the dog, the chain jingled. 'César, come here.'

The dog barked and didn't move, barked again. When Andrea got closer, he snapped his head round.

'Good boy, it's just me.'

'He's fucking mental,' said the brother.

'Come here César, it's me.' He kneeled down and extended an arm, waited for the dog to come, let himself be sniffed, stroked his neck, slowly moving towards his head. 'Hey, friend,' he said, and moved his hand. The dog bit it. The girl screamed from the glass door, the others picked up the club.

'Andrea, Andrea!'

'It's nothing!' Andrea looked down, he'd bitten between thumb and index finger, a hole in between spraying blood. 'Leave him alone, it's nothing.'

They dragged Andrea to one side of the courtyard and she went to fetch cloths and disinfectant. 'Stay still, let me see.' She cleaned his wound and applied pressure to it.

'My job,' he said.

'It's OK.'

'My job, what am I going to do?' He moved his thumb, his finger. The pain was manageable. 'What am I going to do?'

'Let's get you to the hospital.'

He just held the cloth to the wound and hurried inside; his

top and trousers were splashed with blood and soil; he reached the bathroom and let the cold tap run. He plunged his hand under it and saw that the tooth had torn it in two places. He touched his hand: the tendons were fine, phalanxes too, the thumb abductor was not. He kept moving his fingers, one at a time, then all at once, as the blood pooled into a black mass.

'Hospital, come on,' she said. 'Don't be difficult.'

'Listen to her,' said her brother from the bathroom doorway. 'That fucking mutt, this was the night for it too.'

'You beat him.' Andrea removed his hand from the sink, went up to him. 'His side is swollen.'

'Look at you defending animals when you're the first to—'

'You beat him.'

'You're the first to enjoy it! Am I wrong?'

Andrea pushed past them to the fridge, opened the freezer and found César's steak. He wrapped it in a cloth and pressed it onto the wound. He sat at the table, told the girl, 'Get them out of here.'

'They're taking you to San Donato.'

'Please get them out.' He raised his wrist over his head; the bleeding slowed a little. 'Get them out.'

She listened and asked the others to leave. The group stood in silence, then the brother suggested using the wolf in their boot for the ring. They filed away in front of him; he didn't look up, only heard 'You've pissed on everyone's parade, even God's.'

His hand was purple and the wound was bleeding much less now; she took a clean cloth and continued tending to him in silence. Then he stood up.

'Where are you going?'

No reply.

'Where are you going?'

He was going to settle things.

54

The courtyard was a grey square, the fog still thick, and César was curled up under the shelter. He got up and trotted from one side to the other, his chain a snake reflecting the light of the street lamp.

Andrea peeled off the bloodstained top, the outline of his muscles tracing his back and shoulders and stomach, his skin almost pearlescent. He squatted down, hiding the wounded hand against his leg, and waited. The dog came. Huffing from his tightened jaw, he barked.

'Come here, friend.'

The girl stepped back, she was holding the club, ready.

'César, boy, come here.'

The Dogo limped on his injured paw, walked a wide perimeter, stopped in its centre. He moved closer, at arm's length from his face. Andrea started shaking. Then he reached out with his good hand. César sniffed him and he started telling him that he'd only hurt him a little and the one he should've bitten was Giulio; they needed to come up with a plan to bite him together, right, César? Right? How about one of these days you and I teach Giulio a lesson? He stroked his neck, then his back, down to his tail. He continued when he felt at peace with himself. César looked at him, his breathing a purr in his throat, sat like he did when he was about to get fed. Andrea told him, 'I'll be back soon,' slowly got up. He walked backwards and the fog separated them.

'You're crazy,' the girl told him as they stepped back into the house together.

'I need to take the car back to my father.'

'I'll come with.' She paused. 'I'll spend the night.'

He was still bleeding and the pain had become constant. 'Don't.'

She lowered her arms to her sides. 'Fine.' She sat down at the table, her gaze lowered to the plastic tablecloth.

'Cristina.'

'We did give him the rabies shots,' she said, without looking up from the table.

'Cristina . . .' He shuffled his filthy top back on, started moving towards her.

The girl pulled away. 'Keep your phone on, at least.'

Andrea kissed her on the cheek and waited for something even he wasn't sure about, then he left.

That night he missed her as he lay in bed, in his two-room flat in Via Porpora, shuffling towards the second pillow where he'd rested his wounded hand. He kept squeezing it, pinching the pillowcase, pretending to have her there with him, and tried to calm down. Cristina lifted him from what he was unable to be, and for a while he had even been able to take her where she needed too: fleeing from her parents' divorce, to second-hand clothes shops, swimming in the sea, London – they'd gone to Wembley Stadium – light-hearted conversations. They'd found some form of peace together. He'd realised it on the farmstead's sofa, after she'd stripped him and he'd gone along, after they'd been together and Cristina had asked him what he wanted in his future. He'd said, 'My own physiotherapy clinic.' She'd stared at him and asked him again. He didn't answer a second time.

'You a queer or what?' the others had said, out of the blue one day. With physio he'd learned to close up when dealing with pectorals and triceps, wide backs and strong shoulders. 'You're a queer.' Cristina distracted him from the truth. That's why he hadn't let her spend the night, she would've interfered with thinking about how much César's bite would compromise his job. As morning came, he removed the dressing and confirmed it: the tissue was swollen and the holes were still fresh, they oozed at the slightest movement. He cleaned them and wound the gauze tightly around his wrist. It took him twice the time to shave. He had a yogurt for breakfast and took a painkiller, swallowing it

56

with some orange juice directly from the bottle. He was shaking, his head was swimming, his bones hurt. He got dressed slowly, folding his work clothes into his bag. He walked down the three floors of his building and cold overwhelmed him; he got to the metro and wondered if his father had found the car keys in the letter box, checked his phone and found no missed calls, which reassured him. He texted Cristina, *Feeling better, going to work.*

He continued his commute, thinking about what he'd say to FisioLab. He could still take care of the machines, or move to the weights area, only rescheduling the full treatment sessions. He stepped into Via Cappuccini 6; the receptionists greeted him worriedly, he replied it had been an accident at home. He crossed the waiting area into the changing rooms and heard someone call his name. He turned to the seats, saw Margherita.

She stood up. 'On the dot, see?'

He didn't reply, then lifted his bandaged hand.

'Oh God! What happened?'

'I was chopping something.'

'Did you get it looked at?

He nodded, bags under his eyes.

'You shouldn't have come in.'

'I shouldn't have.' Andrea lowered his head and she felt as though he'd just confided in her. She finally saw him. Was he a boy in her eyes? He never had been. A man more mature than his years, now vulnerable. She'd woken up intolerant of her own doubts, wanting to feel confident – it was her right after having spent most of yesterday planning strategies to buy a house that she and her husband could not afford. Then she'd gone to bed early, lain awake; when her husband had joined her, she'd asked him if he was happy. They'd already turned their lights off and had got used to the darkness; she had seen Carlo's shape rest his head against the headboard and heard him answer, 'I think so.'

Think was right. She loved him for that *think*, because it was a *think so* for her too. Being uncertain together, being in a bed that sailed where it needed to sail – a marriage, a luxury flat for the future, a worthy profession – and that was taking on water in the tides of time. How many bodies, huh, Carlo? So many possibilities. So many female students and male physiotherapists let go, so many books dreamt and left halfway, so many. They'd left it at that and they'd fallen asleep. The moment before sleep she'd thought of her father – who knew what his thoughts had been.

As soon as Andrea left the changing rooms, her gaze followed him; they nodded at each other, then he reached the reception and chatted to the girls, stepped into the doctor's office, where she had also had her first visit. Fifteen minutes later he still hadn't come out and she was already forty minutes late on her schedule. She pointed this out to the receptionists and told them she'd be waiting outside and she ran through the day's appointments leaning against the building's wall. She'd have to postpone Buzzati – she would warn her mother. She leafed through her diary and calculated the timing to call the owner of Concordia. She'd check in on a regular basis, keeping her updated on promising visits that would all fall through due to the high price. She would wear her down, step by step, suggesting sudden delusions, without ever leading her to despair, trying to reinforce their friendly complicity. She started noting down the fake appointments in her diary, then saw Andrea walking towards her. He apologised, told her one of his colleagues would be taking over her therapy.

'What about you?'

He raised his hand, now haphazardly bandaged though his face had changed. Emaciated, where earlier he looked livid.

'What did the doctor say?'

He attempted a smile while one of the receptionists buzzed

the door open. 'Andrea, the doctor is looking for you.'

'I know, I got it.'

The doctor joined them and greeted Margherita, brushed Andrea who shifted away from him slightly.

'You need to have that looked at, I'm serious.'

'I get it.'

'Grazi or Cappelli will take you.'

'I'm fine.'

'Sure you are.'

The doctor and the receptionist stepped back in, Andrea turned to Margherita. 'Talk to them about your appointment, they'll slide you in somewhere else.'

'Don't worry.' Her hand moving to his forehead. 'You're burning!'

He seemed to falter. He pulled away. 'Sorry.' He headed towards the exit.

Margherita followed him, keeping her distance up to Corso Venezia, waiting for him to cross the *bastioni*, and sidled up to him in front of the railings of the Via Palestro park.

'If you don't slow down you'll have me on that table of yours for the next ten years.' She panted.

He turned around. 'I'm going home.' He held himself against the metro entrance's wall; he was drenched in sweat and shaking.

'Hang on . . .' Margherita rummaged in her purse and handed him a tissue. 'Where do you live?'

'Near Piazzale Loreto.'

'So does my mother! Where?'

'Via Porpora.'

'Let me call you a cab.'

'What do you want from me?'

Margherita brushed her fringe from her eyes. 'I want to help you home, and then I promise I'll get out of your hair.' She pointed towards the taxi area by the road.

'I'm taking the metro.'

'I'm headed that way anyway, the office is in Via Spontini.'

'That's before my stop.'

'Not an issue, really.'

They reached the taxis and got in, Andrea staring out of the window for the entire Corso Buenos Aires, his bandaged hand on his lap, his head tossed about by the car's vibrations. Halfway he told her he might have an infection, that the FisioLab doctor had given him some antibiotics.

'Why did he want you in the hospital?'

'Paranoid.' His temple was resting against the glass, his skin shiny with sweat; he seemed stunned and she had to wake him up when the driver turned onto Via Porpora and asked for the number.

'One thirty,' he replied.

The taxi pulled up. Margherita paid and got out, opened the door on the other side, helped him stand up. She'd inherited it from her mother, helping people towards what was best for them, while also favouring her own needs. Carlo called it man-ipulation – she thought of it as compromise, or something she didn't really want to dwell on for too long. She made Andrea sit down on the doorstep, spotted a chemist's on the other side of the street, asked him for the prescription and picked up a pack of amoxycillin. When she got back, she found him as she'd left him and got him to give her his house keys. They stepped into the dust-smelling building, took the lift to the third floor; he took the keys out of her hands, unlocked the door, and she saw him scuttle into the room directly next to the corridor.

'Your medicine!' Margherita carefully stepped in and fol-lowed him. She found him already in bed.

'You need to take the antibiotics.' She looked around, then headed to the kitchen and rummaged around the dirty dishes in the sink, found a glass, washed it and filled it with water from the tap. She brought it to him, handed him a tablet, waited for him to take it and lie down again. 'Can I call anyone for you?' But Andrea's breathing was already the regular rhythm of deep sleep. Only then did she realise where she was.

The ticking of the wall clock, his viscous breathing, the hard corner of the mattress where she was sitting. She was staring at the strong, sick body, the pillows — one of them covered in blood. She wanted to take off his shoes, to tuck him in up to his neck. The walls were bare except for a Japanese haiku print next to three shelves, piled with books. Anatomy manuals, Marvel comics, the first one on the pile sporting the Human Torch on the cover. Clothes were draped over a chair, the open wardrobe door revealed two solitary hangers. She could feel her heart leaping and knew that the feeling could've been called youth.

She stood up and removed his shoes, tucked him in; he shifted a little then resumed the same position. She looked in her bag for her phone, pocketed it and stepped out, headed into the kitchen. There was a small two-seat sofa and a cupboard topped with the smallest TV set, a stuffed toy dog on top of the fridge. It was a German shepherd with shiny fur, with a red ribbon collar and a tag that read *To the silent one that lets stories be told, C.* She stroked the toy — it was soft — then she placed it so it could watch over the house. She headed to the sink and washed the mugs, the cups, the plates, and laid them out on the counter. She dried her hands on the tea towel hanging off the French window's handle, opened up her contacts list and looked for *Domenico Pentecoste* — medical consultations were a good common ground with her father-in-law — she gave up, looked for her mother, she gave up. She stood there. Out of the window there were two buildings, on one of the balconies someone had installed a multicoloured pinwheel. She joined her hands, raised them to her mouth and told herself she could do this. She tiptoed back into the bedroom, reached the empty side of the bed and slowly sat down. She lay down.

She kept her eyes on the ceiling, then turned her head and looked at him, his muscles and his face closed into sleep. This was it, then. A different man next to her. The mattress unbalanced with a new weight, a more pungent smell, little time to enjoy it. Could she do it? She inched her head closer to his. She held it there, listening to him sleep and aligning her breathing with his. Then she pulled herself up and left the room; she could do this. She locked herself in the bathroom, cream tiles and a plastic curtain around the bathtub, and called her mum.

When her phone rang, Anna was airing the Persian rug on the balcony.

'My darling, don't tell me you're skipping the Buzzati appointment?' She rested the carpet beater on the chair. 'What do you mean, something came up? Do you know how long it took me? It's your future, for heaven's sake.' She suddenly fell quiet. 'What kind of something? No no no, you're going to tell me, you don't call your own mother and throw around the *something came up* excuse and then expect to leave it at that.' Quiet again. 'Fine, fine, let me know, then, I'll sort out Buzzati, but you promise me you're OK, can you promise me that?'

She'd grabbed one of the curtains and was now scrunching it. She said goodbye to her daughter and stayed with the phone to her ear, then put it down on the table. 'Of course,' she whispered.

She headed onto the balcony and dragged the rug back in, dumping it next to the couch, and ran to the bathroom. She touched up her mascara, powdered her cheeks and slipped in her pearl earrings. She looked like Jessica Fletcher – Franco had said so one evening as they were watching *Murder She Wrote* – and was proud of it. She picked out a man's shirt and comfortable trousers, slipped an old tank top of Margherita's into her bag. She took the trip to the metro station to figure out her plan. The address was in the Navigli area, it would take her twenty minutes: she'd be late to the appointment by fifteen. *Franco, your daughter put me in a pickle.* She and her husband had always been punctual. A railway worker with a Swiss spirit and a seamstress who met her deadlines a day early. They'd had their daughter at the age of thirty-six, the only lateness in their marriage.

She quickly left the house, taking Pasteur station, watched over by the graffiti-adorned houses and Chinese shops. She took out the book on the escalators, started reading as soon as she was on the train. It was a short story collection recommended by a radio programme. The writer's name was Andre Dubus and he'd lost his legs to help two brothers whose car had stopped in the middle of the road: he'd been run over by another vehicle. Then his wife had left him; then he'd stopped seeing his children, and other writers had decided to pool together to help him financially. She'd bought it at the Libreria del Corso. Andre Dubus, a French name in an American body on a wheelchair, he wrote short stories without any twists. Who said you need plot twists? She'd talked about it with her daughter, but her daughter got bored easily; a mother always knows when she brings into the world little patience.

When she resurfaced, Porta Genova station was empty. She started along Via Vigevano, pulling herself away with some effort from the small shop of handmade silver rings, and hurried over. The building overlooked a parking area that had been a dock once. The address had been given to her years earlier by a woman who worked for the same fashion designers and she'd noted down the name *Landi* and the phone number in her diary, but had never used it until Franco's death. Two months after the funeral she'd booked an appointment; the waiting list was three weeks long. When she'd finally been received, she'd been asked if she wanted to know how her husband was faring on the other side. But she didn't want to know that. She wanted to know her own future, darn it. And every time she rang the doorbell – she'd been there a dozen times now – she'd feel a jolt of excitement.

She'd insisted with her daughter because in the last session Ms Landi had asked about her specifically: she needed to tell her about some intuitions. To convince her, after having been dismissed as a sucker for months, she'd told her about Dino Buzzati – he always went to see Ms Landi when she was still a young clairvoyant.

'And what did Buzzati ask the cards?' Margherita had asked.

'I don't know, my dear, I think maybe his love life? And think about when he was told he'd marry Almerina.'

'Was he really foretold that?'

'Yessir.' That was, of course, a lie. Small white lies forged good destinies – she'd always done the same, even with her husband.

She took the lift to the fifth floor; the door was slightly ajar and this time the young woman kept her on the landing. 'I'm so sorry, my daughter had something come up, we both just found out.' She strangled her bag. 'I came in her place, I'm so sorry I'm late.'

The young woman welcomed her to the lounge with flowery wallpaper, with three ink drawings of Milan – the courtyards and the Conca del Naviglio – and a framed *Lady and the Tramp* jigsaw. Living in the corner was a 1940s radio, briar-root dial and golden linings – she always imagined Tenco's voice coming out of it. She stood waiting; they called her as she was trying to call Margherita again. She followed the young woman into the corridor and the small kitchen: the woman was smoking at the corner of the table, the glass of *chinotto* next to the ashtray and the tipping plate. The scarf covered her up to her chin.

'My daughter was held up at work. Thank you for seeing me.'

Magnets were spread all over the humming fridge door.

'So you want a wide spread?'

'One on my daughter, please.' She pulled the tank top out of her bag and handed it over.

The woman put it on the table and rested her elbow on top of it, shuffled her playing cards. 'You know, I never got a name.' She kept shuffling, cigarette between her fingers, then on the ashtray.

'She's Margherita.'

'I mean yours, not your baby.'

'Mine's Anna.'

'You can read it both ways,' she said, eyes partially closed. 'Useful name.'

'Yes . . .' She grimaced, embarrassed.

'How are your hands?'

'They're OK.' She joined her hands, let them fall into her lap.

The woman stared at her, then handed her the deck. Anna cut it with her left hand and moved closer to the cards; the woman started laying them out in a pyramid, twelve plus one at the top. This time, it was the Knight of Discs.

'Does that mean money?'

She gestured her to be quiet.

Anna bit her tongue and listened to the hum of the fridge; she remembered when, a year earlier, the woman had revealed a Four of Swords and said she could see a sadness. Can you explain? she'd asked, her throat tightening. The woman had said that Anna's life had gone as planned, but she hadn't fully realised herself because something had restrained her. Anna hadn't held back her tears. She knew that the *something* was having had to look after all of them, the stool and the corner of the table, the cutting of fabric like impulses to shape, the male complaints in the background. It was this, when *something else* kept insisting she run out of Via delle Leghe, head to the Radicals' local office to join the party, without Franco making her feel guilty in some way. And give up sewing at home: she really wanted a shop with her name on the front window. And St Petersburg, even just strolling in the birthplace of revolution and forbidden loves, and Milan, the clubs of Brera, the singing and the glasses of wine. Was it wishful thinking? Maybe. What was it, exactly?

The woman cleared her throat. 'Margherita is fine, but I can see a change coming.' She brushed each card, one by one. 'A place. Maybe the office.'

'They're looking for a home. They found one they like.'

'It's the right one.' She picked up her cigarette and took a long drag. 'This house reads well.'

'And her health?'

'By health, do you mean that thing about you becoming a grandmother?'

'I don't care about that.'

'All mothers of daughters care.'

'I just want her to be happy.'

'She is.'

'Then that's enough.' She took a deep breath. 'And her leg? Remember I told you? She hurt herself.'

'Just a nuisance.' The woman isolated the Ace of Cups, left it in the middle of the table, shuffled the deck again, spreading twelve cards around it.

'One last thing on Margherita, Anna; if she has any pets, she should give them away. Cats, dogs, parrots.'

'She doesn't have pets.'

'Really?'

'Not that I know of, no. Why?'

'Let's say . . . accidents.'

'Oh God. What kind of accidents?'

'Just tell her not to get any and she'll be fine.'

She nodded. 'And my son-in-law?'

The woman put out her cigarette and looked harder at the cards, pointed to the Ace of Swords.

'He's fine too. He's not what I'm worried about.'

'What worries you then?'

'They need to start a family, they're a couple that need it, see?' With the edge of the Two of Clubs she raised the Knight of Swords.

Anna let herself lean against the backrest. 'That's up to them.'

The woman looked at her, brushing against the cards like piano keys. 'Do you pray, Anna?'

'I don't, no.'

'Doesn't hurt, once in a while.'

'I'll do what I can.' She rummaged in her bag, pulled out fifty euros and one cent from her purse. She put the cent on the plate. 'Sorry again for being late.' She stood up and was about to leave, then stopped. 'Ms Landi,' she took another deep breath, 'is the Buzzati story real? Dino Buzzati really used to come here?'

The woman nodded.

'What was he like?'

She grabbed the cigarette. 'A *bel'òm*. A handsome man who loved the King of Cups.'

'The King of Cups?'

'Improvisation.'

Anna started walking backwards out of the kitchen, followed the young woman and left the house, giving the old radio one last glance. As she waited for the lift, the scene from *Bicycle Thieves* came to her, the one where the protagonist is so desperate that he goes to see a faith healer. Him skipping the queue of women, the healer calling out to God, the despair of the man without a clear response. She pulled out her phone and called her daughter again.

She heard her pick up as she reached the ground floor, said, 'Your mother is an idiot and she wanted you to know that. Hello? Hello, darling? Can you hear me? Where are you?' She stepped out of the lift. 'What do you mean the Fatebenefratelli? The hospital?' She froze in the hall, 'Are you OK?' She stepped onto the street. 'I'm coming over! No no no, I am, even if it's about a friend. Tell me the room number. No no, I'll tell you later, I'm an idiot and that's that, I'm coming.'

She hung up, remembered a taxi stop under the oak tree in Piazza 24 Maggio, headed over with her heart beating in her throat. The King of Cups and improvisation. Margherita and Carlo need to start a family. No pets. Buzzati was a handsome man. Need to pray. My daughter is at the Fatebenefratelli. She

68

was under siege by thoughts; she'd always been a woman who pondered over the sewing table, now she kept holding them back with the same trivial image: the spread of *mignons* at the Cova patisserie. The shiny glaze, the marzipan's texture, the jellies that were like jewellery to her. They'd have them on family occasions, with Franco scrambling for the fruit baskets and Margherita the cream puffs. What was left for her were the *diplomatici* – how she'd learned to love them. Once a week, if she had errands to do in the city, she'd head to Monte Napoleone and sneak into Cova with the fur-wearing ladies, order a coffee and one of those *mignons* with a double coating of Alchermes liqueur. The bar smelled of sugar and she'd nestle into a corner and take a bite and a sip, pay with a note and let the change fall into her bag.

She regretted calling Margherita, and she was now rushing despite knowing it wasn't her daughter who was ill – she'd just given priority to *something* over her own desires. And so, as the taxi took her to the Fatebenefratelli, she told herself her wish list for the day, three items as always, from the least to the most coveted. Third place, a chat with Carlo. Second place, avoid her co-mother-in-law's birthday. First place, still: throw out her husband's leftover stuff.

It had been hard to find them. He'd been buried for a day and she'd opened all the wardrobes and dragged out everything, Margherita and Carlo trying to stop her, then letting her continue way into the night. She'd gone to sleep with the house a tip and when she'd woken up, three hours later, realising that the space next to her on the anti-bedsore mattress was empty, she'd got dressed and taken everything into the cellar. The jumpers and the shirts and the coat and the shoes, the Panini albums, everything except for the *Tex* comics, the vinyls, the pipe and the watch. It took her nine trips, dumping most of the stuff on her sewing table; she'd put away her tool bag and had bumped into a fruit crate wrapped in a bed sheet. She'd opened it up and found the older comics, mostly *Diabolik* and *Capitan Miki*, and between the pages of one of them she'd discovered twenty-one postcards sent to her husband's office. Milano Marittima, Viareggio, the Alps, even Madrid, even Budapest, and a different sentence each time.

She remembered all of them but only repeated *You would've loved the lodges with their pine scent, yours, Clara*. It was dated 8 August 1976, came from Bormio. Margherita was two years old. Each postcard was signed by the same person, the last one was dated 7 July 1986. After reading them, she'd stayed in the cellar for a good forty minutes, sitting on the floor. Then she'd put everything back and had gone back upstairs, somehow able to ignore the fact that five metres below there was a fruit crate that needed to be thrown out. She'd postponed it day after day after day and eventually had come to coexist with those wooden boards that held twenty-one secrets. She'd been tempted to know, to ask his long-time colleague, or call the Hotel Doge in Milano Marittima from the postcard from 6 July 1979.

But what would knowing bring her? She'd tried searching in her own memory too: other than the Turin training course, Franco had never left home. And the phone? Bills were regular, always low enough, except when middle-schooler Margherita would spend half hours giggling with the receiver in hand. What else? Franco was a man of sporadic touches, had always avoided expensive gifts. On Sundays he'd go to the stadium, sometimes he'd take the bike for a ride. He couldn't spend more than two hours a week outside of the house – were those for his Clara? She hadn't cried much for his death. And while everyone was waiting for the rivers of tears to come – of course they'd come – no one could imagine how much the discovery of those postcards had helped stave them off further. She'd been on alert since, expecting to find more, opening drawers, emptying the wardrobes in their entirety, and cleaning out the house, trying to picture all the people who attended the funeral: not even a hint of unknown women. She'd married a good man, and *good* was an adjective that soothed her. She'd repeat that to herself. This Clara had been – if she had been at all – an evasion. Maybe just like the student for her son-in-law, or maybe for her daughter, or anyone at all – *she'd* never had the chance. Her years of marriage, giving birth, the finely tailored clothes, the enthusiastic meals she'd prepared, her repressed politics that she still followed with watchful affection – she had plenty of antidotes for her regrets, really.

She stepped through the doors of the Fatebenefratelli, asked for the short-stay area.

'Anna.' She turned around; Carlo was at the coffee-vending machines, phone in hand. 'Why did you come?'

'Why did *you* come?'

'I couldn't understand what was going on.' He hugged her.

She liked when her son-in-law hugged her; she'd prepare by tilting to one side.

'Where's Margherita?'

'Come on.' He took her arm and headed to the lift. 'It's her physio. Dog bite, infection, something else I didn't catch. She found him.'

Anna clasped her mouth. 'Dog bite. You hang around pets!'

'What do you mean?'

'Stop it. No pets.' She stepped out of the lift and followed him into the wing, the second room to the left. There were six beds; Margherita was sitting next to the one closest to the window, a boy with a bandaged hand was asleep under the blankets.

'You actually came.' Margherita smiled at her.

She shrugged.

'I'm sorry about the appointment, Mum.'

71

Anna touched her arm and rested her hand on her. She shuffled behind everyone else, back against the window, watching her son-in-law texting and her daughter staring at this unknown young man. She asked her what had happened and Margherita said she'd tell her everything outside, his girlfriend would be here any moment.

'What about his parents?'

'He didn't want to call them.'

Anna moved closer to the boy. He had opened his eyes slightly, panicked, the eyes of a child, darted to Carlo, then to her, then they closed again.

Carlo was watching him too and looked away embarrassed. He went back to his phone, finished typing *if you want* and pressed send. Then he got up and said, 'I have to go, my father asks to be kept updated.'

And after kissing Margherita and her mother goodbye, he hurried down the stairs: his hunger for Sofia was becoming an uneasiness that the family hearth prevented him from living fully, half of himself fighting the other half. He wanted to know how far he could go. What was this obsession? Her ass. Then? Her voice, hearing it in the throes of passion. Then? The pill, he'd spotted the pack in her purse: the idea of coming inside of her unsettled him. Then? A new body available, an able body. Understanding if he could do it this time. The terror of being caught had dissolved, as if it were now his right. He could allow himself a connection, going all the way with his wife and doing the same with a lover.

What an awfully wrong word, lover. What an awfully wrong word, betrayal. What exactly was he *betraying*? Why did sleeping with another girl have to mean a loss, taking a fleeting moment of joy and perhaps giving a moment of joy. Getting up, getting dressed again, without any of those romantic or affectionate rituals, maintaining the liturgy he had consolidated with his wife through their years together and which he would never question. Care of the pact, building of the relationship, devotion: a lexicon that, in literature, was synonymous with naivety but that nailed him to the reality of the facts. He had a suspicion it was guilt, for him too, that kept him on the brink. How many times had he pictured himself coming home, three or four hours after having given himself to another woman, awakened by the new feeling and still excited by the unprecedented release, opening the door to the familiar, kissing Margherita and taking time to get used to the idea of his own marriage again.

Getting used to it again, that was the concept that threw him into doubt. Those who are getting used to something again have been somewhere else, subverting an equilibrium. Subversion, equilibrium: the legacy of a solid education, the Pentecostes, the Catholic schools, the opening of the presents on Christmas Eve with her mother lighting candles all dressed up. He was a man looking for familiar alibis, even when his own sister had told him that betrayal had been, for her, an opportunity to find herself again.

'Meaning you'd lost yourself?'

'Meaning I wanted to enjoy it.'

But then, she'd had a child with the first available suitor and happily lived off the Pentecoste fortune. He wanted a particle of that same enjoyment.

And so, that morning, faced with the dog-bitten guy, he'd messaged Sofia three times. She hadn't answered, he'd insisted. He'd asked her to talk about her story – it wasn't fair to leave things halfway. With the second message he'd asked her out for a drink and a chat. In the third he'd used *if you want*, adding a line about him currently looking after a hospitalised stranger. The more he was confronted with her silence, the more he couldn't help himself. Sofia Casadei's butt freed from her jeans, white and out of proportion, her flat stomach down to her

73

mons, how small her sex must be, how welcoming. It was true, he really was all the men from the books he loved, so predictable, Margherita was right. He left the Fatebenefratelli behind, checked his watch and realised he had ten minutes to get back to the office, felt his phone buzz in his pocket, pulled it out and read *I'm dropping the course. Thank you for everything, professor. I'm going back to Rimini.*

After she'd sent it, Sofia rested her head against the train window. Milan and the Master's and writing and the idea that in the north her paths had got stuck: a text message sealed all of that. She'd lived an adventure, that's how she'd explained it to herself, clearing her head — she was a girl with no talent who'd said how things were in a short story. She was a work in progress, as Khalil had suggested, saying goodbye at the café after she'd told him she'd made an impulse decision. He'd tried to convince her otherwise but she'd confessed that she really missed her father. Khalil had gone quiet and hid behind the coffee machine, set off the steam nozzle and cleaned it. Then he'd come to her and given her a bear hug.

At the end of her shift, she'd removed her apron, had called the manager, telling the truth: she wanted to move back to Rimini. She'd started walking home, Milan had followed her for the last time. The Missori buildings, the gargoyles peeking between the spires, the metal tramcars on the tracks heading to the Duomo, the rushing souls, the chance to hide away in any alley, she'd miss all of it. She'd realised that later, as she was packing her suitcase in her bedroom in the Isola, piling up her clothes, the laptop, trying to fit in all the books she'd gathered in those months. She'd left them out in the end, she'd come back for them before the end of her contract. She'd sat on the bed. That empty room: now that she was leaving it she was certain her decision was to prevent her from giving in. Starting to love the big city, forgetting from one day to the next the Adriatic sea and her father dragging his flip-flops across the floor. Becoming vulnerable to a professor's charms, allowing herself the cliché. And all of those complications: finding him at the café after finding his wife at the café. How had she *found* herself in that situation?

She did have the story, though. Being able to write what had happened that afternoon with her mother in the Fiat Punto, with as much precision as her words could muster: this was her reward, she'd told herself trying to get to sleep, on her last night in Milan, folding the seven sheets of 'How Things Are' into her notebook, dragging her suitcase to the metro station, buying a ticket for the 10.35 train, sitting in a window seat and replying to the last message from her professor. Listening again to the recording of their meeting, where Pentecoste stroked her neck and she offered him her nape. His hold at the base of her hairline, the tilt of her neck muscles. She would've liked to let him have those fifty-one minutes and thirty-seven seconds, the proof that they had had something.

She stopped pondering after Bologna, travelling through the countryside of the Emilia with its farmhouses and the tidy yards. She got another message as she reached Faenza, *Is this a joke?* Then another, *I'm trying to call you, please pick up.* The phone started buzzing, she put it away. She could still hear it buzzing. She plunged it into her backpack pocket and dozed off. In her sleepy state, her bones started to ache; she touched her legs and arms, they were warm and heavy. She straightened up in her seat and looked out of the window, recognised her Romagna. After Imola, the flavour of the fields changed, became sweeter; farms were scattered and took on a different cadence, almost melding together, as if people wanted to be close to each other while sowing or harvesting. Then the train crossed the Rimini docks and she held her breath: returning home was still difficult.

She let someone help her with her suitcase and as she stepped off the train she knew she'd escaped Milan. What hurt her the most was the calmness taking hold of her, revealing just how under siege she'd felt. She walked through the underpass out of the station, checked her phone and found three missed calls and four messages from Pentecoste, one said *Call me when you can, I just need a minute. Thanks.* Waited at the bus stop for the no. 1, which would take her to the Ina Casa. It was a 1950s-60s neighbourhood for families with intelligent and cheap architecture, grandparents and parents and grandchildren in the small squares between dairies and cafés and card games over improvised tables, next to the Lambruschini school and the public preschool. Now grandparents were dying and their place was taken by outsiders, but the neighbourhood had not lost its sweetness. Each time Sofia came back terrified of not finding it, she always did. The bus followed the walls, entered the first periphery and the closer it got, the more anxious her heart grew.

The hardware shop was open; she disliked going by it ever since they'd found a new manager. She stayed on the bus a little longer and got off at the Bar Zeta stop, walked up the cobblestone streets around the school, reached the small square and the building she had always lived in, noticed that her balcony had some new flowers. She stepped back a bit; they were yellow. She took out her keys and opened the door, walked up the stairs dragging her luggage against the steps, opened her door, hurried into the kitchen, burst open the glass doors and realised that violets had been planted in the three pots.

'Sofia!'

'Who did that?' She didn't look away from the balcony.

'Me. I bought them across the street.'

She turned around and saw her father. Her dad, in a T-shirt, Bermuda shorts and flip-flops, holding his cigarette so the ash wouldn't fall. 'I would've come to pick you up.'

'It was a surprise.'

Her father had bags under his eyes and his recently cut hair was white and dull. He shook his cigarette into the kitchen sink and moved her suitcase into her room. 'Did something happen?'

Sofia hadn't seen flowers on the balcony since her mother used to grow tulips. She sat down, the Frate Indovino calendar still showed March and she changed the page to April. She looked around. The kitchen cabinet was straight again, the tiles had been cleaned, the radiators had been painted. The wooden part above the French windows had been changed. The ceramic pig with the wooden spoon was still next to the fridge.

She stood up, went back out onto the balcony. There were seven violets per pot and some had been planted too close. She pressed her hand onto the soil: it was wet and smelled of woods; she lowered her head and saw her mother's bucket and tools in the corner. The miniature rake and the shovel and the shears and the gloves.

'I fished them out of the cellar,' her father said, and smiled.
She nodded.

'Did something happen in Milan?'

Sofia was staring at the tools in the bucket, Nothing happened, she said quietly, while moving closer to her father. As she got in front of him, about to brush past him, she wobbled, landed a hand on his shoulder, and stood there, a child badly grabbing onto her dad, and him, being unable to embrace her, replying however he could: he stroked his daughter's shoulder blades and her neck.

'Come on, I'll take you,' he whispered, and heard his daughter crying. He kept holding her. 'I'll take you there.'

'I don't want to go see her.'

'I'll take you to the yellow lighthouse.' He moved her away from him to look at her. 'It's good for my smoking. I'll go change, too ugly like this.'

It took her being alone, drying her eyes on her sleeves, to re-alise she had come home. She thought about when there were still three of them and the hardware shop and her father offering his skills as part of the purchase, her mum behind the counter noting down the jobs her husband would have to do for the customers. *Mirror for Assunta, two days. Drilling and plaster for Ceschi, move painting location.* He'd always be out and the shop did well even after they'd opened the Obi DIY store in Via Marecchiese, with their wider selection. Her father had been so happy in the hardware shop. And her mother, so hidden away in that life.

Sofia went to her room, opened her suitcase and rummaged through the clothes. She found the folded paper with the story, the title 'How Things Are' copied out with care in the top left corner. She joined her father in the bathroom and found him in his jeans and a beige shirt, tidying his hair by carefully combing the tufts. He saw her. 'Let's go.'

She handed him the papers.

'What's that?'

'For you.'

Andrea signed himself out of the hospital and asked Cristina to take him home. His hand was throbbing and his fever had broken but the doctors said he'd need a night of rest. He had an infection – nothing affecting the bones, there was a small issue with the tendons. But he knew that already. He left the Fatebenefratelli after filling out the paperwork with how things had happened: the stray dog had attacked him in the area of Parco Sempione – light fur – without being provoked or with any prior contact.

He waited for Cristina to bring the car round; it was dusk and he thought he could hear the swallows. She arrived, he got in, fastened his seatbelt and kept looking at the sky through the window. Then said, 'Thank you.' He looked at her.

'You could've called me straight away.'

'It wasn't urgent.'

'I mean, you had all of those people around you, and they don't mean anything to you.'

He held back; he'd started holding back with her too, recently. He'd have something to tell her and he'd stop himself, increasing the strain between them. This time he'd wanted to confess: the people that don't mean anything meant a lot. Waking up in a hospital bed to Margherita's family had made him feel good. Margherita, her sprightly mother, those two female presences at his side had changed the invasiveness into a natural caring. Even her husband . . . for a second he'd seen a hint – his posture or his tired beauty or something – of why he deserved his wife.

They reached Porta Romana and drove past the arch; new hyacinths had been planted in the grass and she was about to turn onto Via Crema when he said, 'Let's go see César first.'

'What?'

'I want to see the dog.'

'That makes no sense!'

'I want to see him.'

'He'll react badly!'

'I want to see him.'

'It's dark.'

Andrea went quiet; he'd lowered the window to let some fresh air into the car, had breathed it in as he'd left the hospital and he'd felt better. 'I know it's dark, I still want to see him.'

She turned on the emergency lights and stared at the wheel. Then said, 'They've taken him.' She turned to him. 'They said he could fight; they waited until today because the Latinos are going, and they've got cash.'

Andrea was cradling his hand, like a parcel he'd learned to protect; he gestured her to keep driving.

'Andre—'

'Go.'

'Promise you won't do anything stupid.'

He stopped looking at her until San Donato. One of the group's cars was parked on one side of the street; the boys had left with the other two cars. Andrea walked through the gate, let Cristina open the door and headed for the courtyard, where César's chain was lying on the ground. He checked the sand where the dog had been and couldn't see any blood.

'He didn't beat him,' she said.

'How do you know?'

'I was here.'

Andrea couldn't see the club, or the mace.

They headed back to the car and reached the overpass in ten minutes. It was five hundred yards from a construction site, with its half-built concrete pylons. They parked the car off the road and walked the rest of the way. Before heading out, he buttoned himself up; his legs were strong enough and he managed to keep up the pace. He slowed a little when he reached the crowd. Two Ecuadoreans nodded towards him and he nodded back, positioned himself to the side to take a look. The ring was empty, the owners getting the dogs ready in the two corners, and the generators had been turned on and plugged into the lights. They'd planted some metal sheets in the ground to mark the ring, propping bricks on the outside. He moved in closer. Two people were scattering some soil on the marks from the fight that had just finished and there was a nasty mark on one side of the arena.

One of the Ecuadoreans was staring at him.

There were some new faces and the Italians were huddled in a corner, betting their money. They were watching the dogs being riled up; one of the owners was raking a chain over the back of a Rottweiler, making it clink. The Rottweiler pulled and was choked by its chain, raised on its back legs, the other dog – an American Bully – was also held down by its back legs. The Rottweiler had filthy fur and two scars on its side, giving it white stripes. The American Bully was groomed, a strange grey hue, ear docked to the roots and watery eyes clearly due to an infection.

'My brother isn't picking up.' Cristina shook him from behind, Andrea was still staring at the arena; the truth was that he couldn't stop staring. The bets were sealed in the jar, the jar was taken out, left in a hole between the weeds to keep it safe in the event of a police raid. One of the two Ecuadoreans repeated the rules of the match: animal removed before time's up is one third of the fee for the owner, winning animal is a third of the fee plus three hundred flat rate to the owner, dead animal is whole fee to the owner.

When the dogs were unleashed, the Rottweiler stayed quiet and low, the American Bully was on it for a short while, was thrown down quickly and started gurgling from its throat. Beneath them, the old bloodstains emerged like black branches of a river. Andrea stared at them, pulled himself out of the crowd and headed towards the Ecuadorean; he kept behind the ring and had never stopped looking at him. As soon as he got close, the man gestured with his head towards the overpass exit furthest from them.

Andrea set off and was joined by Cristina and the echoes of the crushed American Bully. He'd readied himself for César's death four months earlier, when they'd saved him by paying a third of the fee, after a Cursinu had almost gutted him. He'd wanted to free him, hadn't done it because he loved seeing him in the arena. There'd been only one fight in which César had ripped out part of a Pitbull's throat and had pinned it to the ground, fifteen seconds from the start of the match.

Andrea held his bandaged arm and didn't speed up, he was light-headed from the recent fever and he couldn't feel his own pulse.

'Did he tell you where he is?' She was on his heels.

He kept marching towards the direction that the Ecuadorean had pointed to, using the torch function on his phone to see ahead.

'Did he tell you where he is?'

They found him in the small tip, a couple of metres over the ditch. The body was badly hidden in a dip, half covered by soil and plastic bags. Andrea knelt down and started digging with his good hand; she helped him and started crying. They freed him and pulled him out, dragging him a little further out. He cleaned his muzzle, stroking him gently, and saw that he had been bitten on his chest and back and on his femoral muscle. César's eyes were open and his tongue lolled out of his mouth. Andrea hid it back inside and put his hand on his docked tail.

He asked her to go fetch the car, and when he was alone with his dog he crouched down next to his still-warm body. She came back and he lifted him up on his forearms, placing him with some difficulty into the boot. Blood spattered his dressing and trousers and top.

'I want to bury him in the field,' he said.

She nodded and wiped her face; they got in the car and drove back to the farmstead. Then he wanted to do things himself. He planted his feet firmly in the ground and picked up César, started carrying him over to the field and his legs began shaking until he had to stop. Cristina joined him with the shovels and helped him hold up the muzzle. They walked together to a clearing with a walnut tree and a dried-out irrigation canal. The night was pale and the street lamps and the moon outlined everything. It took them over an hour to find the right depth because he was digging lopsidedly with his bad arm. He laid César down and together they made sure that his head was looking towards the farmstead. She was stroking him and he stroked him too, pressing his fingers on his wounds. He covered him up with care. They flattened out the fresh soil with the shovels and he quickly headed back to the farmstead. She found him in the courtyard. He'd already undone the chain, moved back into the doghouse and thrown out the water and food bowls, he'd erased César's shape in the earth under the shelter with his foot. He let her hug him and said, 'Take me home.'

'Stay.'

'I don't want to see them.'

'Yours, then?'

They headed over to his place and showered together – she helped him remove his dressing only after. The wound had opened up again at two points and the antibacterial had crusted over. Andrea took it all off and asked her not to look at him while his hand was undone. So she stepped out of the bathroom, but not before handing him the medicines he should've taken hours earlier.

As soon as he was alone, he stretched his arm out under the light, clenched and unclenched his fist and saw that the bite was still oozing. He blew on it and finished medicating it, dressed it in loose bandages and headed to the bedroom, finding her lying in darkness. He lay down next to her.

'My brother isn't answering. I'll deal with him tomorrow, you stay out of it, OK?'

Andrea had already tuned out Cristina's voice and let himself tune out César, though he knew it'd be different in the morning. Now he needed to focus on something that would soothe him and was surprised when he realised it was Margherita. Her looking after him in hospital. He reached out to her, and she did the same.

83

She sought after Andrea as soon as she got in bed, his strong shoulders appearing from under the hospital sheets. And his way of sleeping, as if afraid of being an inconvenience. After leaving the Fatebenefratelli and arriving at the agency, she'd written down the phone number she'd demanded from him before parting ways, writing over the threes and eights while she thought about how to stage the sale process for Concordia. But instead of calling the owner, she'd just sat at her desk doing nothing. What would her father have said? He would've used that word, *Scharfenberg*, meaning a light coupler for trains – *light*, not as stable as the old make according to him – through which each car is linked to the other. She was Miss Scharfenberg, that's what Dad used to call her when he'd catch her zoning out in front of the Andrea Giani poster or when she'd abandon studying in favour of procrastinating. It was thanks to her father that she realised she was trailing a carriage with *lightness*. She'd get back on track, putting the distraction aside – her mother's words this time – and would grab onto the tangible. Pay the energy bills, the Pam supermarket shop, buy a house for her family. So she'd finally called the owner of Concordia and she'd been brilliant and stubbornly natural. She required it of her collaborators, spontaneity, and it didn't matter that it was the result of training. She'd told her that the visits had just begun, they had eleven lined up, only two had given up when they'd heard about the non-negotiable price.

'What do you mean, Margherita?'

It was the lift, ninety-six steps were a burden. She liked the word 'burden', it was elegant and unmistakable. Then she'd added, 'But trust me.'

How did she feel? She'd felt strongly anchored to the next carriage of the train, her family project. That afternoon in Sevilla when she'd said yes to Carlo's proposal: after he'd asked, she'd sat down on the patio's low wall in Santa Cruz and asked him if it was real, admiring the silver ring he was sliding onto her finger. She'd been a woman like *all* the others and she didn't mind in that case. Then something had happened, as soon as they'd told their families: she'd felt something start to bother her about the Pentecostes as they'd started making suggestions about the ceremony. She would've been happy with a small church, ten guests and the flowery dress from Twinset she'd bought the year before, eating pheasant on Lake Como or in a countryside restaurant. She'd said so to her mother, one evening over dinner, and Anna had immediately replied with wanting to contribute to the wedding however she could, maybe making a throw and a bow tie.

Margherita had swept away her plate, throwing the risotto over the table. 'You too! Jesus!' She'd burst into tears and her mother had come closer, dragging her chair. Then Anna had whispered, 'I got a really bad rash. It cleared up a month after the ceremony, but it never really goes away.'

She dismissed Andrea from her mind and let herself fall back into her bedroom, dipped as it was in night, the tall ceiling, New York on the walls, her insomniac neighbour's wanderings, the moon infiltrating the blinds. She slipped her hand under the bed sheet and brushed her husband's side – she always knew when he wasn't asleep. He took it. Carlo always became forceful whenever he sniffed the chance of having her. She also became forceful whenever she decided to have him. Every time she'd take him in her mouth – a regular occurrence before penetration – she wanted to feel him touching her throat, with the absolute conviction of it swelling to the point of gagging. She'd suck until she felt him tremble, stop without allowing him to come, letting him take care of her.

Once her husband's head was between her legs, she'd offer herself up to imagination. That's what she called it, imagination, it took the shape of majestic men that she fantasised about having around and above her, together or one at a time, a circle to protect and take her. Some were from the past, too: the way they'd touched her, kissed her, how they'd learned to move inside her, traces from which she'd gain a surprising immediacy. Being on top of her husband at the end of that day in the hospital with Andrea: it put things back in their place. Seeing him moan beneath her, after she'd demanded someone else: it blew open their complicity. He ordered her to reveal her fantasies. In those moments preceding climax, Carlo would always ask her the things he'd never wanted to ask her and she'd tell him the things she'd never thought of telling him.

She slowed down, he insisted. Margherita resumed, he squeezed her hips.

Then she said, 'The physiotherapist.'

As she said it, Margherita tried finding her husband in the darkness, his profile, his heavy breathing, his hands tightening their grip, the erotic heaving and the annoyance at that revelation. She kept moving. 'The physiotherapist,' she said again, and rode him with force. They came, she stayed on top of him until they'd both calmed down.

They'd always be discreet, after, as to what they'd told each other, as if their libido had put words in their mouths that they didn't share. Realising she had that power over him always aroused her immensely. It had been a risk that led to a form of complicity, and an idea that their relationship was somewhat special. Since the misunderstanding, however, everything had become harder.

She pulled away from him, didn't regret telling him about Andrea. She looked at him, and saw her husband was watching her. 'What?' she asked him, heading to the bathroom. When she came back, he hadn't moved.

'Do you know the exact moment when your youth ended?' Carlo pulled up the bedsheets. 'And I mean the exact moment.'

'Oh God, how does fucking always lead to one of your philosophical questions?' She got under the sheets and searched for his legs. 'The end of high school, maybe?'

'No no no, I mean the *exact* moment.'

She squinted. The answer could've been 'When they told my father he was going to die.' Instead she replied, 'I think the day I opened the agency.'

'So three and a half years ago.'

'We only had desks, you'd brought over a couple of boxes and I'd started emptying them. I chose my spot and I placed the plastic turtle with the bendy neck on it. Remember that?'

'You were scared.'

'A little.'

He shifted the pillow around. 'I was on my bike, I was going to work at the Mincio swimming pool. I was on the overpass in Ripamonti, the one heading down to Porta Romana. The last day of September, five years ago.'

They fell quiet, and he heard her fall asleep not long after. He stayed awake and remembered the moment when he was pedalling and had felt the spell. On that bicycle, panting on the Ripamonti overpass, still without an actual job – he was sure the editor position would be temporary – he still hadn't given up the presumption of writing a novel, living with Margherita as his fiancée, still not a teacher thanks to his father's recommendation. He *still* wasn't. He could be anything. On those pedals, arching up as if close to the finish line, he'd felt joy spread through him from his sternum. He'd ridden down the slope with the certainty that that was his apex and farewell to a season, and that he would soon be entering his new life as a man. He fell asleep with that same melancholy, or maybe he could've called it happiness.

His first image on waking up was Margherita and the physiotherapist. Her on the medical table, legs open, the boy massaging her inner thigh. Her muffled pleasure, the boy unable to help himself – how could he, after all? – lightly touching her where he wasn't allowed, the muted erection, maybe let off in the changing room, later. He snuck out of the bedroom and into the bathroom, quickly washed and headed to the kitchenette and prepared the moka pot for Margherita. He set it aside and took a bite out of a wholewheat cracker, chewing calmly while staring at the corner of the table, the recently paid bills to be filed away, the reading glasses and the bottle of antihistamines, a succulent, his wife's phone charging. His wife's phone. He got distracted by composing a hypothetical shopping list, shoving into his backpack the edited drafts on Morocco, then left the house. How would he have reacted if he'd seen in her phone the same messages he'd sent to Sofia? He walked slowly down Via Montevideo, skirted Solari park with its euphoric dogs let free after a night inside, followed by their still sleepy owners. He noticed the joy in those unleashed yet still loyal animals.

How would he have reacted if he'd known Margherita had another? He left the park behind and avoided the question, yielding to the certainty that his alertness towards Sofia was now taking a different shape. Her return to Rimini, not seeing her in class in three days from now, it was a defeat he was now able to take. As long as it didn't mean finding shelter in Margherita. He had extended his desire beyond his marriage, if he tried redefining those borders he would end up living his wife as a rebound. Margherita was happiness, he knew this with certainty. But he now could also sense a grey area emerging in tangible ways, capricious and incontestable: this part of his mind emitted energy any time it grazed the idea of Sofia. Sofia now, who knows who else in the future? The other happiness. He'd asked himself if the cause had been a tiredness in his marriage, and he'd reached the conclusion that he wanted to be done with this thing about emotional compensation. His wife brought him joy, a marvellous joy; Sofia brought him joy, a marvellous joy.

When he reached the Naviglio, he pulled out his phone and typed *At least let me know if you're ever coming back to Milan.* He plunged his hands into his pockets and walked up Corso San Gottardo; the office was in the ivory building on the corner with Via Lagrange. He nodded to the receptionist and Manuela smiled, shook her brunette bob. Carlo had worked there for six years and still used the same chair with armrests that he had when he'd signed his project contract: one thousand four hundred euros a month, no time sheets. It had been his second position after his literature degree, the first had been an advertising agency. He'd left that one because he was terrible at it and it was hindering his writing. Everything was hindering his writing. So his father had *thought* about it – 'I'll think of something' – offering him the opportunity to manage the staff in his private practice. He'd refused and they hadn't spoken for the entire summer. If anyone now asked Domenico Pentecoste what his son did for a living, he'd reply, 'He teaches literature.' Sometimes he'd go back to that evening, when his father had asked him, 'Will you ever write a novel?'

Carlo took out a water bottle from the pack under his desk,

took a sip and waited for the computer to wake up. He'd always shared the office with Michele Lattuada, a forty-year-old graphic designer of few words who lived near Bergamo and got to the station every morning at around six, an hour before his train left, because the parking spots were scarce and the traffic wardens ruthless. He'd park the car, throw down his seat, set his alarm, and take a nap. For months Carlo had thought about writing a novel about this colleague of his and his reclining car seat, the supermarket points, the lunch Tupperware and the affection he felt towards him. Michele Lattuada had taught him how to be content with a chair with armrests, water bottles under the desk, a wife, maybe a child.

He shuffled towards the keyboard and took a quick glance at Michele: he was working on Japan, adjusting his glasses and clicking the mouse, every now and then grimacing in concentration. They spent some time on Mount Fuji, laid out a double-page spread on the Hokkaido thermal springs, started researching *okonomiyaki*, the Japanese savoury pancake, then the phone buzzed. Michele noticed and turned around, Carlo picked up his phone and read: *I'm heading back tomorrow to pick up the last of my things. Do I have enough attendance for the course certificate? Thank you. S.*

He got up from his desk and headed to the window; the trams in San Gottardo clanked over the switching points. He squeezed his phone. He read the message again and waited for the relief to extend to his shoulder blades. When he looked up, he saw Michele staring at him. He moved back to the desk, replied to Sofia. He reassured her about the certificate and asked her again to meet up. He placed the phone on the desk and got back to work on the double *okonomiyaki* spread.

I don't have enough time, professor, sorry.

He tried finishing the part on Osaka, keeping the designer hotels on the Yodogawa Riverside Park for last.

How about just a coffee?

Maybe tomorrow, if I finish packing my books but I don't know.

He started working on Nara, its deer and the night lantern path.

Let's try, Sofia. Let me know?

Tomorrow, professor, have a good day.

He liked that she'd ended with *good day*. He told Michele he'd finished, that he'd be back soon, and headed out for lunch. He knew he'd be late. It wasn't a Thursday and he didn't like surprising his mother-in-law, but he still took the tram to Porta Venezia, took the metro to Pasteur and stepped into the Scaringi patisserie. He picked up a *diplomatico* and a *babà*, as he did every Thursday. Before ringing the doorbell in Via delle Leghe, he checked to see if the blinds were open. He rang and waited for longer than usual, was about to head back when Anna answered.

'It's me.'

'Me?'

'Carlo.'

His mother-in-law was waiting for him on the landing, holding her hands together. 'What happened?'

'I was in the area.' He hugged her; he always touched cheek to cheek and took in her rose perfume. He noticed she wasn't wearing foundation and her dress was untidy.

'You scared me!'

'No stray dog for me.' He handed her the cakes.

'Have you eaten?'

He shook his head and followed her inside. The TV was off and there was a blanket on the sofa. 'You were sleeping!'

She was already at the fridge, fixing up a plate. 'A mother-in-law always has some *vitello tonnato* ready.'

'My mother is of the same opinion.'

'Speaking of . . .'

'Don't come.'

'Your mother will be disappointed.' She smiled. 'But I don't know what to get her!'

'You're already included in the Swarovski thing.' He sat on his stool while she set his place. She served him the veal and a glass of red wine.

He took a forkful. 'I'd defect if I were you.'

'They used to say the same to the Allied forces just before Normandy, too.' She smiled and nibbled a corner of her *diplomatico*.

They fell silent for a bit as he enjoyed the veal, keeping his eyes on his plate. He chewed with care and took a gulp of wine. He told her about Concordia.

'I'm only worried about the no lift thing.'

'We're young!'

'But Margherita's leg?'

'A temporary inflammation. She'll be fine.'

Carlo attempted to carry the plate to the sink but she snatched it away from him and started washing it, along with a mug and some cutlery. 'You know? I'm still reading that Dubus guy. He's an author that makes me think of silent daughters going to see their mothers, and sons-in-law going to see their mothers-in-law, and mothers-in-law washing the plates because they're on the side of both their daughters and their sons-in-law.'

'You should be on the daughters' side.'

'You sound like a priest.'

'It's a difficult moment, Anna.'

'You don't have to tell me . . .'

He stood up and headed to the French window, the rug was draped over the balcony railing, next to the birdfeed holder. The fog had settled on Via delle Leghe.

'So why are you here?'

'I've become an idiot.'

'All men do, at some point.' Anna sat down and focused on her dessert. 'I would've loved having been born a boy.'

He looked at her.

She was chewing small bites, smoothing out her dress with one hand. 'Margherita never believed in Father Christmas as a child, did you know that? Once, she went up to her father – she must've been five or six years old – and asked him if she could have her present before Christmas Eve.'

'She figured it all out.'

'She figured out you have to go that way.'

'It's a mistake.'

'The word mistake has many hidden meanings.' She felt like putting on some music. She reached for the shelves and picked a record out without choosing, removed it from its sleeve, switched on the device and tried three times to get the needle onto the vinyl, then let Carlo help her.

'Modugno,' she announced.

They'd play music on Thursdays, every once in a while, and even if today wasn't a Thursday and they'd talked about bad stuff, they could be free. Modugno or Aretha Franklin or I Camaleonti . . . the records would play and they'd faff around. Sometimes her son-in-law would peruse the bookshelves or work on the round table, she'd read or make something in the kitchen, or iron some clothes. Often she'd squint, perched on her stool, and imagine that the shape on the sofa wasn't Carlo but a husband. What was he like? Squatter? Or really tall? A wealthy man or an artist? Maybe French, or from Piacenza – men from Piacenza eat horse meat and are strong and kind. She'd find herself imagining a man she'd just met . . . she liked the idea of being a woman in her dressing gown with a stranger in her lounge. She was easily scared of her fantasies, she always had Franco in her heart. Dusk especially marked her loss. The empty bed, being on the sofa and noticing the dents in the cushion where he used to sit. On the other side of the wall were the Soldatis, mother, father and two growing, fighting, loving teens; she'd listen to them through the bathroom wall. The eldest, Fabio, had just got his driving licence and the entire family had celebrated with some warm Prosecco – the father had forgotten to put it in the fridge. Once she was taking a bath and had heard the wife crying about something big, sobbing in despair: she'd got out of the tub with her chest tightening, because she'd also cried like that. Who hadn't? Marriage can be nasty.

She glanced over at her son-in-law, he was tapping on his phone while Modugno sang 'Come stai'. Carlo was a boy who couldn't lead. In seventy years she'd learned to spot them, the deceptive boys who could, and the suspicious boys who couldn't. He was one of the latter; he turned red if he was excited and his behaviour was not very brave. It worried her that he might mess up her Margherita and himself. It hurt her to see him in front of his father, his ears and voice low, the way he'd been that one Christmas when Domenico Pentecoste had told him off at the table, during dessert, an interrogation about his plans, what was he going to do to make things add up?

'What do you mean, add up?' Carlo had asked.

So Pentecoste had turned to her and asked, 'What do you think, Anna? What could your son-in-law do to finally become someone?'

She'd replied with 'What he's doing already.'

'And what's that?'

'Being a reliable man.' She'd bitten her tongue: she might as well have said a boring man. She'd never been good with adjectives.

'Why don't you take out one of my books?' she asked him now, as soon as she saw him look away from his phone.

'Not in the mood for books.'

She went to the bookcase and fished out the wrapped *Tex* from the third shelf. 'This one's a good mind cleanser.'

'Franco will get mad.'

'Franco's underground. And gunslingers always give good advice.'

They headed to the door. She loved her son-in-law for this reason too: he left right before becoming part of the furniture. She watched him head downstairs with the comic book under his arm; she and her husband had found that *Tex* on a stall in Bergamo – flea markets were one of their outings and when Franco had seen it, his jaw had dropped. He'd turned it around in his hands and had asked the seller how much, had checked with her about spending sixty thousand lire for an issue worth one hundred and thirty thousand. She'd never been used to seeing him as a child, his eyes flaring, a comic book held with both hands.

She picked up the blanket from the sofa and folded it, shifted the stools back, and cleaned up the crumbs and leftovers from lunch, switched off Modugno singing 'Musetto' on the record player and opened up the sewing-kit cupboard in the lounge. She unrolled it and took in her needles and spools and reels and fancy threads, the satin, blue and vermilion, the three pairs of fabric scissors, the fabric samples, her surgical tools. Even though she hardly worked any more and her knuckles hurt more often, she knew that her artistry and speed of execution had remained: handling deer skin and jersey, silk – never fold it twice – risking a pattern on denim, and organza, and brocade – the hardest for her tiny fingers – she had adapted everything to the vanity of her ladies. Her customers had come to Via delle Leghe for some small talk too, asking her about a purchase in Via Monte Napoleone, telling her about children, crimes and punishments. They really had been her novels.

She pulled out the large-eyed needle, chose the blue spool,

cut the thread with her teeth – never do that in front of someone – switched on the light above the stove. She closed one
eyelid and pierced the eye on the first try, she always raised one
corner of her mouth when she did. She went to the bedroom
wardrobe, took out the satin and the *rebrodé* lace she hadn't
used, sat on the edge of the mattress, stared at the seams she'd
match together and moved her gaze to the photo on her bedside
table. She sewed without looking down, her digits harpooning
the fabrics while she observed the faces of her early wedding:
Franco spooked in front of the camera, her holding him under-
arm, enjoying herself. She turned to the reverse of the fabric,
without losing sight of those two twenty-year-olds in love, on
Lake Como. She lowered her head and looked at the stitching:
the two fabrics were now one, and she was still an excellent
seamstress. She stood up slowly, sighed, and went to the writing
desk they all used as a general surface at the end of the corridor.
It had three small drawers; she opened the last one and looked
for the keys with the frosted ring.

She opened her front door, headed past the ground floor
into the cellars. Theirs was the second-to-last on the right, and
in the dim light it took her two tries to get the key into the
lock. The damp smell stung her nose and she raised a hand
to cover her mouth, reached for the switch under the jam jar
shelf. The light came on in the room she hadn't been in for a
year and a half. She could hardly see the lower shelves, and she
remembered they held vases of buttons by colour and folders
of manuals to old electric appliances. She moved forward, her
conviction growing step by step: take the fruit crate out, remove
the blanket, drag it into the middle of the room, right under the
light, and crouch down to leaf through the first comic on
the pile, *Capitan Miki* no. 217, find the Bormio 1976 postcard
hiding inside its cover – *You would've loved the lodges with their
pine scent, yours, Clara.*

97

There it was, in front of her, she read it again, and knew she could continue. She pulled out the second one and the third and all twenty-one of them and she felt angry again, because he'd never thought of getting rid of them. She collected them, stood up again and held them against her as she switched the light off and headed out. She left the cellar, took the stairs and got back home. She placed them on the writing desk. It was weird, she felt excited: was this freedom, then?

Sofia was staring at her father reading the story, bent over the kitchen table, with the cigarette smoking from the ashtray. The fog had come in from the north and had taken over Rimini. He finished reading, folded the seven pages over and took them into the bedroom. The cigarette was left to air on the table, its trails almost merging with the haze outside the window.

Her father came back and said, 'Let's go to the sea.'

They stepped out, the Ina Casa swallowed in whiteness. Sofia held him close and they reached their car, still the Renault Scénic they'd used to load up the hardware stock from the last move before handing over to the new managers. That had been right after her mother's death.

They drove slowly to the town centre, along the walls where the Saturday morning market was held and past the Ponte di Tiberio. They crossed the station underpass, took the street with the villas and the hidden gardens and reached the promenade, parked in front of the public beach.

They got out and walked along Rimini's last concrete strip; two fishing boats were docked and a man was washing their bows. Her father's steps were light and she kept at arm's length, felt as if she was walking by herself. As they reached the dock, they could hear the Adriatic crashing against the rocks and sat at the base of the yellow lighthouse. Her father touched her chin, then stared across the water.

She was also looking at the water. Then she asked him what he thought of the story.

He was wearing his cotton scarf over the denim jacket, did up two buttons. 'Was Mum really singing Vanoni in the car that day?'

She nodded.

He smiled.

'What's so funny?'

'In 1987 Vanoni played a concert in Piazza Cavour. Your uncle was with us and your mother made us climb over the fence to get in.'

'You, trespassing?'

'Did you know she chose the overall for the hardware store after that concert?'

Sofia shook her head.

'She had a black one before that. But that night Vanoni wore a blue coat that looked just like a working overall.'

She was staring at him.

He loosened his scarf. 'Your mum has been happy too, Sofia.'

'With me?'

'Especially with you.'

She was tempted to sit closer to him, slide her arm under his; she used to and now she'd forgotten how to. She listened to him breathing, the long, cavernous breathing, the smell of his aftershave overpowering the fog; she smelled him like she did back in the shop. She must've been seven or eight years old and she could smell her dad climbing up the ladder and saying to her, 'Will you look after the shop when I'm an old man?'

Andrea would reply, 'But Dad, you'll never be an old man,' only to immediately go back to colouring the *He-Man* album, finishing off the leftover focaccia from his school break. Even

99

now, every time he'd sit on the newsagent's stool, the image of his young father would pop up.

He watched him as he rearranged the bi-monthlies in the display behind them, his precise fingers making sure the ones with pictures had their title visible from behind the others, while his mother chatted from the doorway.

Andrea held his wounded hand in his lap and served a customer with the other. He'd left home at dawn.

'Where are you going?' Cristina had asked from the bed and he'd replied that she had nothing to worry about.

'I'll deal with my brother,' she'd said.

He hadn't replied.

'Andrea, promise me you won't go?'

He'd nodded, then he'd gone to the bathroom and washed the soil out of his fingernails until his skin was raw. He'd taken the antibiotics and carefully changed his dressing, shoved the bloodstained clothes into a plastic bag, thrown them out in the communal bin outside the building and had headed off. He'd never stopped thinking about César.

He helped his parents until lunchtime, then they took shifts to grab some food at the Bar Rock. He went with his mother, invited her to sit on the bench, and sat opposite her, terrified of her already knowing – she always knew everything. His mother, her ruddy cheeks like a *montanara*, despite being from Vigevano, told him her worries about her husband's heart condition – 'your father is so stubborn and you're just like him' – and asked him why he hadn't called them from the hospital.

He told her Cristina was there.

'I just want to know that you're OK. Are you OK?' she asked, lowering her sandwich onto the plate.

He did the same. He really wanted to buy her a cocktail dress and see her beautiful and tell her she deserved all of that; he stood up and walked around the table, sat down next to her.

'I'm OK,' he said, and he let her hug him.

He wanted to ask her for the car and leave immediately, but instead, after they finished eating he headed back to the shop and moved the comics closer to the car magazines, reorganised the used books crates, his hand throbbing; he served customers and helped his father with the newspaper sales. He asked him if he could take the car. His father told him he'd got petrol the day before, asked him how he could change gear with the bandages and he replied that it wasn't an issue and took the keys out of the small drawer.

He drove to Corvetto, barely able to manage the gear shift, clenched and unclenched his hand at all the red lights, to get used to the pain, stopped as he reached the ring road. He got off it at San Donato, slowed down and saw that the football pitch was empty. He kept going and reached the farmstead; none of their cars were there either. He called Cristina, telling her he was just at the doctor's to check on his hand, though it was already hurting less, then he'd be at his parents' for dinner.

'What did you tell them?'

'A kitchen accident.'

'Did they believe you?'

'I don't know, probably not.'

'My brother isn't picking up . . .'

'I'm going in now.'

'I'll talk to him before tonight.'

They hung up. He got out of the car and hurried towards the farmstead, climbed over the stooping side of the fence and reached the courtyard. It was a dusty arena, the shovels they'd used to bury César still there, next to some buckets. He looked inside the doghouse and saw the chain spiralled up. Two chains, really, linked by a snap-hook; he unlinked them and took the shorter one. He dragged it outside and wrapped it around his strong hand. He headed back to the road and the car, started the engine and reversed, parking it just before the bend. He turned on the radio and waited though he had no idea if Cristina's brother would come. He often spent time at their father's; an old man, they took turns to look after him. He gave himself until sunset and started listening to a news programme then a Carboni song, he'd liked Carboni since the Assago concert. He reread Margherita's message. They'd chatted a bit, then she'd called him and out of the blue invited him out for a coffee at the weekend. He turned off the radio and lowered the reclining seat a little.

When he later spotted the Ford Fiesta, he'd almost dozed off, his hand was throbbing again and he had two missed calls from Cristina. He waited for the Fiesta to move onto the property and be parked and the boy to step out of the car. He left his car, the chain dangling by his leg.

He knocked three times and as soon as the door opened he was on him. He knew how to, he'd already done this, and the truth was that his body admired subjugation. The resistant muscles, the speed in his joints, the precise reflexes – something helped him in moments of cruelty. He shoved and the other fell through the kitchen doorway; he let him get up again, heard him say, 'The fuck!' and hit him on his side with the chain. As soon as he was on the floor again he whipped his legs. He saw him foam at the mouth, turn around, push on his arms and collapse. He smacked him hard on the shin and stood over him, watching this boy his own age hardly moving and hearing his strangled screams, trying to touch his knee and lift his head to look at his broken bones. He hit him again, leaned against the table.

The dressing was fine and his good hand was burning from the chain's bite. The other boy was moaning and holding his broken leg. Before Cristina, there had been him: meeting up at the Magnolia for a gig, getting involved in coke to raise some funds in the days that followed, grabbing a couple of beers while researching the internet for MMA fights, splitting their bets, getting used to animal wounds.

'You broke my leg!' He'd been able to prop himself against the wall, breathing again.

Andrea let the chain loose onto the floor and spotted the sofa, with its cigarette burns and an empty ashtray on the armrests, a pack of cards and a pack of biscuits on the cushion.

'You broke my leg!' The light sank in his eyes. He dragged himself to the cupboard and grabbed on to the surface, first his fingers, then his forearm, pulling himself up, one of the two legs still holding his weight. 'You killed that dog as much as I did!'

Andrea wasn't looking at him.

He was still holding on to the cupboard, an uneasy flamingo. He let himself slide down with a groan. 'You killed him as much as I did.'

Andrea moved past him, stepped outside. Cristina was sitting on the first step. She was staring at the road, her hair tied up to one side. She raised her head but didn't look at him, stared at the open door. He said nothing, headed to the gate. He was tired. Before he reached the road he looked back at her; she was heading in to her brother and he felt a pang of fear, just like every time he'd had to say goodbye to something.

Margherita weighed up the loss of her husband as she headed into the office. She was sure that if she kept this up with Andrea, her marriage would be exposed to a violation. Inebriation, Némirowsky would've said. She unlocked the door, then turned off the alarm and went to the bathroom. She said it out loud to her reflection, 'You're a cougar, going after twenty-six-year-olds.'

She felt different, more grounded, and knew that her actual fear was that of losing Carlo from inside her, a fraction at a time.

That was why she had told him about Andrea just before the orgasm, hoping that their intimacy would link their separate compartments. After all, what would a new body take away from her marriage? She might even not like it. She might even find that it would rekindle the spark in their relationship. She really hated cheap psychology: linking betrayal back to unhappiness. She would've betrayed anyone for Andrea's broad shoulders. For his behind. Because he was young. Because he was shy and she could help him discover something about himself. And most of all: because of the desire the boy had for her. Seeing herself be wanted in a primitive way, the way it was before engagements and altars and mortgages. Her undoing was not the admission of turmoil – she was admitting it, after all – but rather that of not being able to accept compromises, that she could touch the physiotherapist but her husband could not touch any other woman. She had revealed herself as a despot of a woman, and she had no intention of going back on it. She had sandpapered the annoyance at the bathroom misunderstanding, but she was far away from having forgotten about it. Was Andrea a reward? Andrea was a craving.

She had messaged him and he'd replied in a restrained way, except for the ellipsis that ended the sentence where he told her he'd see her on Monday for her session. Carlo once told her that ellipses are a weakness: writers use them when they're hesitating on a page. Then she'd read *The Bad Girl* and had realised that those three dots meant something else entirely. Vargas Llosa's souls used them as foreplay to revolutions. Three dots for a loving intimacy. Three dots for a political uprising. Three dots for a seduction. And so she'd called Andrea. They'd talked about his wounded hand and her leg, she'd invited him out to a coffee at the weekend. He'd replied that yes, he would . . .

She opened her notepad, tore out a piece of paper and wrote down the list of priorities for the day. Number one: Concordia.

Number two: coordinate three visits (NB the three-room flat in Via Morgagni). Number three: focus on her mother-in-law's birthday the following day.

She went over her notes for Concordia from the previous night: a white lie leading to a win-win situation. She'd shown it to Carlo and she'd found it extremely comforting to discover herself so daring and that he supported her with no preaching. She scrolled through her contacts to the owner's name, sat on the edge of her seat, got a reply on the third ring, greeted her warmly and found a tinge of coldness in the woman's voice. She changed her strategy, and instead of reading out the negative list of failed visits, she lied about having some good news: a couple was really interested in the flat.

'Oh, that's such a relief, Margherita! I had a really bad feeling.'

'Why? Don't you trust us?'

'I do trust you.' A pause. 'It's just that, the sooner the better. Who's this couple?'

She explained that they had no children, he was a lawyer, she was a primary school teacher – who knows where she got that from, primary school – and that they'd had the same doubts about the lack of a lift and that the roof was a terrace, their fears were that it wouldn't insulate well enough – but the light in the flat had charmed them. Halfway through the visit the teacher had said, 'This is it, this is my home.'

As soon as she'd said it she feared she'd gone too far, but the owner let out a tiny yelp of happiness.

'But still, I can't guarantee anything, especially on the price.'

'No lower than five thirty, you know that.'

'I'll do what I can, you just think about it some more.'

'I have thought about it.'

Before hanging up, Margherita had risked a comment about Majorca: was there a strange fog over the island too? No fog, just the wind sweeping the coast from east to west.

She hung up, held a hand to her head and decided to cross off that other nuisance too. She looked up her mother-in-law's number. On the first ring, she reached the edge of her seat again.

'Marghe,' said the voice from the other side.

She'd called her Marghe since their first meeting – who would've thought from a cashmere-clad, one-quarter-English lady. Her mother-in-law could make small talk about Breton oysters and construction works, the tenderness towards older women pulling out a shopping cart and finding out one of the wheels didn't work: it was a liveliness that didn't convince her. She'd never fully opened up with her.

'We're ready to celebrate; how are you feeling Loretta?'

'I heard about your mother.'

Margherita fell silent.

'I just heard from Carlo, he told me. But I don't understand: what does it mean that she *doesn't know* if she'll make it?'

Margherita stretched her leg out under the desk, it was itching in bursts. 'She's not feeling too well.'

'In what way?'

'Bit of a flu, mixed with some melancholy, I think.'

'It would do her good to spend some time together with us.'

'I'll see what I can do.'

'I'll call her.'

'Leave it to me, Loretta. Mothers still listen to their daughters.'

Her mother-in-law laughed. 'Sure, like Simona did with that guy.'

'Mamadou is a good man.'

'But how are you, dear? I heard about the house in Concordia.'

Margherita apologised, told her she had to go as someone had just stepped into the agency. She promised she'd be on time tomorrow for the party – though she knew she wouldn't be, reassured her that she'd call back in the afternoon – though she knew she wouldn't. Even more so now, after realising that Carlo was keeping Loretta informed about things that she shouldn't be informed about. Her husband's excesses towards his mother were his excesses in university bathrooms and the excesses that had allowed her to fall in love with him: an uneasy landscape of a man, full of sudden route changes. Carlo's contradictions . . . she'd always trusted Carlo's contradictions. After the death of her father, she'd seen the same in her mother, too: she'd moved the Singer aside and stepped off the kitchen stool, into a season of further gentle settlings, learning how to say no, sighing out loud, keeping her feet on the coffee table in the lounge. She should try too, at thirty-five: a good investment for her later years.

When Margherita's colleagues got to the office, they held their weekly meeting in the small conference room, then Gabriele headed out again for two visits and Isabella hid away to deal with some recalls, and she lowered her head back to her computer. Margherita started typing up two descriptions for properties they'd been assigned, opened up Facebook and looked around a bit – she didn't check it often, her profile had no photo – both she and Carlo agreed to care too little about that stuff. She clicked on Sofia Casadei's profile. Her final post had been last week's photo of the roofs of Milan – twenty-seven likes. She closed everything down and paced back and forth for a bit; it helped her leg. She sat down again, adjusted the settings of the online ads and studied her notes for the Morgagni visit. It was a spacious three-roomer, ninety square metres and if it looked anything like the photos she could sell it for three hundred thousand, about a twelve-thousand share for the agency. If 2009 continued according to plans, she could afford herself a salary of two thousand one hundred euro a month. Carlo brought home one thousand four hundred, plus the pocket money that the Pentecostes gave him in secret and that she refused to consider in the family budget. They could get a mortgage of eight or nine hundred for

Concordia, using the thirty-two thousand in savings as a down payment.

She ate a sandwich at her desk and got ready in the early afternoon for her visit, holding her coat under her arm – she wanted fresh April air and no family budgets for a bit – said goodbye to Isabella and headed out onto Via Spontini. She walked into the Morgagni gardens and along the boules area, past its players. She stopped to look at them for a while and they lifted her spirits. She rested her back against an acacia and showed her neck to the sun.

How are you doing, Margherita? She asked herself that whenever directions could suddenly change, like a train track on which her father used to work, deciding the train's route. He'd warn her: choose the right track for you. The right track for her had always been the direction of others.

A player launched his boule and she set off again, crossing the gardens. She spotted the owner of Morgagni waiting for her at number 9. She was capable of forming a connection on a first meeting, letting the owner vent, letting them guide her on all fronts, only speaking up to reassure them they were in good hands. When the moment came to establish the financial request for the property, she'd tear down all illusions, formulating the real estimate plus the negotiating margin and adding her catchphrase, 'Trust me.' The important part was her tone of voice: calm, spontaneous, no exclamation marks.

It took them half an hour to complete the visit; the flat was worth the three sixty and the owner was a docile seventy-year-old. He shared with her that he'd use the money to move to Liguria and help his grandson through university. They agreed upon a formal meeting back at the office, said their goodbyes. She would get him Liguria and his grandson's studies – she could see the outcome with relative ease. Having a good deal in hand always lifted her mood for the day and, as she had no other appointments after this, she called to check that someone was actually in the office then hurried along the gardens with a current that ran from her heart to her head. Any other moment, she would've called it foolishness.

She walked up to Piazzale Bacone, past the swimming pool where she used to swim before joining the gym, took in Buenos Aires with its windows reminding her of teenage afternoons with friends she didn't now see often, almost all swallowed up by engagements and marriages. She stopped for a coffee in Piazza Argentina, bought a pack of chewing gum, then headed towards the buildings in Piazzale Loreto, with their red neon clocks. She turned onto Via Porpora – and that was when she admitted she was going to see him.

Going to see him, going to see him, with this breath of *arabica* and mint. She felt the urge to slow down but not due to her leg, not out of fear. She watched the delivery vans finishing their rounds for the day, the lights in the entry halls starting to come on, restaurant staff on the doorsteps, Milan's hive buzzing: these souls chasing normality just as she was about to confront it. She surprised herself with how calm her heart was, an impatience rising from her stomach instead.

She reached the door, looked down at where he had sat while she had gone to buy the antibiotics. She crouched down and waited: bumping into him on his way home would've made everything more natural, but he didn't return within the following ten minutes, nor twenty. She should've lost her nerve, should've called him, but instead she stayed where she was, legs closed and head resting against the door, holding her hands and rotating her engagement ring and her wedding ring, then she stood up. She looked for the name on the doorbell. Some just had numbers, the only one possible had AM written in pen on a slip of paper under the glass cover.

She rang and waited on her toes, her cheek against the

intercom grid. No answer. She lowered herself back on her heels as a voice came through, and she lurched closer again. 'Andrea? Is that you?'

'Who's this?'

'Margherita.'

'Margherita,' he said back.

'The leg, the hospital, the coffee this weekend that is actually now, without warning,' she listed, calmly. 'That Margherita.'

The intercom was buzzing and he could hear the traffic from Via Porpora. Andrea pushed the button to open the door. He went back to the bedroom, slipped on a pair of jeans and a sweatshirt, picked up the clothes from earlier that afternoon and chucked them into the washing machine. His head felt heavy; he checked his bandages and noticed a stain spreading. The other hand was marked by the chain at the wrist. The farmstead was no more and Cristina's brother and Cristina were shadows . . . he opened the door and moved aside, waiting on the landing: Margherita appeared on the stairs of the floor below, breathing heavily with her coat on her arm.

'Hi,' she said.

He gestured to her to come inside and headed to the kitchen, took the dirty mugs out of the sink, rinsed them out and started making some coffee. He could sense her behind him, scraping a chair on the floor as he filled the moka pot and lit the hob. He turned around: she was sitting with her bag on the floor and her coat on her lap, her fringe covering one eye. She was staring at his dressing, and his face, and he felt as if they shared the same embarrassment.

Then she stood up, moved close to him, caressed where his wrist was still marked by the chain, then his mouth; he raised his arm and held her close to him and for one moment he felt that Margherita was his girlfriend.

*

When Carlo got under the bedsheets, his wife's breathing was already deep with sleep. He'd found her quiet over dinner, but so was he – the Pentecostes' gathering the following day always shut them down, as if having to save up the energy needed.

He waited until his eyes got used to the darkness; Margherita's shape was small and curled up and he wanted to tell her that he'd spoken to his mother about Concordia that morning, tell her about his visit to Anna that afternoon: he was hiding a lot from her by now. Same with Franco's *Tex*, slid between two photography books on the bedside table. He turned to look for it; his phone was next to it and he imagined it light up, finally something from Sofia, *Let's meet tomorrow in this place at this time*. He'd be able to fall asleep content, planning all the little tweaks for tomorrow's schedule: a longer shower, choosing an outfit, coming up with an excuse that would allow him a couple of hours out of the house.

When he woke up, around eight, he saw no message had come in. He lingered in bed. He wanted to message Sofia, de-sisted, went into the kitchen and called his sister to remind her to bring the gift and arrive on time.

'I will, but Mamadou isn't coming.'

'He has to!'

'He says he might pop in after lunch.'

'Put him on.'

'Let it go.'

'Simona.'

'Anna didn't want to come either, right?'

'But she is now.'

'Let it go, Carlo, come on.'

When Loretta Pentecoste had found out that her daughter had been impregnated by an African – her words, *impregnated* and *African* – she'd run over to her baby to bring her back to reason, with no success, only to stop talking to her, then trying to make amends only after holding her grandchild – 'He's a little latte, isn't he cute?' – and had finally accepted things as they were, realising her husband was internalising the anger towards their rebellious second-born.

He hung up and waited for Margherita to rise before getting things started. They'd looked at each other in passing since waking up and she'd hummed a song by Cesare Cremonini in the bathroom – he always liked hearing her sing. They headed out towards the florist with the radio on in the car.

'How are you doing?' he asked her as they waited for their lilies.

'Good!' She smiled. 'How about you?'

He nodded and took the lilies, they got back in the car and reached Città Studi with the windows lowered, Milan's sky was cobalt blue, and the radio only played ads. He turned down the volume and told her about Mamadou not coming.

'Want me to call Simona?'

'It's OK, thanks.'

Margherita got out in front of the Pentecostes' house, with the lilies, and he headed off to find a parking spot in Piazza Aspromonte. He found one on the short side of the square. He tapped on his phone *Can you make it today then?* and sent it as he walked back to Margherita. He saw his mother-in-law step out of a taxi in front of the entrance. Anna waved at them, clutching her bag and covering her perm with the other hand.

'These taxi drivers keep racing, but I told him I was scared this time.' She kissed her daughter then came over to him: 'I thought I'd add something for your mother.' She rummaged around in her bag, pulled out a wad of tissue paper and un-wrapped it: it was a crocheted bracelet framing an antique brooch.

'You shouldn't have.'

'Of course I had to!' She nodded. 'Just to spite those who believe seventy-year-olds can't wear bling.' Margherita had already rung the doorbell and was holding the door open with her foot. They got in the lift and Anna straightened out her daughter's jacket and her own. 'I got this,' she whispered.

His mother greeted them, said his sister and Nico were in the lounge, and Carlo headed for the sofa as he felt his phone buzz in his pocket. He didn't check it; he lay down on the geometrical pattern of the rug, grabbed his nephew's ankles and pretended to bite them, dragging him over himself. 'Whose is this little man? His uncle's, or his mummy's?'

The kid whined; he picked him up and kissed the curls on his neck, stood up, and they wandered around the flat. He could feel the joy of having a reply on his phone; they lingered over the red glass table – the shrimp appetisers were already out, as was the *nervetti* salad.

'Nico, do you know where we could go now? Let's go to uncle's teenage bedroom.' The kid whined again, and they moved into the bedroom area, sliding through the second-to-last door. 'Here we are!' He showed him the desk wedged between two wardrobes. 'Here we are! You know what happened here? Your uncle here was killing himself trying to make Grandad happy by studying to become a lawyer.' He walked him around and sat on his old bed, shifting the kid to his knee and bouncing him up and down. Nico arched his back, and he moved him to the floor and held his hands, helping him to walk between those empty walls. He'd never hung up any posters, except for a world map, which was still there. He stared at it and with his free hand he got out his phone. She'd asked him to the café three hours from now.

He looked at his nephew. His tiny presence soothed him. As soon as his sister had got pregnant everyone had told her, 'You know what you have to do.' And when she hadn't, they'd said,

'Your problem now.' And he'd also told her, 'Your problem now.'

The same words of his father, head physician Domenico Pentecoste, the tall man with the kind voice, mild eyes – and irreversible imperatives. He'd actually been a caring father, too: staying up late playing with train sets, enacting Orient Express scenes, letting him drive the Lancia Delta when he was practising for his driving licence, sandwiches for dinner after seeing Inter play at the Meazza Stadium. He'd voted for Craxi and Occhetto and D'Alema, he collected pipes but never smoked one. Of his grandson, once the storm had passed, he'd said, 'He'll be a bold little thing.'

Nico headed for the top drawer of the desk, trying to open it. Carlo helped him and they found some coloured pens and a stapler. 'Let's go back, huh, Nico? What do you say? I think you might be hungry.'

'He's already eaten three times today.'

He turned to see his sister in the doorway.

She stepped forward. 'You should try bringing one into the world.'

Nico noticed his mother and stretched out his arms; she kissed him but left him with her brother. 'I know, I know, your jobs, your books, your houses, your careers.'

'The moment's not right.'

'Scared, huh?'

'Always am.'

'Your wife's never scared.' His sister moved closer to the Smurf figurine collection on the shelf, flicked Brainy Smurf off it. 'She's doing pretty great in the lounge.'

'What do you mean?'

'Concordia.'

'Jesus Christ.'

'They had it ready.'

116

He nuzzled his nephew. 'I'll head through.'

'Let Dad roast a bit too, I beg you.'

'I already have my own stuff going on, Simona.'

'Still?' She put Brainy Smurf back in its place and shook the Eiffel Tower snow globe. 'Don't hurt her, Carlo.'

He stared at her. 'Easy for you to say.'

'It is easy.' She flicked her hair from one side to the other; her small mouth took away from her looks. 'Unless, of course.'

'Unless of course what?'

'Unless of course you're falling in love.'

'No.'

'Say it again.'

'No.'

She picked up her son. 'Don't hurt her.'

'You're telling *me*?'

They stared at each other, and smiled. She was heading out with her kid when she froze at the door, still staring at her brother. He was also still looking at her. He got up from the bed and hugged her from behind, like when they were younger and they had their own way of fitting and he'd squeeze tighter. 'More,' she said, and he squeezed, then followed her into the lounge. Margherita was sitting next to Pentecoste, Anna was trying to fasten the bracelet on Loretta's wrist.

'Where were you two? Where are your manners?' Loretta was admiring her gift: 'Look at this gorgeous thing she gave me.'

'It's wonderful, isn't it?' Margherita looked at Carlo. 'Your father has very kindly offered to help us out with Concordia, but I told him that—'

'Everyone, to the table! I've made a variation of the shrimp sauce that is to die for.' Loretta peeled herself off the sofa.

'Food time!' His sister headed to the dining room with the kid.

'All I said was that I can help. Carlo, you know that Indian fund?' Pentecoste adjusted his glasses onto his nose.

'No, of course not.'

'I put some spice in the shrimp sauce.'

'It's a stable enough fund, but I'm worried that the dollar will struggle. A bricks-and-mortar investment is profitable for us too.'

'And the *nervetti* salad, of course!'

'I explained to your father that we want to try sticking it out, even with a significant mortgage,' Margherita said, nodding to herself.

Pentecoste moved to the window. 'A 95 per cent mortgage isn't *significant*. It's a mortgage on your lives.'

'I'm telling you the same thing, Dad: we want to do this ourselves.'

'Such foolish pride.' His father was observing Piazza Aspromonte. 'It's not your fault that your jobs are not worth much.'

'I love my job, Domenico.' Margherita had stood up too. 'And I happen to think it's worth a fair bit.'

'You have ambition and outlook. Carlo does not.'

'My husband loves teaching.'

'OK, enough, all of you: it's my birthday and I'm asking you to come to sit at the table.' Loretta took Anna by the hand; Anna graciously freed herself.

Pentecoste moved closer to his son. 'I know that you love teaching, but six hours of love a week are not enough. And your travel brochures, how much can they ever make you? I mean,' he stared at him, 'you have to face the truth. That's all.'

Nico's shrieks were coming through from the dining room. Simona called them and Loretta joined her.

Carlo sat on the sofa. 'And what exactly is the truth, Dad? I'm curious.'

Pentecoste opened his arms and let them fall back down to his sides. 'Anna, help me out here?'

'Free.' She had an answer ready and was surprised at herself. 'Our kids are free.'

'To become hostages to a bank!'

'To do this one day, and something else another.' She showed him her fingers. 'They can avoid being a seamstress and a doctor all their lives.'

'They're high-risk capital.' Pentecoste removed his glasses and rubbed his eyelids. 'We also had bullshit plans in our minds, but at least we saw them through, is all I'm saying.'

Anna moved one step closer to him. 'And what I'm saying, Domenico, is this: you do not make your wife wait on her birthday.'

'Go sit down, Dad, go on.' Carlo looked at him from the sofa.

Pentecoste looked back, took off his glasses and put them back on, and headed to the dining room. Anna followed him, but first raised a corner of her mouth to her son-in-law.

Carlo didn't move. His father's glasses, taking them off and putting them back – it was bothering him: he was right. Off and on: he could've easily talked about literature with a law degree. Off and on: he shouldn't tell anyone he wanted to write a novel, so that he wouldn't lose face in the case of failure. Off and on: that evening, still a teenager, when Inter had won two-nil against Roma in the UEFA cup, and in front of the screen his dad had said, 'Rather than scoring a point you would kick it out of the pitch to avoid hurting your opponents, even though you have the skill of Matthäus.' A son with a natural instinct for quitting: the high-risk capital.

Margherita said they had to head to lunch and attempted a smile. He reached to grab her hand, letting her know he'd stay there just a minute longer. Just now, as she left, he looked at the linden tree in Piazza Aspromonte that appeared in the window. The tree where he'd had to make himself be found whenever his mother called from the balcony, in school-free afternoons, when he hung out with the other neighbourhood kids.

He stood up and joined the others. They were standing around the table, nibbling: the mother had two rhythms for holiday meals, buffet first and table meal second, assigning seating with care. He'd been reserved the outside corner, close to the door, next to Margherita, and opposite the birthday girl, almost obscured by the lilies now put into a vase. She was his mother, a woman so buried into manners that she allowed herself minor subversions: tapping her foot under the table, twisting her watch around her wrist, winking at one of her two children, hoping to hold back any potential rudeness, serving food to interrupt heated conversations. She had the gift of placating any hint of revolt. She did so for a good part of the meal, ensuring it would be a smooth birthday, starting with silencing her husband – and with Anna next to her, and Margherita, and her sister and Nico serving as catalysts for everyone's attention.

All Carlo cared about was the phone in his pocket and the passing of time. He would be there on time; he would tell his wife he needed to be alone for a bit, go for a walk. It wouldn't be the first time after a meal at his parents. As he was being served a plate of risotto, as they cheered to Loretta Pentecoste and another hundred years of good health, the idea of Sofia built up and started burning in his chest. What if he gave up on her, if he messaged her that he wouldn't make it, that something had come up, removed her number from his contacts, imagining her in Rimini forever, limiting the tingling to his fraenum and the tachycardia to his neck? What if he redirected all of this energy onto his wife, fucking hard and good as they knew how to do, going out to the cinema and a meal, validating their family plans, maybe a child, definitely a child? What if he did that? The truth was that he had come to understand how much their erotic urges transmigrated at times: it was a limited, exact quantity and giving to one woman meant taking away from the other; giving to both meant half each.

He helped his mother clear the table of the risotto plates, brought the stew onto the table, along with the sauces and the mustard ice-cream, then headed to the bathroom. Margherita's gaze followed him and he noticed; he chose the one with the grey tiles and locked himself inside. He stood in front of the granite sink, undid his belt, and pulled down his trousers. He checked he was tidy, the smell, the resting but ready shape, hiding back into the cotton and the denim, checking himself in the mirror, the heavy bags under his eyes, his ruffled hair, the hint of redness in his cheeks. And the cake and his mother blowing out her candles, the clapping, twenty-five minutes later: the moment when he decided he couldn't stop himself.

He looked for Margherita while he was handed his slice of raspberry cream cake. She was sitting lopsided on her chair, her fringe held at bay by a clip, laughing with Nico in her childish and sensual way, God how he loved her. He slowly ate his cake, then his sister handed him Nico and disappeared into the lounge, came back with the gift for their mother. Loretta unwrapped it not without some effort, her hands hesitant. She sighed and found some scissors to help out. A round of applause, and he breathed onto Nico's neck and whispered, 'Uncle's going now.'

He calculated he'd be a little late, allowed himself not to warn and let things happen, while in the lift he told Margherita he needed a walk.

'Alone,' she finished for him.

He nodded.

Anna snuck a hand into her bag, removed it and closed the zip, asked her daughter, 'Can you take me for a ride?'

Margherita held the door open. 'What if your father is right?'

'My father should've been the party secretary.'

Anna took her daughter's arm.

Margherita patted her mum's hand. 'How long will you be, Carlo?'

'Just until I walk it off.'

She lingered over that, then headed with Anna to the car.

He set off between the low houses with pastel walls, the neighbourhood of families and students; it still looked like the one where he'd grown up, with its shoemakers and haberdasheries, the wide streets and the sudden inlets; but everything switched off at night and it became the phony Milan he didn't love. He'd realised that the first time he had moved out, when he'd settled into a flat in Porta Venezia, taking in the new architecture, hanging outside while others slept, following the echoes of a party, the ones for the road, resting against the corner of his street and seeing a city as worried as him.

It took him ten minutes to reach the taxi stands in Piazzale Piola and the closer he got the more he felt a trepidation that was the bitterness of not being able to escape who you are. He asked to get out just before the San Nazaro basilica, squeezed past the Indian rotisserie and headed quickly for the Statale. The café was there at the end, its windows half lit and no one in sight. He got closer and saw her. She was inside, sitting at one of the tables, leafing through a magazine. Her hair was amber and her tight jeans ended in two wide-heeled boots. He tapped on the glass.

Sofia stepped outside and he apologised for being late, thanked her for coming. She told him she had a train at six and she still had to go via her place to send off her books with MailBoxes, they were already in two boxes; she'd leave the keys for the owner – at least he'd found another student so he'd only lose one month in rent. She kept drawing a curved line with the tip of her boot, looking up every now and then. Her hair fell to one side – to smell it while holding her from behind as he'd done in the bathroom. He asked her if he could help her with the boxes. He got embarrassed as he was speaking to her and his voice took a strange accent.

'Thanks, but I'll just do two trips.'

'Sure.'

He invited her for a walk; she said yes. They ended up on the square; he asked her again if she needed help with the boxes.

She laughed.

He laughed too. 'I have strong arms,' and he showed her.

They walked for a bit without talking, side by side, she'd got ahead of him by the time they reached the lights in Piazza Diaz and he'd watched her walk; he would've done anything to have her. He took out some chewing gum from his pocket and offered her a piece, asked if she wanted to take a taxi. She stopped, considering it, then nodded and as soon as they were inside the cab she told the driver the address – Via Pollaiuolo 2, Isola neighbourhood – she said it twice, Via Pollaiuolo 2, Isola. She settled in the seat and crossed her legs. They spoke very little during the ride. He was looking out of the window, thought he saw Anna and Margherita in the Polo just around the corner of the Chinese neighbourhood; he looked again and saw it was a Lancia Y with no one he knew on board. When they arrived, he paid the driver. She tried stopping him, he pretended to push her out of the car; it worked, and Sofia laughed. They got out of the taxi and found themselves in front of a straw-coloured building.

'It's the first place I found.'

'The Frida was one of my clubs.' He pointed to the inner courtyard opposite where there was the patio of a café with dark, wide windows.

'There's no lift.'

'See? You did need a hand with the books.'

Step after step after step admiring her hips, her calves in the tight jeans, the boots pointing into the steps, feeling uncertain and driven by her. He helped himself up with the handrail and they stopped at the second landing to catch their breath. This time he preceded her and reached out his hand to heave her up. She grabbed it and they reached her floor entwined. She let him go, rummaged in her bag for the keys, opened the door, and said, 'Come in.'

They found themselves in a small hall with a tree-shaped coat stand, its branches empty, a small wrought-iron table, a kitchenette.

She stepped into the next room; the window overlooked the Isola roofs and let in the April sun and she'd planted some beautiful primroses in a pretty pot. The two boxes were at the end of the bed, open, a roll of tape and scissors next to them.

'Let's close them up,' he said, and crouched down, picking up the tape, and thought of nothing else but doing a good job of it. He caught sight of a Fenoglio, *La paga del sabato*, and other books from the course, felt her looking at him from the middle of the room.

'Go back to Fenoglio, if you get a chance.' He closed up the boxes, then sat on the edge of the bed and undid his jacket, Sofia was still staring at him.

'Thank you,' she said.

'Come here,' he said.

Sofia kept her eyes on him.

'Come on.'

She did, her head slightly to one side and her hair in her face; he reached out his hand to find hers, like they'd done on the stairs. He pulled her to him; she stayed on her feet and he hugged her to him from the bed. He stood and caressed her nape and let his hand fall down her neck, his other hand

124

between her shoulders, holding her. She curled up against his chest.

'We can't,' she said.

But he plunged his nose into her hair – it smelled clean – he lowered his hands to her waist, embraced it, that small, taut waist, he turned her around so her back faced him, like that time in the bathroom, and he held her hips. She pulled her shirt up just a little and he could feel the warm, smooth skin, her short breath. He grabbed her butt, its shape and feel. He pressed it against him and just then, as he could feel her press back against him, she whispered, 'We can't,' and stopped.

'Sofia.'

She turned to face him. 'We can't.'

He moved closer with his mouth and she opened her lips and he had her again, her mouth and soft tongue . . . he was kissing her, then she pulled away from him.

'It's fucked up, Carlo.'

Her face was red. She flicked her hair onto the other shoulder and reached her hand out to his face, to his burning cheek, she caressed it. He tried kissing her again, but she stepped back. He sat back down, his limbs felt like lead, he rested his hands on the bed. Then he stood up, he was looking down at her now, and she was looking back at him.

'It's fucked up,' she said.

'It's not fucked up.'

'It's fucked up.'

'Let's go,' he said, glancing over at the Isola roofs outside the window, the primrose plant. 'Come on.' He hauled up one of the boxes, moved past her and she squeezed his arm, a touch he wouldn't forget. He freed himself and headed to the door, opened it with difficulty and heard his name, started down the stairs with the books, the fucking books straining his arms, reached the ground floor and opened the front door, all in vain, all in fucking vain. When she reached him he gestured her to go in front and they set off, he stuck behind her until they reached Via Pepe, with the screeching of the trains from Garibaldi. She slowed down and he overtook her. They stepped into MailBoxes; there was one cashier and he abandoned the box in a corner and helped her set hers next to it.

Then he left the shop without turning around, walked away down Via Pepe, turning at the metro station, crossed the street and reached the other pavement. He stopped with his back against a building. This is what he was: stopping one moment before the act; this, enjoying fantasies, skimming the reckoning and immediately seeking refuge in his hearth. He pulled out his phone, found his wife's contact and started the call; he cleared his voice, the phone rang.

Anna told Margherita that it was Carlo calling.

'I'll call him back.'

She was regretting having asked her daughter, she was regretting having attended the birthday, she was regretting having sacrificed herself for smoother sailing. She squeezed her bag's handles. 'When we get to the cemetery, I want to go in alone.'

Margherita took the Centrale underpass. 'And what about me?'

'You go in first.'

'Mum, is everything OK?'

Having to explain herself, at over seventy years old. She kept quiet, her bubbling thoughts comforting her. She was going to see a dead man in the place of the dead and she wanted her share of peace. Ends bring about beginnings – a customer who'd asked for an Astrakhan coat had told her that, and for one moment she felt her daughter would've felt that wisdom more than her. She looked at her. Margherita was driving with one hand in her lap, her head a little tilted on the headrest: it felt like looking at her for the first time today. More beautiful, not because of her pendant earrings, or the light in her tired eyes, it was something else: she had the look of someone abandoning everything to themselves, just like she did when she'd day-dream while listening to cassette tapes on the bed. She wanted to tell her that, 'You look more beautiful today,' but she stayed quiet and enjoyed her baby with her something different. She touched her ear, played with a lock of her hair; they didn't talk for the rest of the drive. As they reached their destination, she handed her back her phone and her purse and waited for her turn in the car.

She lowered the window and could now smell the cy-press trees and the wilting flowers; she looked up and saw the wrought-iron gate and the deep red of the entrance. She waited until her daughter was walking back on the cemetery path. They passed each other on the threshold and she took the gravel path and walked among the tiny chapels, skirting the grass, and down the external stone corridor until the second-to-last headstone where she placed herself in front of the photo. 'I'm here, *Franchin*.'

She was quiet for some time; she missed him, and they both knew that. She moved closer and touched the bunch of fake roses, took it out of the metal cone. Some of the leaves had faded and she ripped them off – not without some effort, she had to use both hands – let them fall, and left the bunch on the ground. She peered into the cone; it was empty and deep, she and Margherita had chosen it so it could hold medium-sized flowers and they'd been satisfied with that practical, if not re-fined, choice. She raised her bag and took out the postcards, the Bormio one on top, set them down and went to pick up one of the watering cans from the small fountain nearby. She filled it up a third, came back, and watered the postcards.

She waited for them to soak it up, watered them again and again, until she was sure they were drenched, then she tore them up, made them into mulch. She picked up the mulch and stuffed it into the cone. She did everything with care and it took her a couple of tries not to leave any trace. Then she took the roses and placed them back; they were jutting out more now, she shoved them down with irritation, then collected herself.

'Here's your Clara.'

She'd count the ninety-six steps to Concordia every time she went to visit her daughter. Just one month after the move, she'd started breaking down the cost of that flat for each of them. She'd used a calculator and it turned out it was more than four thousand per step, plus the interest from the thirty-year loan that Margherita and Carlo had taken out with Deutsche Bank. The amount went up to five thousand every time one of her feet touched the ground. Anna climbed up to the fourth floor, her legs tied to her daughter's financial burdens, to Carlo's, to all of theirs, it was her way of partaking in the efforts of a family that had invested in bricks, as Franco would've said.

The truth was that she had insisted on the purchase, and was now atoning four hundred and sixty-five thousand euros for almost one hundred and twenty square metres without even a service lift to help them out with the luggage or the push-chair: she'd seen her daughter so happy about all that light in the lounge that she hadn't been able to say no. Climbing up Concordia put her in a bad mood, going back down brought her relief, she felt like she was freeing Carlo and Margherita, removing some of the debt and going back in time with each step: when she'd reach the ground floor, she'd imagine them at the start of their love story, light and full of adventure in their studio. Gone were the one hundred thousand they'd accepted from the Pentecostes, gone were the thirty-five thousand she'd been able to offer – at least she had been able to help with the furniture and the curtains, getting back to sewing despite the pain in her hands.

The fortune-teller had told her that 2018 would be a good year for each of them, especially for her grandson: he would've been lucky especially because of his silent behaviour. She loved children who knew their place – she was still convinced that Lorenzo had taken after her husband and still hoped that it wasn't entirely true. As she passed the second-to-last flight, the staircase light went off and she couldn't be bothered to step back down to the landing to switch it back on; she squeezed the handrail harder and thought about what her grandson left her with after those two hours in the afternoon together: it was happiness – not unexpected, almost obvious – dying without having experienced it would've been like going through the French Revolution without taking the Bastille. She smiled in the dark, placed her foot badly on the step but was sure she could catch herself. She didn't. She tried to stop herself with the palm of her hand and when she opened her eyes again she realised that, at the age of eighty, she was going through the most bothersome pain of her life.

Upside down, she was looking through the dim light at her legs on the steps, the back of her neck resting against the mat at the foot of the stairs. She tried moving, but the pain was sharp. She couldn't feel her left leg and right arm and she pushed on her right hand to slide down onto the mat. She wouldn't scream, never. She pushed again and slid a little more; now she had the handrail just within reach, she could grab on to it and pull herself up, maybe sit up. The pain in her leg made her groan. She could let out tears but not sounds. She pointed her elbow against the mat, pushed and moved towards the wall; she pushed again on her hand and was able to arch her back, pushed even harder, and found herself with her back against the wall; she managed to sit up straight.

Her leg was throbbing. She lifted her skirt and saw that her hip wasn't straight, and that her arm wasn't straight. She let it fall into her lap and listened; everything was quiet. It was like being in a farmhouse. She'd thought the same thing when Margherita and Carlo had brought her to visit Concordia for the first time, a building sheltered by bigger buildings in the centre of Milan. There were four flats inside, one for each floor; she considered which of the tenants might find her first, then she remembered her phone: her bag was halfway up the flight of stairs. She tried moving again, fell over herself and said, 'Help', with a sob.

'Please help.'

She was annoyed by her old-lady voice, echoing in a fancy building's staircase.

'Please help.'

She pushed the back of her head against the wall, closed her eyes and fell quiet for what felt like a long time. When she heard the front door unlock she was a little out of it. Someone switched on the light, the lawyer from the third floor. She tried smiling at him as he bent down to help her and she felt embarrassed. She told him her daughter was home and the lawyer ran up the stairs while she tried straightening up. She tidied her skirt and wool jumper, but the pain made her cough. She listened to the footsteps and the doorbell, the voices, then Margherita was at the top of the stairs, staring at her with fear in her eyes.

'I'm OK, it's just this leg.'

Margherita was beautiful. Her hair was long as it had been when she was a child, and worry softened her features. The weight left from the pregnancy looked good on her, and after the child's birth they'd started gossiping over tea like friends.

131

'And also the arm.'

'I'm coming, Mum.'

Her daughter came down and hugged her; she checked her leg and pulled out her phone, called the ambulance.

'I can do it, I'm OK.'

'Please don't move,' said the lawyer.

'My back hurts.'

They helped her lie down and she thought about when they'd moved Franco onto the anti-bedsore mattress; his jaw set and his eyes rolled back during the move: she didn't hold back her tears.

'Mum, Mum, it's OK, it's nothing bad.'

She nodded and grabbed her daughter's hand, strong and warm. Margherita was surprised at how strong and warm her mother's hand was. She had a brave mum who hid her fears. She was shaking as she stroked Anna's hair and only stopped when they moved her onto the stretcher and put her into the ambulance because she had to go and check on Lorenzo.

She rushed back up the stairs, stiff from the cold of that insistent February Milan was stuck in. She held onto the handrail, angry once again at the lack of a lift. The tenants of the building next door had opposed the project due to distance regulations and she'd taken it as bad karma for how she had tricked the previous owner of Concordia. She'd manipulated things with such cunning that even nine years later she still felt a tinge of pride, even now, as she ran up the stairs and through the door to her lie. She found Lorenzo in the corner, colouring his *Pimpa* book; she told him that grandma had hurt herself and they had to go see the doctor. The boy looked at her, put the cap back onto the pen and stood up. She helped him get into his coat, his scarf, and he waited for her at the end of the corridor wearing his bunny rabbit backpack. They hurried down the stairs while she pulled out her phone to call her husband. 'Carlo, Mum is—'

'I'm about to go in, I'll call you back.'

'Mum fell down the stairs.'

She bit her tongue for having told him that just before his interview. She had to insist on stopping him from going straight to the hospital, worried that her husband would never get the job if he did so. She often underestimated him. Many times he'd been strong and capable of making decisions for both of them. His ease, when the doctors had said that they had to keep an eye on Lorenzo's reluctance to speak. For her, it had been an obsession, it still was, even though her son's calm behaviour gave her a secret relief. They took a taxi to the hospital and she watched her baby stick his head through the front seats, looking at the hybrid car's dashboard, the driver telling him about the blue light and the red light and him just nodding as if he understood everything. Lorenzo understood everything. The tension between his parents, the possibility of finding refuge with Grandma Anna, the way he got to his classmates in preschool.

They got to the Fatebenefratelli and a nurse told her they had to wait.

'Can I speak to a doctor, please?'

'We'll call you shortly, please take a seat.'

They found a spot next to the coffee-vending machine; Lorenzo pulled out his colouring tools and sorted himself out on his knees. She stood, her eyes on the door to the wing. She leaned against the wall and rummaged in her bag to distract herself, realised she didn't have a book with her – she hadn't had one in her bag for some time now – so she sat and opened up her diary, trying to figure out how to postpone her appointments for the day. She wrote an email to her supervisor and stared at her phone until she got a reply: her colleagues would cover for her. She cradled the phone in her hands.

Lorenzo stared at her.

'It's nothing, darling.'

She risked losing a couple of sales; she'd have to be back at her desk in no more than a day. She sat down and stroked her son's head, those locks just behind his ear that smelled of warm milk. She stood up again and paced a little, found the number for the Pentecostes, hung up immediately. She didn't feel like using her father-in-law's queue-jumping to take advantage of a more effective health service, add another debt of gratitude to the list. She'd been the one to accept their money for Concordia, because *she* wanted the house. She'd been aware of her corruption. This must've also contributed to her mother's fractures: seeing her two hours later in the orthopaedics wing brought her to silence.

'Mum.'

Anna opened her eyes. 'It's bad.'

Margherita touched her cheek, it was cold. 'It's OK, you're OK now.'

'They put the thing in.' She pointed to the tube that ended under the bed. 'And also the . . .'

'It's OK.'

'The nappy.'

'It'll be OK.'

'Hey, little man,' Anna raised her head towards her grandson, 'Grandma tried flying, like Superman, but she didn't make it.'

He was serious and he touched the cast on her arm.

Margherita turned towards the other beds. There were five of them and only the one at the back had someone visiting the patient. Coming in, she'd thought back to Andrea's hospital stay for the dog bite: she stared at the window and remembered the same view, but from three floors higher. The works on the building opposite were finished now, and the road had its new pedestrian lane. With time they'd become something, she and

Andrea, almost without noticing; she was still unsure why, and yet she confided in him a lot. She pulled out her phone and typed *My mother just fell down MY stairs and broke her limbs. What was that you said about muscle karma?*

He got the message as he was waiting for the training session of his last student of the day. He read it again, vaguely remembered telling Margherita that the Concordia trick could cause unexpected physical side-effects. He'd learned from working with muscles that forced movements exposed the entire body to painful consequences. The body as judge and jury, she'd replied.

Andrea saw his student walk through the entrance to the Ravizza gardens, his legs were stiff with cold and his eyes were tired from the newsagent's daily routine. He was anxious to finally free his eighty kilos of their 10 per cent body fat. Giorgio had the heart of a cyclist and respected his role as trainer; he liked calling him a student, like the others.

He watched him take off his jacket and tie up his curls into a ponytail. 'How was work?'

'I'm exhausted.'

'Warm up.'

He finished replying to Margherita – he'd call her later – nodded to Giorgio to increase the pace. Every time he looked at him moving he knew why he'd fallen in love. He made him wear the weighted vest and they started the push-up routine: one minute rest, holding a hand on his back to increase the resistance, always his right hand, so he could see the scar going from his index to his thumb. He'd never gone back to César, under the walnut tree. Some time after having buried him, he'd started driving around the suburbs of Rozzano and Barona at night, the wide streets with graffiti-filled blinds, the courtyards with insomniac smokers, and he'd felt better; he listened to Carboni and sometimes he'd get closer to the centre, with its Expo building sites that were like living monuments. He'd turn onto roads that led to nowhere, then he'd felt his curiosity increase and had reached the hairpin turns in front of the Triennale. He'd driven along them slowly, peering into the cars parked by the roadside, some had people in, some were empty. One evening he'd parked, Radiohead playing 'Reckoner' on his radio, and he'd kept his lights on; someone had tapped on his window almost immediately. He'd looked at this middle-aged stranger, his slightly open shirt, well-groomed beard, kind smile. He'd opened the door and let him in, he'd turned down the volume, and had shifted his seat back. He'd leaned back against it, while the stranger placed his hand under his top and unbuttoned his trousers. Milan was so beautiful, even from the window, the soft darkness of summer nights . . . Since that time at the Triennale he'd only let himself be sucked off. Sometimes, with these strangers between his legs, he'd thought about Margherita and when they'd been together, her able mouth, his embarrassment in finding her so unsuspectedly good.

He held his hand on Giorgio's back as he finished the last rep of the fifth series, pushed a little harder, Giorgio collapsed onto the mat and, as he collapsed, he dragged him down with him. They laughed – he still struggled with feeling at ease, but he had got much better. They ended up on the floor, around them February darkness and the cold of winter that bit at their cheeks. He'd left FisioLab on a whim; he'd had enough of fixing bodies and had decided to make them stronger instead. He asked for forty euros an hour and his diary was full; he spent mornings in the newsagent's. His father had said, 'Sell it, I'm retiring,' and his reply had been 'I'll take over.'

Sofia started the motorised shutter of the hardware shop in the morning twilight; she'd brought forward the opening time, at the beginning of winter, to half past seven. She was about to push the door open when she saw it and froze: the bakery bag was hanging from a red ribbon in front of the window display. She turned towards the car park of Largo Bordoni, hoping to see the metal grey Golf: one time, Tommaso had waited in the car to see her reaction to his gift.

She took the bag and went inside, opened it after turning on the lights: it was a hazelnut puff. She thought she was getting used to surprises, just as living in Rimini meant getting used to the constant celebrations in the air. She was worried it might have been her hitting thirty, the age of settling down or late-blooming revolutions: her personal one had been a tomboyish haircut and a man who snuck her breakfast at work. She enjoyed her cake in the dim light, her eyes half closed; the shop always smelled of wood in the morning.

She messaged Tommaso to thank him – she sent him an exclamation mark, their secret code – then switched on the spotlights and the radio, gave everything the once-over. She filled the displays with flowerpot plates and watering cans – it was cold and the sea was chucking over a fog that wouldn't lift until the afternoon. She checked the cabinet with the house appliances she hadn't sold over the holidays – she'd put them on sale at 30 per cent off without taking down the display; she never liked taking down Christmas displays. She placed herself behind the counter, the blue overall watching over her from the coat stand; her mother had worn it for ten years and her father had hung it up there some time ago. He would arrive mid-morning and would tell her that a good hardware shop owner needs a good uniform, she would barely listen.

She'd insisted on taking back the shop three years after moving back from Milan. Whenever she showed it on Instagram – the chest of drawers or a corner of the counter as a background, the foreground was always a book – she'd never get less than two hundred and fifty likes. As if others out there could share her feeling that books took root inside her only if experienced behind that counter. Some days, all she needed to feel something close to joy was seeing the name Ferramenta e Casalinghi Casadei on the shop's awning.

At ten to eight the first customer came in, a construction worker looking for some plaster, a handful of German nails and four iron wedges. She climbed up the ladder to reach the higher drawers – her strong legs made her agile – came back down and wrapped the nails and wedges in newspaper. She handed over the change and when the door closed again, she felt the moment had come. She pulled a book out of her bag, *Sylvia* by Leonard Michaels, its brick-coloured cover, a photo of a woman in bed, her breasts exposed, the story of a return home after university. A boy and a girl and innocence, New York, fate looming over them.

She tried a couple of shots to get the light she wanted, then she wrapped the book in the same paper she used for her customers, slipped it into an envelope and wrote the address in capital letters. She always shivered when that happened.

Carlo lifted up the bags and took the road leading to the Naviglio and was out of breath when he reached the second-hand bookshop. He went in and said hi, took out the books, piling them up on the counter and waited for someone to come value them. They could give him eighty-five euros for the lot. He agreed, too shy to haggle. He looked around and felt embarrassed to be there, but he'd told himself that second-hand sales were a fund for Margherita: a dinner, a bunch of flowers, though last time he'd kept thirty-five euros for a woollen tie. He handed over his ID to record the transaction, then filled in the form and handed it back with his money.

He thanked them and asked if they were looking to hire.

'You can leave a CV, but we're not really, at the moment, sorry.'

He nodded and left, crossed the iron bridge, clutching the money in his fist and watching the water steam in the cold. No one else around . . . Every now and then Milan gave him the impression of being entirely his. He checked his watch and folded the empty bags as he walked, reached the bar with them in his hand; she hadn't arrived yet. He chose a table at the back and ordered a coffee, his eyes fixed on the door until they brought it to him. Then she walked in, holding two catalogues and looking busy.

'Hi,' she said, unwrapping her scarf.

'I made you come all this way.'

'It's an easy day, I told you.' She asked the waiter for a coffee. 'How are you doing?'

'My mother-in-law broke her femur.'

'Ouch!'

'Yeah. She'll be out of it for a while.'

'And what about you?'

'Mornings are good.'

'Then nothing?'

He nodded.

'Since you left, Michele has stopped talking entirely.' Her cheeks were red with cold. 'You're missed.'

He didn't respond. 'Why two catalogues?'

'Canada brings you 30 per cent more. The other one, I mean, it's Scotland, you can write it with your eyes closed. Deadline is February.'

'How much?'

'Eight fifty, but invoice upfront.'

'I need three, we'd agreed on three. Can you ask again?'

'No luck with the university then?'

He shook his head. 'There might be something opening up elsewhere, but we'll see.'

'Where?'

'*Bell'Italia.*'

'That would be nice!'

'I also have another interview lined up, better pay.'

'Anything interesting?'

'A marketing thing, beer and beverage.'

'Beer and beverage?'

Carlo reached over to take the two catalogues; she leaned over and touched his hand.

'It's weird seeing your desk empty.'

He looked for his cup; the dregs on the bottom formed a profile with no nose, he would've liked to be able to read into it. They stayed in silence and she tortured the hem of her jumper. The mascara on her left eye was slightly smudged and to him she was still the twenty-year-old who had stepped into the office years ago, introduced as a bright temp; Michele and he agreed that she looked like Audrey Hepburn.

Carlo picked up the catalogues. 'I've always been fascinated by Canada. Thank you, Manu.'

'Do you want to go for a walk?'

'Don't you need to go back?'

'I have a two-hour break.'

She pulled on a woolly hat and it framed her dark eyes. They left and headed for the Naviglio Pavese; they'd taken away the boats in January and they almost felt lost. They reached the crossing with the ring road and they stopped and he told her, 'I'm going to pick up my son.'

Manuela froze before she got to the lights. 'Now?'

'Now.'

'OK then. Bye.' She smiled, walking backwards on the pavement; he smiled back and waited for her to disappear round the corner. Then he headed towards the school.

They'd finished setting up the tree in the preschool's entrance, with its long branches and red leaves, there were squirrels on every branch, a blackcap, then more squirrels. He peered through the big window and saw the kids in a circle around one of the teachers. Lorenzo was sitting cross-legged, his smock scrunched up around his shoulders, swaying slightly; sometimes he imagined him grown-up, a kind, strong young man.

His son ran towards him as he saw him come in and Carlo stuck his nose behind his ear and sniffed him. The boy laughed. Carlo helped him put on his raincoat, told him they'd drop by the university to pick up his post. But first they stopped for a piece of pizza. They always shared a slice, eating it perched up on the tall stools. They drank a Coke between them and Lorenzo told him that Filippo Gattei was now Francesca Vecchietti's boyfriend. Carlo asked him if he was happy they were together – these days he was particularly talkative and they tried to encourage him.

Lorenzo nodded, then said, 'Grandma Anna is dying.'

'Of course she's not dying.'

'Her leg is broken.'

'Yes, but she's going to get better and then she'll come home.'

'Mum said on the phone that she is worried.'

'Who did she say that to?'

'Aunt Simona.'

'She didn't mean it, don't worry.'

The boy left the last piece of pizza on the serviette. 'But I *am* worried.'

He kissed him. 'She'll get better soon, chipmunk.'

During the car ride, Lorenzo kept looking out of the window and Carlo turned on the radio, his son followed the music with his lips and kept going after they got out, but he fell quiet when they reached the university entrance. Carlo picked him up and gave his name and surname to the staff member there, who nodded and looked through a box on the ground, pulled out a padded envelope and handed it over. Carlo saw there was no sender – it was her. He walked away with Lorenzo's hand in his but before reaching the exit he turned towards the bathroom. The tiles and the neon lights, the gurgling of the plumbing, the reflection of the mirrors . . . He held his son tight. 'Do you need to go wee-wee?'

The boy said no.

They went in anyway. They'd changed the taps and the two doors were slightly open: the misunderstanding. This is where he'd known that desire can trespass. But it hadn't been to compensate for Sofia Casadei, the other women. Three months after she'd moved back to Rimini, while he was in the office working on the Martinique catalogue, he'd stood up and headed to Manuela in the other office, asked her to go to see a film that afternoon. He'd surprised her at her computer and had received the shy yes of a soon-to-be-newlywed, a yes that had echoed within him with trepidation. They'd waited for half an hour, leaving separately to then meet again at the Orfeo, sitting next to each other in the dark, legs brushing, watching the film until the end of the credits, then leaving and going on a walk with the terror of being seen together. They'd said goodbye and he'd headed home, hugging Margherita with a sense of dissatisfaction already in progress, discovering yet again how stepping outside the boundaries impacted the family's hearth.

'I need to go wee-wee.'

'See? I told you.'

He stepped into the cubicle with Lorenzo and helped him with his trousers. He listened to the gurgling of the stream, the smell of ammonia, and the smell of his son. He flushed and they stepped out again, washed their hands. Back in the university courtyard he chose to wait a little longer before opening the envelope. He looked at his son; he had a self-restrained way of communicating his wishes – rubbing his fingers together, the strength of his hugs, sometimes his posture. Lorenzo never demanded anything, as if wishes being granted were something unnatural. Together with Margherita they'd learned to discover what made him happy.

'You want to go see Grandma Anna?'

The boy smiled and clambered into the car. His hair was chestnut brown and his irises had streaks of soot; they flashed when he was colouring or watching a cartoon, or when he'd run through the rooms in Via delle Leghe. Anna always let him dress up as a musketeer even outside of carnival, and challenged him to duels from her sofa. They arrived in the area of the Fatebenefratelli and drove around looking for a parking spot. Then he opened the envelope. Inside it was a book wrapped in newspaper: he read the author's name, Leonard Michaels, and the title, *Sylvia*. He pulled out his phone, searched Sofia's Instagram account and found a photo of that same book, at an angle on the hardware shop counter. He quivered.

This was the third book he'd received. All in the past month and a half, never a note or a sender, all in newspaper, his address in all caps. The first one had been *La paga del sabato*. He'd immediately noticed Rimini on the post office stamp. And the more he'd thought of it being from her, the more he'd abandoned all search for confirmation. In nine years, all he'd done was look her up on Facebook – her new haircut had thrown him – and on Instagram. He'd often kept her safe in his fantasies: Sofia, that day in her room in Isola, him fucking her on the bare table, Milan's roofs out of the window, him with her on the bare mattress, him finally. Now, stepping away from the car, carrying Lorenzo and his bunny-shaped rucksack towards his mother-in-law, he was still able to latch back onto that same material.

They reached the hospital wing and found Anna's door almost closed. They waited outside and heard screams from the room. Lorenzo moved closer and tried looking through the crack in the door, pushed it slightly. Carlo ordered him to stop and he froze in place; the doctors came out and found him on the spot.

'Where'd you come from?' they said.

He shot inside and Carlo followed. Anna was awake and with her free hand she held her grandson while the boy looked in his bag for his Spider-Man headphones.

'Thank goodness my handsome man and his music are here.'

'How are you feeling?' Carlo took off his jacket.

'That lady is doing worse, they did something to her shoulder.' She pointed to the last bed where the woman was holding an arm over her eyes. 'Wasn't Margherita just outside here?'

Carlo said no.

'She's down at the café then. She just told me that Emma Bonino is joining the Democratic Party.'

'So?'

'So I won't vote.'

'No second thoughts?'

'I've stopped having second thoughts.'

Lorenzo watched them from his chair, his eyes wide.

'Sorry, darling.' Anna pinched his cheek and offered him her head; he slipped on his headphones and gestured to his father to proceed. Carlo took his phone and handed it over, the boy scrolled through the songs. He pressed play and watched his grandma.

'The English and their whining,' she said.

The boy laughed.

She sighed. 'Couldn't you choose Modugno?'

Lorenzo turned up the volume and enjoyed watching his

grandmother close her eyes, the Spider-Man headphones around her tiny head, her withered paper skin, and her young mouth.

Carlo peered at his phone in his son's hands, he'd opted for Pink Floyd, 'Shine On You Crazy Diamond'. They'd sniffed him out with music. There had been a period in which he'd hole himself up in his room to listen to it and it had lasted a whole winter, then he'd started sharing it back with everyone: headphones and home stereo and the record player in Via delle Leghe, humming, and at the same time he'd started talking more and the psychiatrist had said he'd bloom from there.

Carlo had liked that word, bloom. He sat next to the bed and took out *Sylvia*. He read a couple of pages, envious of the simple style, so simple, just a couple of lines for the meeting of main character and this girl, in a flat in New York, the Village, her with her fringe covering her eyes, giving her an air of shyness or modesty, the falling in love. He thought of his wife every time he read about falling in love. When Margherita arrived, he looked up and watched her: he could break down his feelings for her, Michaels' writing had helped him focus. Sylvia's fringe, sure, and the discreet way of being; she was always smiling beneath it all, her airy demeanour for a sudden thought, her secretive then forceful seductiveness: his wife knew better than him what held them together.

He went towards her and stroked her hair, she asked him to step outside and told him that the doctors were going to get Anna into surgery, they'd just told her. For the first time, her mother was a burden. She asked Carlo for some sort of comfort: she let herself be caressed, she let herself be told that all would be fine. She grabbed his hand, only now did she realise he was holding a book. She moved away a little to peek at the cover, saw the title and froze, then she said she had to call the office.

She waited for Carlo to head back inside, knowing what had

happened. She opened Instagram – she'd made a fake profile to distract herself and followed Chiara Ferragni and Fedez, the Kardashians, Sofia Casadei. She hoped she was misremembering but she found the last post with *Sylvia* and the caption *this hurts*: it had over three hundred likes. A book in Carlo's hands and the same posted by her. The third book, and the third coincidence in the past few months. She'd avoided asking her husband – are you in touch, is she sending them to you, do you cherish her literary recommendations? She was good at breaking down her doubts, though suspicions still took hold. She imagined what had grown in him: some sort of evasion, dithering on the limbo of possibility to relive the time when he was *almost* a teacher and *almost* a writer, relive the time when he could still *be*. Sometimes, looking at him, she felt a little strange: Carlo, his six foot two, his back just a little more hunched – his size that never really changed – his arms defined thanks to the rowing machine at the gym, the few white hairs camouflaged in his beard, and his still thick hair, the same aura of youth, his unchanging nature, in mannerisms and behaviour. She would've liked to see him marked in some way, the signs of time certifying his acceptance of maturity. In all this, she'd been able to hold back the shadow of his potential betrayal. She had the presumption to recognise the erosion of their marriage: there had been nothing that had stopped their family plans. She'd often tried imagining his dick inside other women but the idea destroyed her. Anatomy was still her weakest suit.

She went back to her mother, got closer to the bed and smiled at her. 'Mum.'

'Darling.' Anna cleared her voice: 'You're making that face again. What's wrong?'

Margherita looked at her husband and said it as if she was talking to him, 'You're going to get surgery, they're putting in a plate and you'll be as good as new.'

Her mother stared at her, almost not recognising her, then she turned her head on the pillow and chewed her lips.

'Mum.'

'I always thought that's what you did to people with no other option left.'

Carlo sat on the bed.

Anna's eyes searched his. 'Can I say no?'

They both shook their heads, and she attempted a smile.

Lorenzo put down the *Pimpa* colouring book and stepped forward. He had a green pen in his hand, he hesitated, stopped. Suddenly he moved to his grandma's arm cast and slowly started drawing all over it, from the wrist to the elbow, one of his fluorescent pictures.

'Draw me a heart,' said Grandma.

But he said no and Anna looked at Margherita. 'He's not a romantic one.'

'I'll draw you a heart while you're asleep tonight.'

'I want no one here tonight.'

'Don't be difficult.'

'No, don't you be difficult.'

'We'll see.'

'We'll see nothing, darling. Go back to work, you have a lot on your plate.'

'I don't have a lot.'

'Like Bonaparte said at Waterloo.'

The nurse announced that visiting times were over. The others left and Margherita whispered in her mother's ear, 'Let me stay tonight. We had fun last time, right?'

'I want to be alone, darling.'

Margherita took her hand and held it. She turned towards the bedside table and checked she had a towel, water, crackers. Anna hadn't wanted anything to read. She stayed just a little longer, and as she left the room she saw her mother watching the evening sky out of the window. Once in the corridor, she covered her mouth with her hand; she was about to start sobbing but stopped herself, joined Carlo at the entrance of the Fatebenefratelli and asked him if he could look after Lorenzo because she had to pop into the office. Walking helped her feel better. After the pregnancy she'd got back in shape by walking with Lorenzo in the pushchair, as Milan changed, buzzing with construction sites and greedy for surprises, like a young person who's told, 'Go and live.' Finding herself with her child among the mirror-like skyscrapers and the vertical woods and the feeling of not actually being in a city, or the bikes passing through historical neighbourhoods, all those bikes you could rent at every block, then a bit on foot, and another on two wheels, hop onto a tram and then down onto the new metro crawling into Isola; they said Milan had bloomed all over again, thanks to the 2015 Expo.

She cut through Via Solferino and continued past Naviglio San Marco, then down Corso Garibaldi up to the Duomo. She could see the scars much better here, the shops closed down where they'd been open. All must go for rent, old newspapers plastering the dusty display windows, empty banks replaced by Chinese knick-knack shops overnight, open twenty-four hours; she counted two closed restaurants on Corso Porta Romana, an optician's that was never replaced. It was a bad time for real estate agents too. It started when she had to let Gabriele go from the office, then the Concordia mortgage had dug into the family savings and she'd been forced to sell to a big property group.

She'd traded the agency for a flat with magnificent light and a forecast of a stable future. But for a couple of hours now she'd known this: Carlo with Sofia's book in hand. Carlo, a man who was just on this side of unemployed. A man emptied of his profession, vulnerable. He was worth seven hundred euros a month and a dozen failed interviews. Two pending. He was worth a possible collapse. And yet, he was the man she'd sat down with in a medical centre with grey shutters to listen to the voice of a neurologist speak the words *expected irreversibility* about Lorenzo, her waiting to break down at any point, taken aback by her husband's calm during the visit. Outside of the medical office he'd told her: we'll take care of our son.

Seven words. Seven words well placed, almost a murmur, but clear and irrational, as if he already knew that Lorenzo was an orchestra conductor and that he needed silence to conduct. And they really did take care of it themselves, though the truth was that *he* had taken care of it: organising activities to stimulate him – taste, touch, then hearing; he'd finally focused on music as the way in to unlock his voice. Leaving that medical office with grey shutters, she'd believed in her husband.

She passed the basilica of San Nazaro, the Indian rotisserie where she'd caught her breath after talking to Sofia Casadei was still there. The café had become a winery and she had become a jealous but sensible woman. It was strange to look back at the past and find it looking right. If this was who she'd become, if *they* had become this, everything had had its meaning. She slowed down and tried convincing herself; she stopped and turned back, slipping into the tight alley next to the rotisserie, and kept walking until the entrance to the Statale, the Cortina bookshop in front of her. She walked in and waited for the cashier to finish with two students, then asked for a copy of *Sylvia*. She put it in her bag and when she got back to Corso Porta Romana she waited for the lights to turn green: buying the book had been soothing. She looked at her reflection in the window of a chemist's, tidied her hair on one side and tightened her scarf. She felt as if she'd only aged a little – she even got freckles last summer and their friends had reassured her that freckles were very popular with twenty-something boys.

But she'd already had a twenty-six-year-old, and he was still a memory she held on to. With him she'd come to realise that betrayal could mean loyalty to herself. Andrea. After she'd left his house, that night nine years ago, she'd gone by the office even though it was empty, had locked herself in the bathroom and covered her eyes with one hand. She told herself: you did it. You took in your mouth what wasn't yours, you undressed, you let yourself be undressed, you opened your legs on the kitchen table and demanded him, holding onto him, his strong shoulders, his strong grip; you took him in, you had him take you to bed, feeling young and desired and happy.

She'd stayed in there, in her office bathroom, telling herself this for some time, feeling her sore legs and burning skin, a new smell, and had finally spoken that word: derailed. Her particular carriage had always had too light a coupling, her father was right: it had derailed and hadn't followed its route, she was Miss Scharfenberg and these were the consequences. That evening she'd come away from the bathroom and sat down at her desk, rested her hands on the keyboard and written a paragraph-long description for the Morgagni flat, its airy bedrooms, the aristo-cratic setting and double exposure, and had ended on: *young and desired and happy.* She'd stared at those three pleasing words and had realised that guilt was a banal procedure. The fact of the matter, the real fact of the matter, was that it had been perfectly natural. She'd fucked a man she liked and he'd pleased her. What did that take away from her marriage?

She decided to change roads, left Corso Porta Romana and started down the small street to San Calimero, its starry church ceiling, and the Gaber and Jannacci street art further ahead: it hadn't taken anything away from her marriage. She had a vivid memory of that night, when she'd got home after Andrea. She'd been careful, a little scared. She'd let herself lie on the sofa, feeling a little drained. Incredulity had attacked her on waking up the following morning – she'd repeated to herself as she woke up: I did it – only to then soften during Loretta's birthday. She'd masturbated, thinking about how uncertain yet brutal he had been: as if she'd convinced him with each layer of clothing they'd removed. For a long time she hadn't forgotten the weight of his body on hers; her marriage was in that weight. She'd no longer taken certain issues for granted: Carlo's lustful passion, and his tenderness, his small folly, how much he made her laugh. For just one second she thought she had disavowed it all. After all, she was still the daughter of a woman who'd patched up her own tears as well as those of others.

She let herself be taken by her worry for her mother – what consequences could a broken femur really have? She passed the Gaber graffiti and felt a pang of fear, brought a hand to her stomach, under her coat, where she hid away omens, too. She held it until the Ravizza gardens – Andrea always chose the same patch of grass under the two pine trees, next to the concrete ring. He'd laid out on the bench the dumb-bells, the fighting pads, the bag with the bands. There was a young woman on the grass and he was pointing out a stretching exercise; the student nodded and started running at a good pace. Andrea walked in the same direction – he'd learned to elegantly show off his boxer shoulders and his long beard made him look grumpy. It took him some time to clock Margherita but when he saw her under the lamp post he headed towards her and noticed she was on the verge of tears. He stroked the back of her neck, pulled her to him. Every time he hugged her he was afraid he wouldn't be able to do it. He asked her about her mother.

'Those damn stairs.'

Andrea waited for his student to finish her loop, told her to do two more, then he asked for the whole story and explained what would happen to Anna. The surgery, the rehabilitation at home or in a clinic, the drugs, the recovery times and how they might change. Margherita reached out her hand to touch a spot at the base of his neck.

'Look at this,' she said. 'Your wild training sessions.'

He touched the same spot; he'd treated the bruise with salt and water but it hadn't fully healed yet.

'What does Giorgio say when you're bruised up?'

'He's used to it.'

She attempted a smile. 'Will you take a look at my mother?'

'There's people who specialise in fractured femurs.'

'Just a look.'

'You keep me updated, we'll see.'

He suddenly felt like being alone. He told her that his student was heading back and he had to focus, kissed Margherita on her cheekbone and asked her to tell him when Anna's operation was.

He felt distracted for the rest of the session, checked his neck at the end of it, ran his fingers down his torso, inhaled deeply until the pain in his rib stopped him. He'd underestimated the blows, wondered how he would make it that night. He dispelled his doubts and enjoyed the fog. The traffic around the gardens faded away and he watched some dogs and their owners in the fenced area next to the grass. He picked up his bag and weights, walked by the fence. It was a Maremmano and an American Bully playing; the former was old, with a good gait for his age, the other was a pup buzzing out of its skin. He walked slowly towards the newsagent's, lowering the weights every now and then to straighten his back. He pulled up the shutter and went in. The space was half taken up by the display stand and he stuffed his bag under the counter, the smell of paper making him feel better. It was dark and the warmth of the heater had stayed a little.

He'd never regretted removing the *For Sale* sign against his father's wishes, and he'd met Giorgio there too. He bought *la*

Repubblica and *Vanity Fair* and seemed like a kind customer. They'd chatted a bit at some point and he'd found out that Giorgio was a shoe designer just got back from four years in Stockholm. They'd warmed to each other, and Giorgio picked up his papers from the side door. One afternoon he'd waited around to ask about training times – he wanted to try – and they'd started that Monday at the park. In one year Andrea had helped him increase his muscle mass to 12 per cent and they'd fallen in love. *Jag älskar dig* . . . the first time he'd been told 'I love you' in Swedish. He was still embarrassed, thinking about his father and mother knowing their son was being fucked by another man. He'd never told Giorgio about the dogs.

He called him now and told him he wouldn't be back, that he was heading to the gym to loosen up his muscles. He was not allowed to keep watching *Game of Thrones*, but *The Crown* was OK. Giorgio replied that he'd make do by eating beans and would wait up for him. Andrea told him not to, he wanted to use the gloves too, he didn't want to force anybody to lose their sleep.

'I'm not anybody.'

'I said anybody meaning *you*.'

'I know I know, your usual illiterate self! Avoid the gloves, enjoy your workout, love.'

'Enjoy your English crown jewels.'

He closed the shop and searched his phone for a gym session photo he hadn't yet sent, held it at the ready, reached his car and checked his clothes and shoes in the boot. He had an hour left; he could feel his stomach closing up but forced himself to eat something. He opened the Tupperware as he drove north, gulping down two boiled eggs and a bite of chicken sandwich left over from lunch. He sped up and tried enjoying the trip; he'd kept driving by the Triennale in those years, imagining parking his car with his lights on, waiting for someone, but the turns were empty and Milan had changed with him – his complicated city now welcomed him as he prepared to deceive Giorgio, sliding away into the outskirts of town.

He took the road towards the furniture-making district, the terraced houses and the gentrified squalor, turned off the radio and listened to the wheels on the tarmac. This was his preparation – he thought of anything but his opponents. He'd focus on his students and the training changes, tweaking each of their protein intakes, then on Giorgio. And Anna: he'd try focusing on that little old woman with a blazing face from the day he'd been hospitalised for César's bite. And Cristina: he hadn't heard anything from her since, hadn't wanted to; she was working at a driving school in Melegnano, and that was that.

He drove along the Novedratese, he saw the Nigerian prostitutes in the parking lot behind the Carrefour and the deer crouched down in the park behind them. Fifteen minutes later he passed Carimate and parked along the gravel road. He turned off the engine and picked up his phone, sent Giorgio the picture of him in the gym, wearing his boxing gear, the ring behind him, typed *the eye of the tiger*. He messaged him that every time he headed into the ring. He waited for an answer, *Come back in one piece*, put away his phone and checked his ribs – the pain was manageable. He pulled out his bag from the boot. The fog was a veil and the warehouse a blurred shape. There were three of them watching him come closer. He greeted them, kept going along the length of the warehouse and pulled back the metal door; there were thirty more inside.

Many had come straight from work, builders and labourers, some unemployed; they changed on the spot, fishing their shorts out of plastic shopping bags, helping each other with the tape, mostly North African, Italian and some Belarusian. Each time there were more; they had to be introduced by someone who was already a member. There were also the safes, as they called the guys that bet high and had different odds from the others. He'd got there through the dog fights, he'd started with a handful of small bets. Then he'd plucked up the courage and had waited his three rounds to fight. The ring's ropes were tied to the columns of an old industrial woodworking factory, the owner was paid off with a percentage of the winnings. The warehouse fights had started with the first business closures. They had three rules: no aiming for the bollocks, stop if the opponent taps more than once or passes out, fixing a fight meant being beaten up and kicked out.

After a round of hellos he said he wanted to fight and the Italian who organised the billings asked him about his neck.

'It's fine.'

'Let me see.'

Andrea undressed. He was much bigger than most present and they had to bring in the Egyptians for a fair fight, all over eighty kilos, or the Argentine, or a couple of Slavs. The worst were the Polish and the Ukrainian guy who always went below the belt, holding the other hand up to hide any dirty move.

He stood topless, the Italian ran his finger from his neck to his pecs, to his ribs. 'Is this it?'

Andrea nodded.

The Italian pushed and he shuddered.

The Italian shook his head.

'It's nothing serious.'

'Maybe not, but you'll go down in under a minute and folks will get angry.'

'It's nothing.'

'You'll go down.'

Andrea rolled his eyes – the others were watching. He got dressed again and stood aside. He went back to the Italian, asking to take the middle.

'You won't hold up with that rib.'

'Let me try the first one, then we'll see.'

The Italian was silent at first, then told him he'd do the one.

Andrea got ready. Being the ref was different. He'd been in the middle every now and then and the others liked him because he only stopped a fight a second before one of the two passed out: a body and a body and his body, grappling through limbs and cruelty that ended up being his own; some had started noticing how much he enjoyed it. His chest would swell and he stood like a dog, poised before the hit, the semblance of a smile coming across the mouthguard. After the fight, win or lose, he'd move to one side of the warehouse, awash with a peace that lasted him until the next day.

He placed himself in the middle of the ring and waited for the two fighters, an Algerian in his thirties and a Ghanaian; he knew them well. The Algerian was reckless and had a good pain threshold, the Ghanaian messed up fights because he always pulled himself out of submissions: he'd got to Italy three years earlier and had found a job as a carpenter around Bergamo but he'd lost his job the previous summer and all he needed in there was to make seven or eight hundred euros. He had good character, talked a lot; he'd told Andrea he was caring for his only uncle, back in Ghana. When he saw him on the ground, the Algerian had swiped him and had straddled him to hammer down. Andrea bent over, almost as if to protect him: nothing could be further from the truth. There, between the Ghanaian's face, under his shielding forearms, the neck muscles flexed to take the blows, his nose drowning in blood, he'd fall back into his trance. The black man's eyes, wide, and focused on the beating, the eyelids shutting: that overwhelmed body brought him back to César and the time when he was still complicated – he would've given everything to have that back.

*

The same for Sofia: she would've given anything to be desired like Pentecoste had wanted her. While she used her lunch break to take a walk, she calculated that *Sylvia* should've reached Carlo around then, if not the previous day. She took the bus to the Arco d'Augusto and walked along the Corso as far as the Ponte di Tiberio, slipped into the streets of Borgo San Giuliano, between the old terraced houses of the local fishermen, their pastel walls peeling, and here she imagined the good side of her gesture: Pentecoste receiving the parcel and spotting the stamp with the sender's origin, another novel from her; he enjoys a good book and accepts the intrusion, nothing wrong with that. She imagined him leafing through the first page with the excited – and sly – expression she used to see on his face during class, his hair slightly ruffled. She'd looked him up on Facebook over the years and from the few photos of him she could find, he hadn't changed much.

She kept wandering the *borgo*, stopped for a half plate of tagliatelle; the waiter knew she had to be back at the shop and served her immediately, her dad claimed these were the best *tagliadeli* in Romagna, alongside the Renzi di Canonica ones – rough and hard. She enjoyed them with her phone on the table, checking Instagram, reading through the comments, the reactions to her stories, she kept in touch with some of her friends this way, they'd all started families and never left the house now. They sometimes met up at the beach, shared a happy hour and chatted about husbands and the next holiday trip, some were doing yoga now. They talked about kids, and she felt ashamed for her thirties and missed pregnancies and missed husbands and added books. Jogging on the shore, going to the cinema alone, baking a cake for her father at home, meeting someone on the internet for a date, she'd been waiting for something she didn't even know, and had picked Tommaso without even realising.

'You get bored so easily,' he'd told her, touching her left hand.

'Why do you say that?'

'If you get bored with me, raise this finger . . .' He'd touched her index.

'Then what?'

'Then I'll disappear.'

The disappearing boy. Since then, she'd looked at her left index finger as if it could tell the truth. She left the *osteria* and touched it the way he'd touched it. She walked down to Parco Marecchia – it was empty in winter and the gravelly footsteps echoed – and she enjoyed her stroll towards the Ina Casa, hoping for the other consequences of her gesture: Carlo Pentecoste receiving the package, checking the stamp's origin. He's already seen the other books on her Instagram account, he's anxious, he fumbles in opening it because he knows; he takes out the book and sees a never forgotten want. She'd asked herself if pulling herself away from him, before moving back to Rimini, had been a way of planting a regret. She'd accepted the risk that the regret could take different forms: an innocent memory, remorse, indifference. The two of them indifferent to each other – time had very much eroded Milan – but something kept resurfacing whenever she met a new man. She'd think back to Pentecoste, almost automatically. After him, she'd held back a bit. An intangible holding-back, stubborn, but she'd noticed it. The professor's legacy had been a handbrake and, eventually, an impatience – '*You get bored so easily.*'

She'd had her confirmation when she'd had the idea of sending the first book. The excitement had struck the afternoon when she'd got the boyish bowl cut: the following morning she'd bought Fenoglio in Piazza delle Poveracce and taken it home like carrying a treasure in her bag. She'd smelled it, fanning the pages, she'd wrapped it. Fenoglio and *La paga del sabato* and the kitchen where the protagonist seeks refuge; Pentecoste's lessons about that kitchen – it wasn't that much different from her hardware shop with its screws and plaster and brass hinges. So much resolve came to her from fishing nails out of a drawer with her fingers, the *clack clack* of the rollers of the rivets drawer, climbing up the ladder – and looking at her father rearranging the window display, this well-aged man with a cigarette pack in his shirt pocket.

They'd always lived there, between the shop and the house on the other side of the square. And that Friday evening he'd insisted, 'There's some good ads for places in Padulli, you can get your own place.' She'd shaken her head and seen him give up immediately, make dinner, lay the table with care; every Friday he made her spaghetti with *puràzi* and she made trifle. Sometimes he'd say, 'Let's go see Mum', and she'd answer, 'You go.'

Margherita took some extra break time to finish the last few pages, got back to the office and placed the book on her desk, staring at the reddish cover and its bare-breasted girl: *Sylvia*, a novel about an obsession. If Carlo really hadn't had Sofia, if he really hadn't fulfilled his desire for that woman, if that woman hadn't granted Carlo's desire, then Sofia Casadei was part of the present. Because she knew this: she had contained her desire by demanding to have Andrea, and then demanding nothing else.

She was tempted to talk to her husband, call him directly from the office, her colleagues around her, a tension that was getting tangled with her worry about her mother. She stopped herself and scrolled down her contacts to the number of the person who'd introduced her to Carlo. She still remembered the centrepiece candles from that dinner and in her husband's sister she still found some form of contact. It was weird; sometimes all she needed to do was talk to Simona to feel at peace

159

with him. She waited for the phone to ring and Simona picked up just as she'd lost hope.

'Simo, you're out of breath.'

'Nico forgot his football shoes and I had to run and there we go.'

'Is it all sorted now?'

'I wanted to drop in on your mother in hospital but can you believe that—' She panted.

'She told me you called her.'

'I got Carlo to put her on for me.' She tried catching her breath. 'She seemed in good spirits.'

'I'm worried, Simo.'

'She'll be out of there soon, you'll see.'

'If you can, drop by the hospital and take Nico – she loves him, says he makes her happy.'

'She should be around him for an hour and see if she still thinks that! Rap and Cristiano Ronaldo, rap and Cristiano Ronaldo. At least he comes back happy from weekends with his father now – last time he swore Mamadou made him carbonara.'

'Mamadou actually cooking?'

'Meh. Petrol station worker to chef – I might consider getting back with him.' Her laugh sounded like a hiccup.

Margherita had put on her coat and left the agency. 'Would you?'

'Get back with Mamadou?'

'I think you probably would.'

'Want to know something? Strictly between us? I sleep with him, like twice a month. We just sleep. At my place, when Nico is at his grandparents'.'

Margherita put a hand in front of her mouth. 'Tell me more!'

'I like listening to his breathing as he sleeps. He's that type of man who stays in the same position all night; he wakes up early in the morning and you don't even notice him. You open your eyes and he's gone to work and everything feels like a dream.'

'You miss him.'

'I miss that. But anyway.'

'Never say never – maybe with time.'

'It's gone. Nico is fine, except for school. And I'm happy enough with those two nights a month and the other happy nights.' She laughed. 'But what about you?'

'I'd like a small part of yours,' and she dropped silent.

'My what?'

'I dunno.'

'The day, Margherita. You need to seize the day.'

'I'll show you my daily schedule.' She was pacing now. 'Never mind seizing one.'

'So maybe plan a nice visit to your sister-in-law. I'll make you black cherry cupcakes. We can't keep up with the requests down at the workshop.'

'You really sleep with him twice a month?'

They had to hang up because a colleague of Margherita's had gestured for her to come back into the office. When she sat down at her desk, she imagined the double bed, Mamadou calmly sleeping and Simona listening to him breathe.

She waited until the end of the working day, then left and took the metro to Via delle Leghe, went up to the flat and opened the desk drawers. She found her mother's address book, looked for *Buzzati (Landi)*, headed to the lounge and sat down on the sofa with the book on her lap. She took out her phone and typed in the number, asked for an appointment. There was one two months later and she said it was urgent.

'They're all urgent, madam.'

'My mother is ill. She's known Landi for years.'

'Madam.'

'Please.'

They snuck her in the following morning, just for fifteen

minutes. She slept badly that night and when she reached Via Vigevano in the morning she told herself she'd never want to seize the day.

She waited in the lounge, looking at the framed *Lady and the Tramp* jigsaw. Then she was shown to a small kitchen with a buzzing fridge. She greeted the smoking old lady with her eyes half shut.

'My mother broke her femur.' She sat haphazardly on the chair.

'Is this why you're here?'

Margherita was quiet, then nodded.

'What do you wish to know?'

'Everything.'

The old woman took a drag and put out the cigarette in the ashtray. She shuffled the deck, with difficulty, asked her to cut it with her left hand. She laid out the cards and said, 'Ask.'

'Will she die?'

'You don't have to worry.' The old woman kept staring at the table

'She's getting surgery.'

'Don't worry. About her, or your son.'

'My son? What about my son?'

The old woman raised a Knight of Wands. 'Don't get in his way.'

'We're in his way?'

'You are.' She showed her the Knight of Swords.

'Not my husband?'

'Not your husband.' She took a card, put the deck back together and shuffled, laid out a pyramid. Then she raised her head and opened her eyes. 'Don't worry about your mother and say hi to her from me.'

Margherita stood up suddenly, realised she was strangling her handbag and unclenched her fists and rummaged in her purse for the cent and the seventy euros, placed them on the plate. She got up to leave, and stopped at the fridge.

'Can I ask what you saw about my husband?'

'What do you wish to know?'

'He had an interview.'

The old woman took out another cigarette, lit it. 'This one will fall through.'

'Really? Again?'

She nodded. 'You need to be patient.'

Margherita inhaled sharply. 'And the rest?'

'The rest?' She looked closely at the cards at the base of the pyramid. 'There's nothing else.'

'There isn't?'

Madam Landi raised the King of Cups. 'The rest is fine.'

Margherita let her bag hang from its strap on her arm and turned towards the fridge; there were some magnets on the door, one with the Tower of Pisa, one with the Colosseum. She thanked her with a nod of her head, then slowly left the flat; her clothes clung on to the stench of cigarette smoke for the rest of the day.

She got home and she and Carlo fucked. She thought of nothing else when they fucked; sometimes she listened to herself moan and moan and forgot that she was a mother and a wife and wanted to be a slut. In the meantime, it had happened: a dull burden had been dissolved for seventy euros and one cent, given to a clairvoyant who had certified her a decent fate. She hadn't asked anything else – what would she ask the stars about?

'Tell me if I will ever start my own agency again, if I'll orgasm until I'm ninety. Tell me if I'll love my man and my son as I love them today.'

Even though she didn't want anyone around the night before the operation, Anna found all of them there, Margherita, Carlo, Lorenzo, the Pentecostes, uncaring of her discomfort. She had two pillows beneath her head, she was stiff, almost paralysed all the way down to her groin and it was giving her a hint of claustrophobia that she kept in check by looking out of the window, at her Milan and its aluminium sky. Her sole respite was her grandson, doodling on her cast; for a second she'd thought she was back home with him, listening to her records. She could feel her fear growing in the presence of all of them.

She told Carlo, 'How about you all leave?'

But Loretta was arranging a vase of anemones on her bedside table, Domenico was chatting to the primary physician. He came over and reassured her that the deputy would conduct the operation – he was a good one, they would let her go home in ten days, maybe sooner.

'Ten days?'

'I asked them to, so you can recover better. You might just need a week.' Pentecoste smiled. 'But we'll all be here for you anyway.'

He'd softened with age – she agreed with Carlo when he compared him to brandy, the older he got, the less sharp. He should've retired a long time ago. He'd confessed to her that he'd rather die on his job than spend sixteen hours out of twenty-four with Loretta. They'd laughed – strange how one minute someone can be so grating and the following you'd happily have a picnic with them. She stared at him at the foot of her bed, then shifted her gaze to Margherita and Carlo at the centre of the room. They were still beautiful together. Their bodies knew how to be close and this made her happy every time. Carlo had lost his Thursday visit routine – he appeared whenever, now, with Margherita too. Both of them would make themselves at home on the long side of the corner sofa, resting their legs on the small table and their heads back on the seat; it was funny to see two people ending up choosing the same position.

'How about you, you finished colouring me up?' She peeked at Lorenzo, who was drawing a fish on her cast. Now she was a sharp-finned grandma. Lorenzo used a sky-blue pen for the eyes and told her, 'It's you.'

'Am I a turquoise fish in a tank or a turquoise fish in the sea?'

'In the sea.'

'Good answer, dear.' She strained her voice and had to let herself back onto the pillow. She stroked his head, then they all turned towards the door; a man was asking to come in.

She stared at him. 'I'm not a believer.'

'I'm here for those who do and those who don't.' And he stepped in. He was a middle-aged priest with tortoiseshell glasses, and she noticed some product in his hair.

'We'll wait outside,' said Margherita.

The priest greeted the other patients, asked if he could sit in the chair.

'Are you here to bless me?'

'Just a few words. You're having an operation and I always come in these cases.'

'Oh,' she muttered, and tears came to her eyes. She changed them into a smile.

'What's your name?'

'I'm Anna.'

'Anna, if I'm bothering you, I'll leave.'

She shook her head. 'It's just that, I thought of my husband.' She looked at the window. 'When he was about to die, someone came for the last rites. Franco was almost gone, but I saw it: at some point he raised his fingers like you do to shoo a fly, you know?'

'But you're not about to die.'

'Who knows, really?' She stared at the priest's hands; they seemed soft, one of the nails was dirty and he kept rubbing two fingertips together. 'And what's your name?'

'I'm Antonio.'

Anna thought about it. 'Like the film, you know the one?' She touched her head as if to access her memory.

'I can't say I do.'

'Main character with the tuft. Excellent kisser.' She settled back into her pillow. 'Antonio, you may continue.'

'May I?' said the priest.

'I mean, you're here now.'

He raised his arm and blessed her in the name of the Father, the Son and the Holy Ghost.

'And the Virgin Mary. Why do you always ignore her?'

'Do you pray to her?'

'Just bless me.'

He did so.

'Thank you,' she told him.

'I'll come and visit you tomorrow.'

'If I'm not here, I'll put it in a good word for you. Though it's probably overkill.'

'Don't be silly.' He touched the turquoise fish on her cast. 'See you tomorrow, Anna.'

When the priest left, she called Carlo and whispered, 'I'm leaving you all of my records.'

He knew that Anna was serious because of her frowning forehead. He stroked her. 'I want the comics too,' and that omen came back to him: her in a wheelchair. The previous evening Margherita had said, 'Mum in a wheelchair.' He'd stayed quiet, she'd cried, then they'd huddled together in the kitchen until the coffee was ready.

'It's this house,' Margherita had added.

'It's the osteoporosis.'

'I played dirty to get it.'

'She's eighty years old.'

'I paid for the hundred thousand we saved with my mother's femur.'

'Come on, that's enough.'

'We need to find nine hundred euros a month for the next thirty years. Three thousand euros a year of housing fees. We don't even have a fucking lift.'

'What did we have before? The same amount in rent and a third of the living space. Can you see us living with our son in seventy square metres?'

'Buying a cheaper apartment with fewer issues, that's what I can see.'

'Don't be one of those, Margherita.'

'One of what?'

'Those who have perfect hindsight.'

She'd pulled away from him, made the coffee and started stirring it in the mug. 'Tell me this: if you couldn't rely on your family's inheritance would you have gone for this place? If you couldn't rely on your family's inheritance would you have continued to refuse a full-time contract at the office, ending up with nothing, bare-arsed on the floor?'

'I didn't let them sign me on because I wouldn't have had time for teaching, you know that.' He'd taken away her mug. 'Everything will be OK with your mother. And this house is a great deal for Milan. And soon I'll be an editor at *Bell'Italia* or a factotum in the beer industry or I'll pass an interview. Jesus Christ!'

'It's just . . . we pay for our sins, Carlo.'

He thought of Manuela. How he'd managed his own sin. That afternoon of many years ago, after having fucked her, he'd come home in a hurry, knowing that Margherita would be out until late. He'd meticulously showered and had realised that, as of that moment, he was a ticking bomb in their marriage. The asymptomatic carrier of a separation if he were to be found out, if he confessed. If the deed came out for any reason at all, any moment could change everything. He hadn't considered the more indulgent alternatives: forgiveness, reparations, understanding; he'd known that his pact with Margherita did not allow for them. He'd always known. He'd told himself as much the evening of his infidelity, pacing around the house, stepping in and back out of the shower, slowly drying himself off, observing his own body: nothing had changed – it was the same as before, maybe some redness on his penis. His colleague had smooth skin and moles on her back, a more pungent smell than Margherita, her nipples less pronounced . . . the comparison had laid siege to him. He'd wrapped himself tighter in the towelling robe, going over the events of that afternoon. This time it had been Manuela, in the office, inviting him to another film. He'd looked at Michele Lattuada at the desk next to his, told him he had to leave, Michele had looked at him in a way that let him know he needed to add nothing else. Carlo had left the office and reached the end of Corso San Gottardo – it was September and they'd just signed for Concordia. He'd waited for Manuela with the inside flutter of someone who can smell out an opportunity: pressure on his sternum, different from the pressure he'd felt with Sofia, a little weaker, but still very much there, embers that burned independently of whoever stood before him.

They'd set off together, reached the Naviglio Grande, then he'd stopped at the lights, let her understand that he wanted to cross in the opposite direction to the cinema. They'd set off again, chatting, the morning meeting and the publisher's 9 per cent loss in the past six months; they expected cuts across all departments. They'd crossed the ring road and he'd stared at her, this girl-next-door with short-heeled boots, brown bowl cut over brown eyes, their very own Audrey Hepburn. He'd felt he could continue to the outskirts, slowing down at the Mercurio Hotel Milan, stopping at its entrance. A moment of embarrassment, then she'd said, 'After you.'

After you . . . it had made the butterflies worse. They'd got out their documents at the desk and his had fallen; he'd picked it up and said nothing, not even inside the closed doors of the lift, all the way to the fourth floor. They'd walked down the corridor with its cream carpet and he'd thought of his wife, imagined her pretty grimace that he spotted some evenings when they bumped into each other in the street on their re-spective ways home. Then he'd unlocked room sixty-seven on the inner courtyard side of the building – and in the hour he'd spent there, he'd shared the space with the two of them, Manuela and Margherita, on the double bed with the sheets fleeing the mattress's corners, with Manuela grabbing him and guiding him inside her, shifting, trying to enjoy this new body as much as possible. The moaning without Margherita, the force of an orgasm without Margherita – already on the first wave he'd sensed a halo of darkness: what had been urge was now becoming apprehension. He'd felt it lying down next to her, in the silence of the hotel room, and after that, washing himself in the faded blue tiles, checking for hairs on his cotton jumper. He'd lingered by the window, overlooking another building's wall. Then he'd asked her to leave the hotel and they'd walked almost in total silence. They'd slipped into the traffic of a city riddled with building sites, with people walking aimlessly, with freelancers looking the worse for wear, and all those pieces of a free-falling Italy had felt like his own free fall. They'd walked up to where the Naviglio takes on the air of the real periphery, with its locks and bridges; there had been no need to say anything to each other.

When Margherita had come home that evening, he'd had to deal with the estrangement; he'd coped. They'd had an omelette and some salad, she'd turned on the radio, they'd shared a Coke, they'd chatted, they'd stayed quiet. He'd asked himself why he'd stepped into room sixty-seven. He was happy with Margherita, truly happy. Had he done it because of something primordial, because of the mortgage, the Pentecostes, the son they hadn't yet decided to have, the publisher's struggles, the missed orgasm with Sofia? He'd done it. That evening, clearing the table and glancing at his wife doing the washing-up, he'd asked himself if fucking another woman meant that he'd fuck other women in the future.

The answer was yes. Before becoming a father, he'd had other women. A marketing consultant who came to see the publisher every now and then, an ex-colleague from university, a girl who worked in a café close to the office. Manuela again. A couple of meetings with each, then he'd brutally shut down this Pandora's box, avoiding turning adultery into routine. He'd never doubted his future with Margherita. He'd slowly come to see those experiences as necessary – a formation of the self – and he was now going over them as if they were feeble lights, almost captions: he'd needed them, he'd been able to. Now he felt that he had crossed the cliché of betrayal, the biological need of betrayal, the evasion of betrayal, the answer to a dissatisfaction revealed by the betrayal. What if betrayal had been his way of coming back to fidelity to Margherita?

This doubt, even years later, in a hospital room host to his mother-in-law about to undergo a femur operation, still haunted him as he watched the turquoise fish on the cast. He looked at Lorenzo and it came back to him, even though he knew it hadn't taken his son to make him change his ways. He tried guiding him away when the nurses came in to take Anna for her final tests before surgery, but the boy was holding onto the bedsheet and would not let go.

'Dad's taking you to the swings.' Margherita moved closer.

The boy started crying.

'Darling, I have your lucky fish.' Anna showed her cast.

'Let's go to the swings.' Carlo lifted him up and Lorenzo grabbed on to him. They left the Fatebenefratelli and he could feel the boy's tears on his neck, kept walking with him in his arms until Corso Garibaldi. He lowered him again and cleaned his nose and mouth.

Lorenzo was watching him.

'Lorenzo, have you ever seen a lucky fish as good as the one you drew for Grandma?'

The boy shook his head.

He took his hand and they walked towards Parco Sempione. They went in through the Arena side and headed towards a building on one side of the gardens instead of the swings. They went in, bought tickets and he asked the boy if he could cover his eyes with a scarf for half a minute.

'Why?'

'It's a surprise.'

The boy thought about it for a second, then nodded his head.

Carlo tied his scarf behind his head and guided him to a room with a giant arching aquarium. They stopped just beneath it.

'You ready, chipmunk?'

Lorenzo nodded again, under the scarf.

He took it off him.

The lucky fish. Ten, twenty, hundreds of them, everywhere; to one side and above them, and there were some manta rays. He'd seen the rays in a book he'd read with his mum – they had a really dangerous tail spike. He moved closer to the glass, craned his neck and a grouper stared at him, giant mouth gaping. Lorenzo turned to his father and laughed. 'It's a tuna!'

Carlo laughed too.

The boy stuck his finger to the glass. Carlo joined him and told him to suck on his finger and stick it again. They both did and the grouper swam closer.

'It's the lucky fish,' said the boy.

'Yeah, it is.'

For a while he'd been afraid that Lorenzo might've inherited his affective stammer, almost as if emotional behaviour were contagious. He'd thought about it again when he started receiving the books from Rimini. The echo came back, almost immediately: the way Sofia would nibble on her almonds in class, how she had squeezed his arm as he fled her place in Isola. The day he'd unwrapped the first book he thought it was a complimentary copy from a publisher – strange that it would be a Fenoglio novel. He'd brought it home and left it on the sofa armrest. But then Fenoglio had been the most talked-about writer on his course. When he'd opened up her Instagram profile and saw it in a post, he'd chalked it up to a coincidence. The second package had arrived a few weeks later. He'd looked for the stamp and had seen *Rimini*, he'd held it in anticipation of a revelation. He'd unwrapped a copy of *Camere Separate* by Tondelli: she'd posted it on her profile with a corner of the hardware shop showing in the background. He'd felt a tingle throughout his body and through the day he'd been taken over by an excitement that had put everything else to rest, including his unemployment. He'd been waiting for another book. The whole month and a half it took, he'd never stopped asking himself what she wanted with him.

Sofia asked herself why he wasn't replying. Sometimes, having closed the shop for lunch, she'd head home and peek at her postbox or the corner of the hall where parcels ended up sometimes, hoping he'd send some sort of sign after she'd found his address on the university website.

Since her return to Rimini, she'd been tempted to reach out to him. She'd had the chance to head back to Milan once or twice but had eventually refused. She'd never reread 'How Things Are' – she'd stuffed it into a blue folder with the other papers from the course and a USB stick that held the recording of the conversation with Pentecoste about the chick, his voice enunciating *propulsion*, feeble, strong: she was ashamed of having considered sending it to his wife. From that time, she'd also kept up her friendship with Khalil; they messaged with each other sometimes, followed each other on social media; he was working in a Dubai hotel and posted photos of Arab fantasies; he'd taken up kite-surfing and hadn't found love yet. He was *speranzoso* – hopeful. He used that Italian word because the sound amused him, always asked her if she was too.

She was hopeful towards a boy three years older than her, manager of a hotel in Bellaria, with curls that covered his sea-green eyes and who opened the car door for her in the evenings. He fucked her good. *Tommaso* was a name that rang true for a truthful man. She realised she'd think about him during the day, sometimes even looked out the shop window wanting to see him; she felt like waiting for him was waiting for a reply from Milan, particles of an impatience that she would've liked to ball up together.

She got her confirmation that morning, too, when he showed up at the shop with breakfast and she suddenly felt much calmer. They shared the *pistacchio cannolo* behind the counter – he claimed the bit with more almonds – and she was watching him devour it as her father came back saying, 'I'd forgotten the lightbulbs,' and headed to the shelves furthest away.

Tommaso almost ducked, then he raised his voice to say goodbye. He kissed her without smacking their lips as he left.

'He's the Della Motta boy, right?'

'Yes.'

'He's a good boy, you can tell.'

She threw out the bakery bag. 'How can you tell?'

'*Dài che l'è brèv.*'

'I'll give it a go if you say so.'

'I'll stay here, you go with him.'

'He has errands to run.'

Her father put the lightbulbs down onto the counter and started arranging them in a box. 'They've refurbished the Fulgor cinema.' He was a little out of breath. 'Some famous architect. Go see a film with him so you can tell me what it's like.'

'Let it go.' She helped him with the lightbulbs. They both had careful hands and her father's breath smelled of tobacco and mint. '*Bà*, how long has it been since you've been to the cinema?'

'Me?' He did up his raincoat. '*Dis an.*'

'Ten years? You want to go this evening?'

Her father lowered his head; she'd learned to sniff out his happiness from his hands – he'd curl them up in each other.

Margherita saw the same gesture in Anna, days after the operation, as soon as she told her mother she was free to go home.

'My dear, never lie to a dying woman.'

'I'm taking you home.'

'When?'

'Tomorrow.'

Her mother looked away. 'And what are you going to do with me?'

'We'll get a carer.'

'You need to live your own life.' Anna kept one hand closed inside the other. Margherita came closer and cupped them in hers. The leg had reacted well to the surgery and there had been no infections; she told her she'd have to increase her physiotherapy.

'With the boy?'

Seeing them together, her mother and Andrea, had been the most natural of things. She'd waited to call him, a couple of days after the operation, and he'd dropped in one afternoon and sat down on the bed without taking his coat off. Her mother had watched him and Andrea had started asking her very precise questions about her symptoms. At the end of the conversation he'd said, 'Don't you worry, Anna.'

He'd come back the following day; Margherita kept an eye on them from the corridor. Andrea, with one knee on the mattress, had started exploring her mother's muscles, her neck and free arm, even her torso, helping her twist it however little she could. He'd graze her skin and suggest slow movements; she'd execute them holding on to the strong shoulders that had been strong shoulders for her daughter too. Then Carlo and Lorenzo had arrived and she'd regretted exposing something that had been hers. But she also felt like Carlo knew how much a good part of her Andrea had become – she refused to think his homosexuality was the reason for the trust.

She hadn't had any other men after him, only desire and cravings, letting herself be satisfied with an interrupted seduction. She'd let occasions vanish, as if her devotion to herself no

176

longer followed urges but a quiet centring. She'd felt on her skin the desire for a child, the cliché that protected her effortlessly from temptation. Giving birth to Lorenzo hadn't been a repression, or setting a limit, it had been: 'That's it.' It had left her feeling sated. She'd been sated about the misunderstanding too, but now?

'Grandma didn't get better.'

'She *is* better, Lorenzo. She's coming home tomorrow!'

The boy looked at Margherita.

She smiled at him. 'Tell us what you did in school today.'

'The wooden house for robins with Roberta Calcaterra.'

'Is Roberta Calcaterra the girl with curly hair?'

Lorenzo nodded.

'She has a nice face.'

Lorenzo shook his head.

'She isn't nice?'

He shook his head again.

'So why do you play with her?'

The boy climbed off the sofa and crouched down on the rug. 'She says we're inseparable.'

'Really?'

'Yes.'

'Do you know what inseparable means, chipmunk?'

'Friends.'

Margherita and Carlo looked at each other. 'Lorenzo, come back on the sofa, you'll get cold.'

'I'm not cold.'

'Listen to your mum, come on.'

He obeyed and settled down between them.

Margherita left him some space on the cushion. 'Did you make a really good wooden house for robins?'

'She does everything and I watch.'

'You're a cheeky one, you. You don't say much but you're cheeky, aren't you?'

'Roberta Calcaterra says that she wants me even if I don't say much.'

They tucked him under the blanket. 'Of course she wants you even if you don't say much, darling.'

'Is Grandma really coming home tomorrow?'

As she watched her mother being carried to the ambulance by the nurses, then the drive together from the Fatebenefratelli towards Via delle Leghe, holding her hand, Margherita told herself that her own impatience was a suggestion coming directly from this old lady on a stretcher, as if she'd pushed her to be different from who she was. She stroked her hair. 'How are you feeling?'

'I'm going back, darling.'

As they were carrying her into her flat, Margherita felt a surge of sudden strength. She shifted her bag onto one shoulder and helped so that the stretcher would be as gentle as possible. Carlo was waiting for them with the door wide open.

'In the lounge, please,' said Anna.

'Mum.'

'Don't you hole me up like your dad.'

'In the lounge,' said Carlo.

Anna was placed between the sofa and the table and they went to fetch the anti-bedsore mattress from the bedroom and set it up in there. Then they lifted her out of the stretcher. At the moment of lifting she closed her eyes. She was picturing what was awaiting her: worry around her and the certainty of being in the way. Just after they got married, her husband had said he would've liked to take care of her, but it'd only happened one time, for the flu, and getting soup in bed wasn't exactly the same as being offered a chair in a restaurant. She wanted

178

a carer, immediately, no matter if Italian, Ukrainian, Russian, Indian, as long as they were invisible and allowed her daughter to get back home. They'd told her they were looking for one. She turned to face the bookshelves, looked for the *Tex Willer* comics' spines, and pressed her cheek into the pillow – she'd discovered that she could stop tears from falling in that position.

She kept her eyes closed as her daughter and Carlo rearranged the lounge, then her son-in-law left and she was moved closer to the wall. Her heart was beating fast and she had difficulty breathing; she stared at the turquoise fish on her arm to calm herself down. Lorenzo had drawn it with a serious mouth, and she was certain it was a wary fish. It had kept her company in hospital and her grandson had slowly added details – green scales, sharper fins – and when she'd asked him what fish it was, he'd told her it was a tuna. But tuna was the shame of her old age. Whenever she'd see one at a fishmonger, or even just if someone spoke the word 'tuna', she'd always end up at that morning five years ago, when her phone had rung and Margherita had told her she was pregnant. They had squealed like a pair of gossips, hung up, and she'd felt the urge to celebrate: she'd gone to the supermarket close to Corso Buenos Aires to buy some Ferrero Rocher, had wanted to have one immediately, but when she walked past the seafood stalls she'd spotted the fresh tuna and had chosen a fillet for dinner. She'd picked up some Burrata too, and she had a Berlucchi in the fridge – becoming a grandmother was a good reason to open the bottle.

Then, heading to the tills, she'd been taken over by a strange energy: she'd let the bag with the tuna slip into her own bag and had kept the Rocher and the cheese in her hands. She'd walked down the personal hygiene aisle and in this new state of fear, she'd picked up and put back a hair conditioner; she'd wandered a little more, then she'd queued up at till number 5 and waited for her turn to pay. She'd taken out the note, put away her change, and had surprised herself with how cordial she had kept through a fear that was also joy. She'd shoved everything into a plastic bag and had headed towards the exit, where an ordinary-looking man had asked her to follow him.

'I'm sorry?'

'Please just step this way.' He had pointed at the service door where new products emerged.

'And who are you?'

And as soon as the man had shown her his security badge, she'd felt her cheeks flare up and hadn't looked at him. She'd followed him and found herself in a dimly lit space between pallets of products; another man was waiting for them and asked her what she'd bought. She'd opened the plastic bag and waited for them to ask her about her handbag.

'Can you open it for us, please?'

'That's not a nice thing to ask of an old lady, is it?' But she'd complied. 'What's going to happen to me now?'

The two men had looked at each other. 'You forgot about it; it's OK, it can happen. Just go back to the till.'

She hadn't moved; she'd felt the ground slip away, had held on to a pallet and one of the men had helped her up by an arm.

'It's OK, it happens!'

'My daughter is going to have a baby.'

They'd nodded and she'd said goodbye with a nod of her head, had paid at till number 4 and had left the shop with burning cheeks and a cold feeling along her back that followed her home. It had been an adventure, that's how she'd framed it. Just like letting herself be massaged by a thirty-five-year-old with a pianist's hands and monk-like modesty. That Andrea was a boy she could feel safe with.

As soon as the doorbell rang, she straightened up on the pillow and tidied her hair with her fingers. Andrea appeared in the lounge and she smiled at him. 'See? I managed to bring my old skin home.'

He greeted her and came closer to the bed. Margherita said she'd be in the bedroom for some work calls but Andrea kept looking around him and lingered in the kitchen.

Anna smiled: 'You're hungry, aren't you?'

He said he wasn't.

'Why don't you look in the cupboard over the fridge – there should be some rum chocolates.'

He didn't move.

'You really are shy, aren't you?'

Andrea went to the kitchen and opened the cupboard over the fridge; he found nothing.

'They must've moved them. Look in the cupboards around there.'

'We should ask your daughter.'

'Asking takes the joy out of it.'

'Rum wouldn't be a great idea with your medicine.' But he kept looking through the cupboards and he found the box next to the stove and brought it over to her.

She took one. 'Help yourself.'

'It's my mother's birthday dinner this evening.'

'So?'

'I'll be having sweets there.'

'Right, your muscle-man diet.' She frowned. 'How old is your mum?'

'Sixty-eight.' He rolled up the sleeves of his jumper.

'Buy her some red and yellow tulips.' She picked out another chocolate from the box. 'You sure you don't want one?'

He took it and they ate in silence, closing their eyes and chewing until the taste had faded. Then Andrea moved over her, started on the free arm, slowly. He'd come to recognise her by her shoulder joints; he felt them loosen and knew that returning home had relaxed her. He lingered over her shoulder blade, every now and then looking at her tiny eyes, bloated with medication, or maybe with melancholy. He moved from her arm to her neck and back, he made her turn around and sat her up on the edge of the bed, so that her legs would dangle off it. There was the same smell of hairspray from when Margherita had invited him over years ago. She'd told him that her mother was with her family in Como and he'd really enjoyed that version of a teenager taking advantage of a situation. He'd said yes, wondering what would happen, but instead they'd just talked and shared one kiss, standing up and almost distractedly, then they'd made coffee and as the moka pot started bubbling he'd said, 'I like men.'

She'd tensed up and he'd tensed up. The noise of the traffic from Via delle Leghe was coming in through the window and she'd said, 'I like men too.'

They'd laughed, their backs against the counter. She'd reached over and grabbed him; they'd hugged and he'd added, 'I can't help it. I can't help it.' He so wanted to be able to tell Giorgio those same words, to explain about the dogs and the warehouses and the fight he'd be going to again that night.

'Let's try moving this leg.'

'I'm scared.' Anna smiled.

'Ready?'

Andrea bent over and let her latch onto his neck, held her by the waist and prepared himself to help her at the critical movement. Before letting her off the bed, he checked that her nightgown covered her – one time she'd stood up and whispered, 'Please look up.'

They took one step, then another, and when they reached the centre of the Persian rug in the lounge he felt as though he was dancing with her. Strange how he'd got used to this tame body and how he'd get used to the authoritarian body later that night, and the reactive bodies of his students in the coming days, and the welcoming one of Giorgio. The only ones he wasn't used to were the ones of his parents. He'd be heading to their place after this, have some cake, then he'd change the lightbulb in the corridor on a ladder; he'd settle on the sofa with the TV on at half volume and they'd chat about the newsagent's and his training, then he'd leave and would head to the warehouse, but first he'd squeeze his father's shoulder in a gesture of closeness. It was so hard to touch his father . . .

When Sofia took her father by the arm, she sensed her mother there too. When she was a child, the three of them had gone to see *Toy Story* at the Astoria, and all she could remember was the popcorn. She matched her steps up with his and they crossed Piazza Cavour together; it had snowed a little and Rimini was a sepia painting under the street lamps. They took the Corso and saw a small crowd in front of the Fulgor cinema. Her father slowed down and said, 'Maybe they've sold out.'

'Come on.' She tightened her grip.

They queued up in silence, then Sofia wanted popcorn and he wanted liquorice; he liked eating swirls even though they raised his blood pressure. He'd gone for the light wool cardigan and the rough-thread burgundy tie; when it was their turn he already had his wallet out. They walked into the screening room – it had golden gilding and scarlet seats, it really was the 1930s cinema of Fellini. They told each other the story of the director driving around Ina Casa in a Mercedes and someone had seen him and swore that Mastroianni was also in the car. For a second, she regretted not being there with Tommaso; maybe she did know what to do with a reliable partner. She took her phone out of her jacket – but also maybe it would never be enough. She typed the message, *I hope the books have arrived, I reread Fenoglio in these years too. Sofia (Casadei).* She pressed send, then she let herself flop into a seat; it was dark now and she could be a daughter.

The message reached Carlo as they were all in Via delle Leghe. He and Margherita had hidden in the bedroom while Lorenzo slept with his grandmother in the lounge. They were about to choose a film from the laptop – she was suggesting *The Big Chill* despite having seen it over and over again while he was more for *A Special Day*, but he'd put the discussion on pause to check his buzzing phone. He read Sofia's message. Margherita had walked across to the Andrea Giani poster and was pressing against the drooping corner, telling him that *The Big Chill* was one of the films on her hypothetical top ten list – what did he think?

He looked at her and didn't reply.

'Carlo?'

'Hm?'

'Do you agree?'

'Yes.'

'Who's that?'

'What?'

'Your phone.'

'Oh. My sister.'

'What's Simona saying?'

'The interview.' He paused. 'She wants to know if there's any news.'

'But we talked about it for half an hour today already!'

He looked up. 'She's also asking about your mother.'

'OK, but any news about her son?'

'She says . . .' He was still holding his phone. 'I'll call her tomorrow to find out.'

'She says . . .?'

'She told me yesterday they're making him switch classes.'

184

'I'd make him switch schools. They keep shouting Nico the negro at him.'

'They're using the n-word.'

'I mean, it's a good name for a rapper.'

'He told me they actually stuck a note on his rucksack.' He put the phone away.

'You're not going to answer her?'

'Let's watch the film first.' He invited her back to the bed.

Margherita told him to wait, headed to the lounge as he reread the message: he stared at the words and checked that the delivery date and time were indeed three minutes ago and not from a time when he was in turmoil. Now he was just dazed and excitement barely prodded him. He put away his phone again. Then she came back.

'They're fast asleep. Lorenzo is so comfy on the sofa, I don't think we should wake him.'

'And your mother?'

'Exhausted from physio.'

Carlo stretched out on the bed, invited Margherita to join him again and rearranged the pillows behind their heads. He laid his body against hers, started *A Special Day*.

'The dictator hath spoken!' She pretended to shove him off the bed.

'I feel like some Loren.' He waited for the opening credits and the train whistle and Hitler at the train window, the voice off-screen announcing the triumphant march towards Rome, the swastika hung by the custodian on the building's balcony, then he said, 'It wasn't my sister on the phone.'

She shifted her head on his chest. 'OK.'

Margherita was watching the film – or at least facing the other side of the room, the desk where she used to study and the cassette tapes piled up on a shelf corner.

The camera lingers on the building: it's dawn and the windows light up one after the other.

'That book hurts,' his wife then said.

'Which book?'

'*Sylvia.*'

He kept himself against her, stared at the Andrea Giani poster and its peeling corner. 'I haven't heard from her in years.'

'The books you're reading and the photos of the same books in her Instagram posts, are they . . . what are they?'

'She did everything herself.'

'Carlo.'

'She sends them in the post.'

'She sends them?'

'I told you, entirely her own idea.'

'Carlo.'

His wife's body was light and the warmth moved down to the ribcage, Sofia Loren finished ironing a shirt on the kitchen table and made some coffee; he rummaged in his pocket and pulled out his phone. 'I want to show you, nothing's going on.'

She stopped his hand under the blanket. 'I don't care.'

'Read.'

'I honestly don't care.' And she moved his arm away, gently.

He set the phone down on the bedsheets. She'd left her hand on his stomach; now moved it lower and touched him lightly. She undid his belt and the buttons of his jeans, tried pulling them down to his thighs. He wasn't helping her, so she tugged them lower, Sofia Loren and the creased dress and her tired face, pacing the house, all those kids, her eldest caught wearing lipstick.

Carlo's gaze was fixed on the screen and so was Margherita's, then she stroked it, was stroking him. She moved closer with her mouth and closed her lips on it, Sofia Loren alone at home, Margherita sucking and giving it shape while Mastroianni sits at a desk, the red jumper, part of his shirt poking out, Margherita insisting and him staring at his wife's mouth, imagining the other woman being there. It had been a while since he'd imagined her like that, the childishness of men; he returned to his wife and got ready, to moan for her, to get ready to feel pleasure for her, come into her, confused by the arousal and a strange feeling.

Her husband's taste hadn't changed in all those years; Margherita rested her cheek on her husband's groin, closed her eyes, and for a moment her paranoia was back: that the same taste had been in the other's mouth too. She got up from the bed, careful with the computer; Loren showed up at Mastroianni's door and asked to come in, and did; Margherita left Carlo and the bedroom and ended up in the corridor. The lounge was almost dark and she went to see her mother and her son, both sleeping. Lorenzo's leg was out of the blanket – he'd always used his left foot to cool down. She moved closer to the French window – she always called upon her father in these moments – she wanted to go back to her husband and tell him about Andrea. When she turned around, Carlo was in the lounge doorway. She joined him and took his arm, dragged him into the corridor and into her mother's room; the sewing machine had been moved next to the wardrobe.

'You didn't fuck her, in that bathroom.'

'You know that.'

'I believe you when you say you didn't fuck her.'

'So what's the problem?'

'Maybe that you didn't fuck her.'

'Come on.'

'If you'd fucked her, you would've got rid of her by now. Or maybe got rid of me. Or me of you. But you wouldn't still be getting messages that startle you while you're watching *A Special Day* with your wife in her teenage bed.'

'Startle?'

'Startle. Or do you prefer trouble?' She raised her voice.

He gestured her to lower it again. 'You're the one with a problem here.'

'Oh, sure! A wife sees her husband turn red because of a text from a nymphet ten years after she's been dead and buried – but I'm the one with a problem, of course.'

'The text means nothing.'

'Then why tell me?'

'I told you about it *because* it meant nothing.'

'Like that time years ago, right?'

'I didn't realise you were hung up on this.'

'Nor did I.' She took a deep breath. 'That girl is worse than a nine hundred euro a month mortgage, she's worse than . . . hell if I know.'

'Than an unemployed husband.'

'Don't.'

'Don't what?'

'Don't turn the tables.'

'You'll see. I'll get through this interview and I'll get that beer marketing job and you'll see me as another alpha male marking his territory.'

'Please, don't.' She let her arms fall to her sides.

He took them. 'It's going to be OK, don't worry.'

'How long since you heard from her?'

'Since then.'

She squirmed out of his grip. 'Carlo, please.'

'Since then.'

'So those books she sends are a, what, cultural exchange?'

'Entirely her idea.'

'Carlo, I want you to get her out of your head.'

'She's already not in there.'

She took another deep breath. 'I'm tired,' she said, almost

not hearing herself. 'Please get her out of your head.'

'You're the one who needs to get her out of your head.'

'Carlo . . .'

He stayed at the centre of the room, almost invisible in the dark. She stepped closer and rested a hand on his chest. 'I'm tired . . .' And she let herself be held; she'd become small if he held her right.

'Stay a little longer,' his mother insisted.

Andrea hugged her, then he stiffened and had to pull away. 'I need to go, happy birthday, Ma.' The red and yellow tulips were in the glass vase. He waved his father goodbye on his way out – dropping in on them before the warehouse always drained him.

He walked to the car, got in and checked his phone, started the engine. He didn't feel like music and he set off with a heavy head. He pulled back his seat and inclined it a little; his rib was just being annoying, no pain; he felt his work with Anna in the lumbar region, he still smelled of her rose perfume. His stomach was light – he'd limited himself to cake – the important part was the candles and the wish he'd made as his mother blew them out, 'Let her be happy' – it was always the same one.

Then he freed his brain. The road had a thin frost and Milan's night-time made him feel safe; he was hoping for the Egyptian, that colossus of a baker with a newborn son who hit round the ears and had KO'd two fighters. It took him thirty-five minutes to reach the Novedratese; there were three Nigerians in front of the Carrefour and he carried on and took the slope down to Carimate, parked where the road narrowed and unfastened his seatbelt. He went to open the boot; there was another car waiting in the darkness just a couple of metres away, headlights on. He covered his eyes to spot the driver, gave up and opened the boot, pulled out his bag and listened to the car slowly roll closer. It stopped next to him and he recognised Giorgio. His window was down and he was staring, saying nothing, he continued and parked a little further ahead.

Andrea went to meet him. 'Go home.'

'Is that where you're going? Who's inside?' Giorgio pointed at the warehouse. Curls were falling over his forehead; he brushed them aside and leaned out of the car. 'Who are you fucking?'

'Please, just leave.'

'I was downstairs from your parents' for the entire meal.' He looked down at the wheel. 'When I saw you leave I thought, so he isn't fucking anyone else. He's not telling me he's going to see his parents and at the gym and then going to get his cock sucked somewhere.'

'I asked you to leave.'

'But then . . .'

'Leave!'

All that cold clearing the night air, and the humming of the engine, and Andrea who was only looking forward to the Egyptian. Then Giorgio started the car, turned it around, accelerated – and Andrea saw his man in the window, just for a second, before walking off.

They woke up in Margherita's teenage bed, his wife curled up against him. Carlo carefully got up; it was still dark outside. He left the room with a stiffness in his neck and went to the bathroom, sat on the edge of the bathtub and closed his eyes. Bathtubs. The day that Lorenzo had come home from the hospital, a wailing, two-and-a-half-kilo little thing, he'd cuddled and walked him around all of Concordia, had shut himself in the bathroom as it was the warmest room, had sat on the edge of the enamel bathtub and had made up a fairy tale on the spot: his baby had fallen asleep.

He took his time getting dressed, wore his wing tips, decided he'd wear them for the interview two days from now too; they were comfy and well made. On the other side of the wall, the neighbour was humming and he felt as though they were brushing their teeth together – Anna had told him the gossip about the neighbour sleeping in a different room from his wife. He was thinking about the previous night, about Margherita who, after their argument, had said to him, 'Sleep with me.'

He buttoned up his shirt and took his phone, read Sofia's message again, and now thought about the books from Rimini as a definite motive – she really wanted to see him again. About his wife sniffing him out – 'I want you to get her out of your head.'

He felt lacking for not having wanted to sniff her out, back then: the morning when he'd got up and made breakfast while Margherita was still in bed, her BlackBerry on the table. He'd sat down and picked it up; he'd never done it before. He couldn't tell why that morning had been different. He'd scrolled through her messages and had found *Andrea physio*, nine messages in total, the last one sent was *If you want, I'd like to see you one afternoon*, no reply from him. *If you want* – what an elegant hiss; it had rung in his ears for a long time.

Adultery versus adultery: *I did it but you also probably did it.* He'd let the suspicion set in, removing part of his own guilt, feeling annoyed, jealous, holding back. Their marriage had survived the siege of doubt. They had protected each other, somehow protected each other, and he had used their fragility to rediscover the hunger for his wife's body after a hypothetical Andrea. He'd studied her pussy (still the same, compact or more welcoming or less welcoming, different?), kissed her nipples (had *he* also kissed them, had he been better?), heard her moan with pleasure (had she moaned the same with him?).

He'd stopped asking her, while they fucked, if she was lusting after someone else. Having this confirmation heightened the pleasure – Margherita had desired another, maybe still did, but only he could truly experience her. He'd raised his guard again. He was married to a woman demanded by someone else, a woman he could take better care of. He'd stopped thinking of her only as his wife. And so the wonderful legs of Margherita had become the wonderful legs that could only belong to Margherita, and her marvellous brain had become the marvellous brain that could only belong to her, and her eyes and her lips could only belong to her, as did her strength, and she could use all of it as a means of seduction that could go beyond him.

It had been this painful awareness that had allowed him to rediscover her. A woman, and not his routine. Then one evening, at
dinner, she'd told him, 'Do you remember my physiotherapist?'

'The dog-bite guy?'

'Yeah. He's gay.'

'Really? I had no idea.'

'Me neither.'

At that point, he had glimpsed, or thought he had, a wounded woman.

He left the bathroom and moved into the lounge. Lorenzo
was sleeping, Anna was awake and watching the sliver of sunrise
out of the window. 'Is the nurse coming soon, Carlo?'

'An hour.'

'An hour is a long time.'

He moved closer. 'Does it hurt?'

She grasped his hands. 'Maybe you should call Margherita.'

He noticed her fingers were trembling. He went back to the
bedroom; his wife was up and about to open the blinds. She
saw him come in and said, 'I liked sharing this bed with you.'

'Me too.' Carlo hinted at a hug, she pulled away. 'Your
mother wants you.'

Margherita found her torturing one side of the sheet. 'Darling, can you ask the nurse to come sooner?'

'Are you in pain? I'll make something to eat so you can take
a painkiller.'

'It's not pain.' She lowered her eyes to the bedsheets. The
stink was coming from down there.

Margherita nodded. 'I'll sort it out.'

'Can you call the nurse, please?'

'I'll do it.'

'Darling, please, no.'

'Mum, I'm here.' She turned towards the corridor, she
knew her husband was there and that she didn't have to

193

explain how scared she was. She gestured him to be quick with Lorenzo, then went to get dressed. Her mother was waiting for her in the same position, strangling the sheet and looking at her grandson. Carlo was helping him with his trousers and jumper.

'Are you coming back to see Grandma soon, my love?'

'You snore,' said the boy.

'You snore too,' she replied.

'I snore too,' said Carlo, buttoning up his jacket.

'I can confirm,' said Margherita.

'You be good in school today, young man.'

Margherita walked Lorenzo and Carlo to the door. When she came back, she finished opening the blinds and saw that Anna was looking at her husband's armchair.

'I've cleaned up after your father so many times. And you know what I'd think as I scrubbed the sponge?' She scratched her throat. 'I'd think: the state of you, Franchin.'

Margherita reached the shelf with the records. 'Who shall we play today?'

Her mother didn't reply.

Margherita chose a record. 'De Gregori?'

'He's too clean.'

'Rino Gaetano, let's play Rino Gaetano.' She pulled out the record.

'No, don't play anything.'

'Really? Are you sure?'

'Don't play anything.'

Margherita slid the record back onto the shelf, went to the bathroom. She took out the pack of nappies and unwrapped one, took the bowl and filled it with warm water, took the sponges out and the water jug, filled it with warm water, took out the plastic cover and the soap, the bucket, put everything onto the trolley they had used with her father. She carted it to the lounge, moved close to the bed and turned the crank to raise the mattress.

'Are you comfy?'

Her mother nodded.

Margherita touched her arm. She kissed Anna on the cheek, then she held her side and tried turning her over; her mother groaned in pain. The catheter tube was limiting – she checked the bag and it was only half full. Margherita held her mother by the shoulders and moved her onto the right side of the mattress, laid the plastic sheet over the bed and covered it with towels.

'I'm here.'

Anna's head was lying back and her eyes were shut.

'I'm here, Mum.' Margherita poured a little warm water into the bowl, took the sponges out of their wrapper and let them soak, removed the cap from the soap.

'You had a kerfuffle last night, didn't you, darling?' Anna lifted her head a little to see what her daughter was about to do.

'Kerfuffle?' She moved aside the lower part of Anna's nightgown, the stench overtook her. 'We were watching a film on the computer, there was a kerfuffle.'

'Which film?'

'Loren and Mastroianni.' She was breathing with her mouth.

'And what made Sofia Loren raise her voice?'

Margherita didn't reply until she finished undoing the first nappy tag. 'Mastroianni revelling in the past.'

'What sort of past?'

'The *dolce vita* that escaped him.'

'He was a rising star, my dear, now he hardly works any more. When's his interview, by the way?'

The vest was also limiting her mother; she moved it up to her bra. 'In two days.'

'He's got the odds on his side.'

'He's got forty-four years on his shoulders.'

'People have more experience at forty-four.'

'Nowadays, you're half dead at forty-four. And work isn't the only issue here.'

Anna shifted her cast arm onto her chest. 'It's just that I heard the word mortgage, too.'

'Open your legs a little, please.' Margherita held back the instinct to gag and pressed her nose in her top, turned back to look at Anna and undid the second nappy tag. 'You folks from after the war only worry about the money side of things.'

'Because we compromised on marriage.'

Margherita stared at her.

Her mother was serious. 'Compromise was a type of freedom, darling.'

'I can't compromise.'

'You've never liked freedoms that take effort.'

Margherita grabbed the front of the nappy and pulled as she looked at her mother; she smiled at her, lowered her head. The shit had stained the towels and her fingers.

'The state of me.'

'You're beautiful.' She removed the nappy and closed it up, left it to one side and hurried with the bowl. They'd taught her how to wash Anna from the belly button downwards, to avoid infections. 'Is the water the right temperature?'

'Let Mastroianni take the bull by its horns.' Then she nodded. 'The water is just right. The bull by the horns always works out.'

Margherita did a first run. She was hiding her nose in her elbow, ducking to not be seen, wiping the sponge and focusing on a single point to one side. Then she got tired of being scared and looked at her mother. She swore Anna could've been a young woman in her twenties. She cleaned her gently, top to bottom, rinsing the sponge; top to bottom, rinsed again; top to bottom, careful with the tubes, threw the sponge into the

196

bucket and picked up another. 'Mum, did you ever really not believe Dad?'

'Easy darling, easy. Please.' Anna sighed. 'Of course I didn't really believe Dad. I doubted myself too. But had I lived in your time . . .'

'What?'

'The bull by the horns, I think.' She smiled. Her breath was short and she coughed.

Margherita stopped until the fit was over. Then she kissed her on the forehead. 'You're beautiful, you got that?' She'd splashed the leg's dressing; she cleaned up the side of the bandage and her mother wailed.

'Does it hurt that much?'

'A bit.'

'It's a little swollen, but I think that's normal.' She kept cleaning, gently. 'We'll ask the nurse when she gets here.'

'You know I'm rooting for Sofia Loren, in the end, right?'

Margherita nodded and took the clean towels and started dabbing her skin, applying pressure and smelling her clean mum. She'd spilled some water onto the bedsheets, grabbed the hairdryer from the bathroom sink cupboard, dried the sheet and blasted her mother with the warm air before turning it off.

Anna smiled.

Margherita placed everything back on the trolley and rolled it to the bathroom, then locked herself inside. She leaned against the wall and dabbed her eyes. Her hands hurt, she clenched and unclenched them. Cleaning her mother, cleaning is what she would do, clean her well, clean her without fear. She pressed her back against the tiles, waited to calm down, pulled herself up again. She moved to go to the sink but stopped. She took out her phone and called her husband, waited for three rings and when he replied, she said, 'I just wanted to hear your voice.'

He recognised the raspy voice and asked her to tell him everything.

She said, 'That's all, promise.'

They kept quiet for a moment, then he said, 'I love you, OK?'

When they hung up, Carlo felt the tenderness of when, after the other women, he'd get home and look at Margherita – and was overtaken by agony over what he'd done, a deep and visceral sorrow, because now he knew that she was right: he had to get Sofia out of his head, see her again.

He dropped Lorenzo off at preschool and watched him walk towards the other kids; his overcoat was large and made him look smaller. He pulled away and walked to the Porta Genova metro station and stopped thinking of his son. Winter was burning his face. He got onto the train and got off at Cadorna, bought a three-euro ticket and waited for the regional train to Asso. It was on time and he took a window seat. He didn't take off his coat and stared at the warehouses for sale, the bare countryside and the small-town stations, the retired men and women and the small crowds of migrants shivering in the cold, waiting for their train. He got off in Cabiate. One time, he and Daniele Bucchi had calculated that it took forty-five minutes from Milan to the launderette, so less than an hour to catch up: it had only happened once.

He left the station along the road leading to the tiny city centre directly opposite. He wasn't sure about the street, then he spotted the white sign for *Tintoria Aurora*. He saw Daniele on the other side of the glass and stopped. There was a customer at the counter and he was nodding to her as he took a pair of trousers off a hanger, the washing machine behind him was a hive of lights and Daniele placed the trousers on tissue paper, wrapping them without looking away from her. He closed the parcel with some tape, lowered his head only to take the money and give back her change. The customer left and the door tinkled; it reminded him of the bells of old restaurants. Carlo snuck past her, 'May I come in?' His friend was almost in the back, talking to the woman at the ironing board.

'It's me, Lele.'

Daniele had a stapler in his hand; he put it down. 'It *is* you!' He came to greet him. 'Where have you been?' They warmly shook hands.

He could sense the rustiness in the friendship. He stayed quiet and Daniele invited him behind the counter, took his coat. 'How are you, Pente?'

'I feel like before a test with our teacher, Bagli.'

'Latin or Italian?'

'Latin.'

'Ouch. That bad?'

'But you do have the best cheater in the whole Parini school here.'

'Yeah, good times.' Daniele pulled a lever on the washing machine and pointed at the round window. 'We just changed it, consumes half as much and got a great deal on it. Still a mistake.'

'The other one was still fine?'

'Yeah, in a way.' Daniele gestured him to follow him to the corner of the window, pointed the same finger at a blue sign at the end of the street. 'You see that?'

'That's new.'

'It appeared overnight, three weeks after we got the new machine. Chinese family. You know how much they charge for clean and press? Two euros. Me? Ask me.'

'How much?'

'Two seventy, and I barely make a profit. Who'd you go to?'

'You, of course.'

'As fake as Judas.' He pretended to hit him in the stomach,

199

Carlo still avoided him. 'Still in good shape, even after a kid, Pente.'

'I've been training.'

'By avoiding who?'

'My parents.'

'As long as you don't go KO for bullshit reasons, you lightweight.'

'I'm trying.'

They fell quiet; it was the same in high school when one of them snuck in some truth. At their desk, elbows touching, on the football pitch, one defence the other wing, some Sundays at Carlo's place and the next week at Daniele's, following the football on the radio as they did their Latin homework, or sitting on the Piazza Aspromonte benches, secretly smoking and drinking beer, or in Bucchi's kitchen, his father with his vests and his missions into the kitchen to make sandwiches for himself and the two of them.

'And what's the name of this bullshit?' Daniele raised the left corner of his mouth, he still wore long sideburns and his eyes were sunken from tiredness, but they had a glint in them.

'The bullshit has had various names.'

'When you were teaching?'

'Also then.'

'Things get harder with children and Chinese launderettes and age and people can react like that, you know this, right?'

Carlo nodded.

'And you also know that if you can weather the shitstorm then what you've put aside gets stronger?'

'What if it's not just bullshit?'

'Then go through with it.' He wandered around the shop. He still had his weirdly shaped football-player legs and he dragged his pumps. 'I'm a go-hard-or-go-home guy, myself.'

'Says you, with a wife and three kids.'

'Precisely.'

A man came in, hat drawn down to his eyes. Daniele greeted him silently and his movements were now elegant, hand and legs were lighter, a dragonfly; he moved with a new awareness and took a shirt from the electric hanger rail, wrapped it and disappeared in the back. He came back with a jumper that he folded with thumb and index, placed it on tissue paper, sealed it with two bits of tape. 'That'll be six twenty, thank you, Mr Rosati.'

The man handed over the money. 'I'll never betray you, Bucchi.' He pointed to the window. 'The blacks are never going to wash my clothes.'

'They're Chinese.'

'They're all the same to me.' He picked up his change and his clothes, tipped his hat and left.

Carlo croaked his voice, 'I'll never betray you, Bucchi.'

Daniele nodded. 'Don't betray yourself either.'

'Same for you.'

'Just a little.' Daniele jotted something down on a calendar. 'But you know what? Little sacrifices for Agnese and the kids feel perfectly natural.'

The washing machine hummed its regular lullaby. 'You follow Inter. You did ten years of shiatsu. You used to eat frozen pizza. Maybe it's your nature as a masochist.'

'I've been feeling claustrophobic for the last while, Pente. I got shut in a lift for forty minutes, I was in Milan to review the insurance for the launderette. When they pulled me out I pretended I was fine. But since then I've had palpitations and short breath, even in the car if I'm stuck in traffic. Last year we took a plane to Lanzarote and I just couldn't – I freak out if the metro slows down.' He brushed a wool thread off the counter. 'I saw a therapist for a year and he told me that to protect my family I've been ignoring, you know, my own stuff.'

Carlo smiled.

'The fuck you laughing at?'

'Imagine if I'd started seeing a therapist.'

'He'd switch careers.'

'I did start, actually, after they fired me from the university.'

'You should've continued.'

'A failed professor, a questionable husband, a son of a wealthy family in denial? Too much stuff.'

They looked at each other, then Carlo noticed a photo on a shelf and went to pick it up. It was Agnese on a hammock, their youngest daughter on top of her, one leg dangling off, and wearing an ankle bracelet. 'Fucking is a wonderful thing, Lele.'

'You telling me.'

'Different women, I mean.'

'I can imagine.' He peeked at the back, then gestured him to lower his voice. 'But if I think about coming home after having done what I'd like to do, and make Isabella's baby food, and play video games with Manuele, and chase Giulio in the corridor, then watch *X Factor* with my wife's head resting on my legs, I can't, I just can't, Pente. How do you do that?'

'What if your wife did?'

'You think Margherita . . .?'

'I just don't want to think men are the only ones doing it.'

'But how do you even start to come home to your wife after you've been with a twenty-year-old. It's just . . . no.'

'Maybe.'

'And don't you tell me that sort of thing doesn't get you in the heart.'

'I love Margherita.'

'You're scared.'

'Scared of what?'

'Of being there, having your marriage and your family, seeing them to the end like a book.' He turned round, pressed two buttons on the washing machine. 'To see through a book you need guts, right? You told me that once.'

'Or recklessness.'

Two women were coming in, with a mutt on a leash. Daniele checked a list next to the till, Carlo moved closer to the heating, rested his back and let himself warm up. He read her message again. Then he turned to look at the Chinese launderette sign. It was piercing through the winter and he thought he could see a glimpse of spring . . .

Beyond the window, Sofia caught a glimpse of Largo Bordoni freed from ice. She told herself that Pentecoste would never get back to her, that maybe he'd never received the books, that maybe her invasiveness had been too much.

She reached the top of the ladder and opened a drawer. There were enough masonry nails and she could make an order in two days with the glues and the iron wedges. From up there, the shop had its own grace and she asked herself how she expected him to reply. She would never send him anything again.

She closed the drawer and went back to her chair, let her hands fall on her lap and her gaze on a non-defined spot of the counter. She couldn't move. It happened every time she missed her mother. She waited for the feeling to pass, remembering the time around summer when they went to the field behind the primary school in Vergiano. Ten minutes in the car and as soon as they'd get there her mother would hand her the jar with scrunched-up paper and ask her to pick one.

'Choose well, Sofi, choose well.'

One of the last times she'd hesitated; she'd picked one, opened it. 'Yellow.'

'The loser has to look after the balcony for a month!'

They'd closed the car doors and run off into the field. The rule was that any hue, up to orange, counted – never daisies, it was too easy – and the bunch had to be right for the vase in the kitchen.

Sofia had pounced on the dandelion. Pulling and grabbing without pause, she took a breath again as she looked for her mother on the other side of the field, seeing a small and cat-like figure, sneezing here and there. Then she'd lost sight of her. She'd looked again, still nothing. She'd pulled herself up.

'Mum . . .?' She'd headed over to where she'd last seen her. 'Mum!' There had been a felling of stalks to the end of the field. Then she'd spotted her: in the wheat field next to them.

'That's not fair!' she'd shouted.

Her mum had raised her head, coal-black hair and glimmering eyes. 'Yellow's yellow!' She was laughing, wheat ears beneath her fingers.

Wheat and dandelion – they'd kept both in the kitchen and in a corner of the cupboard. After the accident, her father had thrown them out.

She thought that one ear of wheat might be enough; she'd keep it in the shop, maybe in a long, thin vase on the counter. She stared at the coat stand, moved closer to the blue overall. She imagined her going to buy it after seeing Ornella Vanoni at the Piazza Cavour concert, coming back half-singing, happier; she imagined her in the field behind the school in Vergiano, towards summer.

She took the overall from the hook, slipped it on, one sleeve then the other, fastened it across her chest, feared it might be too tight on her hips. She buttoned it up and was relieved to see it fit perfectly. She tilted her nose onto the shoulder; it smelled of dust and she wondered where her mum had gone. Rimini always brings spring forward.

Andrea heard a tapping on the car window, woke up and saw Giorgio staring at him, hands on the glass. He raised his head. He'd parked badly in front of the newsagent's and it was early morning. He touched his split lip: the Egyptian. He'd lost the match after two rounds – they wouldn't let him fight for a long while. He unlocked the doors and Giorgio swung the driver side open.

'Jesus Christ!' He closed it again and went round to the passenger side. 'I called *everyone* last night!'

'My parents too?'

'No, not them. I even went back to the warehouse but it was empty.'

'We need to open the shop.' He leaned over and spotted the Bar Rock waiter watching them.

'He's the one who told me you were here.'

'The papers.'

'He took them and called me. They were about to call an ambulance.'

'I'm fine.'

Giorgio touched his neck and he pulled away. The Egyptian had beaten him on his chest too; he pressed against his ribs and saw it wasn't too bad. He lowered the mirror, opened his mouth – one of his front teeth was missing a corner. 'I have some painkillers in the bag, in the back. Can you get them for me please?'

Giorgio didn't move.

'The bag, please.' He raised the back of his seat.

Giorgio found the painkillers and handed them to him. Andrea popped them into half a bottle of water, drank up and his blood mixed with the now medicated water. Giorgio took the keys out of his hand and opened the shutters, went to the bar and started carrying over the newspaper stacks. They shut themselves inside the newsagent's, he pulled up a stool and told him to sit.

They stayed there in silence, it was cold. Andrea sat. 'I need this.'

Giorgio moved the pile of newspapers. 'I'll take half a day off and sort this out. You go home.'

'I'm fine.'

'Go home.'

'One match keeps me going for a month.'

'Going where?'

'I need this.' Andrea was holding his ribs; he lowered his head, his eyes were wet, and his lungs inflated and deflated, sounding like a newborn.

Giorgio cut the ties holding the papers together, chucked the blade onto the counter. He moved closer, held Andrea's temples between his hands, gently moved his head towards his chest and said, '*Jag älskar dig.*' He dried his eyes. 'Are you at least making some money out of it?'

'Not enough.'

'A shitty version of *Fight Club*, too.'

Andrea dabbed his swollen lips.

Giorgio looked at him. 'What's wrong with me?'

'I did this before meeting you, too.'

Giorgio didn't move. Then he piled up the papers on the counter, checking that the paperwork added up and ticking it off. He stared back at Andrea. He grabbed his hand and placed it on the stack of *La Gazzetta dello Sport*, fished out the pen they used for closing-time accounting, uncapped it and drew a line from his index finger to his wrist. Then a line from middle finger to wrist. Then a line from ring finger to wrist. Then a line from little finger to wrist. Then a line from thumb to wrist.

Andrea watched his lined hand.

'Your roots, your baggage – I get all of that.' He suddenly drew a line from little finger to thumb that cut through all the others. 'But I don't accept this.' He put down the pen. 'The shame you feel for yourself disgusts me.'

Andrea was looking at his hand; it looked like someone else's.

Giorgio let it go. Andrea pulled it back and touched the five lines. Even later, when he got home, in the shower, before putting it under the stream of warm water, he touched them, then scrubbed them with the soft sponge. He stopped: he wanted to remember them.

He finished washing, treated his wounds and put some ice on the bruises. He called his students and told them he'd have to reschedule. He went into the bedroom; there was a nook in which they'd shoved a small table, Giorgio's markers were scattered among pencil shavings and he opened up the drawing pad and took out the top sheet of paper. It was a sketch for an autumn-collection suede shoe, the heel studies in the bottom half – he'd been working on it for the past three days. He picked up a pencil and wrote in a corner of the sheet, *Jag älskar dig*.

He took another painkiller and got himself into bed. He slept for ages or not at all, wasn't sure how long for when his phone rang. He was still groggy. He waited for the ringing to stop, fell asleep again and woke up to another call. It was dark outside. He went into the kitchen and saw it was Margherita. He picked up and she told him that her mother's leg was a weird colour and was hurting her.

'What kind of weird colour?'

'Like after a bruise. The nurse says it's nothing.'

He told her to trust the nurse, asked if she had any other symptoms, temperature, cold, difficulties in breathing. He listened to Margherita ask Anna – no symptoms.

'I'll come by tomorrow afternoon.'

The wind had picked up, the clouds were thickening. He slipped on his shoes and wrapped himself up warm, he didn't wait for the lift and took the stairs, his left thigh twingeing with pain. He warned Giorgio he was headed to see the femur lady because something didn't seem right. Then told him, 'Thank you for today.'

'Are you really going to see the femur lady in this state?'

Andrea reassured him he was fine and told him again, 'Thank you for today.'

It took him forty minutes to get there. He got out of the car and the wind was warm. Margherita opened the door as if waiting for him.

'Oh my God!' she said, as she saw his lips and cheekbone.

'He had a good right hook.'

'You're crazy.' She was keeping him on the landing. 'And you came anyway.'

'Just a quick look.' He stepped into the lounge. 'May I come in? It's me.'

Anna didn't reply, so he stepped in front of the bed: the mattress was down again and she had her head turned towards the bookshelves. 'What are you doing here?' she said without moving.

'I was in the area.'

'Like Onassis who'd take a plane just to have breakfast with Jacqueline.'

'Margherita told me about your leg.'

Anna turned around. 'Good heavens, what happened?'

'I was boxing.'

'You were an idiot.'

'Can I see your leg?'

'Give me the number of someone who cares about you so I can call them immediately.' She pulled at the sheet to uncover her legs.

Margherita switched on the lights in the room and he low-ered his head; there was a clean smell in the air. The skin was poking through the dressing and had a dark olive colour.

'Did the nurse loosen the bandage?'

'It feels tighter to me.'

Andrea removed his coat by letting his arms fall to his sides, grabbed it before it reached the ground, and placed it on the armchair.

'Has your love ever seen you take off your coat like that?'

'Why?' He started undoing the dressing's clips.

'Irresistible.'

'You're being silly.'

'You're like Humphrey Bogart.' Anna clenched her teeth. 'What's your love's name?'

He teetered over the second clip. 'Can you raise your thigh a little for me?'

'Please forgive an old nosy parker.'

He froze. 'His name's Giorgio.'

'Then you must tell Giorgio to wait for you every night on the sofa, and every night you have to – ouch, ouch! Easy, please go easy.'

'I'm sorry.'

'You stand in front of Giorgio and you do that coat thing.'

'Here we go.' He removed the dressing.

She sighed. 'Freedom at last.'

Andrea tested the leg and Anna responded with small jolts. He reached the edge of her nappy and spotted Margherita out of the corner of his eye, in a corner of the room. He felt pain in his ribs and pulled himself back up. He was looking at his hands and could still see Giorgio's lines, his branches climbing onto Anna, then he called Margherita over. 'You need to get her to do this movement every two hours, but without touching the inside of her leg.' He guided Margherita to the stiff muscle. 'Like this, got it?' They massaged together; his knuckles were rough and she covered them with her hand – they were still a boy's knuckles.

They kept going. Andrea closed his hands and Margherita felt the medical table of the FisioLab again, those hands running from her thigh to her pelvis, the shifting of the bikini bottoms and the throbbing pressure, the urge, the absolute need for him to move his finger towards her. She had so demanded the impertinence of his finger. She'd betrayed Carlo with a man who loved men. Had it been weird? No, it had been disheartening, having let herself go with a body that had yielded out of indecision, or distraction. She'd long considered herself just a happy accident. Then she'd re-evaluated herself as a rarity: she'd been able to corrupt an incorruptible nature. She'd got an orgasm out of it and a tenderness that still lingered. A friendship. A man taking care of her mum.

'I'd leave the dressing off tonight. But ask the nurse tomorrow, and if the skin darkens call the doctor. Is she taking the blood-thinners?'

Margherita nodded.

'They said it's going to snow.' Anna spoke without opening her eyelids, her head against the bookshelves.

'There's a strange wind outside.' Andrea shifted her gently to the centre of the bed.

'Snow in March brings change.' Anna insisted on not looking at them. In her mind she saw their four hands on her leg and was putting back together her convictions; maybe her daughter had had a distraction with him. She would be quite shocked. She suddenly had enough of thinking about others: she was a bedridden seamstress who shat herself. But she still had her fingers – she could see them under the sheet, bring them to her face; the tips used to the eye of the needle, following its movement, cutting any hem without hesitation using her finger as a ruler, savouring the damask with her fingertips. She imagined herself perched on her stool in the kitchen, with Franco reading in his armchair, the sweet smell of broth on the stove, Margherita chatting from her bedroom. What once was, still is.

She asked Margherita about Lorenzo and her daughter told her he was coming home from swimming. She was impatient when it came to her grandson – they'd brought him into the world late and now she had to catch up. If she could, she would never have taken off her cast so he could add details to his lucky tuna. She touched its fin, its tail, went over its shape while she listened to Margherita and Andrea whispering in the hall. She dozed off and woke up again to Lorenzo next to her. 'Hello little one,' she said with a sleep-filled voice. 'Did you swim really well?'

He nodded and walked around the bed, grabbed the cushions from the sofa and stacked them up on the chair, settled himself on the throne. 'Massimo Nicolini was first.'

'Who's Massimo Nicolini?'

'My friend.'

'And how did you do?'

'Seventh.'

'And how many of you are there?'

'Eight.'

'Do you like any other sport, darling?'

'Swords.'

The boy fidgeted with his rucksack, pulled out a paper bag with some focaccia, took a bite and chewed. 'But Mum doesn't want swords.'

'Ah, but you're a musketeer with or without swords! You and I are the two musketeers of Via delle . . .?'

'Leghe.'

'Well done, my darling.'

The boy offered her a piece of focaccia. She took it and ate it while she kept watching her grandson, his cerulean eyes and the same fringe as Margherita. She saw Franco in him when he was about to laugh and held it back, just before opening his mouth and letting himself go, the cheeky look that didn't fit with his spiky jawline. She asked him for some more focaccia even though she didn't really want it. The boy fed her and watched his grandmother chewing until suddenly she wasn't chewing any more.

Anna spluttered and tried breathing, she clutched her chest, reached with her free hand to the boy and he let himself be grabbed. 'Grandma, Grandma!'

She coughed and inhaled fresh air, realised she was digging into her grandson and stroked him. 'My love, I'm sorry.'

The boy was staring at her.

'It's nothing, my darling.'

'You ate too quick.'

'I did, you're right.' She coughed again and spat out some saliva. 'I choked on my snack.' She tried covering the spit with her fingers. Her heart was beating too fast and had sunk down into her leg. She touched the hard skin where Andrea had massaged it. 'Grandma is OK now.'

'Dad!' The boy made to get off the chair.

Anna held him down. 'Why don't you draw me another picture on my cast?'

Lorenzo didn't move.

Carlo came in from the bedroom. 'What's up?' Margherita was behind him.

'Do you need something?' asked Anna.

'Us?'

The boy looked at his grandmother; she winked and he got off the chair to open his rucksack, pulled out his crayons.

'We wanted,' Anna coughed, 'wanted to tell you good luck for the interview tomorrow – what time is it again?'

Carlo came closer, brushed some crumbs off her sheets. 'Nine o'clock.' He stared at both of them for a while. 'Don't tire out your grandma, you.'

'He's not tiring me out, I just asked him for a picture and was about to ask him to push me all the way to the bedroom with his musketeer strength.'

'You want to be moved back into the bedroom, Mum?'
Anna nodded.

Margherita crouched down and removed the brakes from the bed's wheels, as if she'd been waiting for that moment forever. She grabbed the side and started gently wheeling it out of the lounge.

Since she'd met Carlo, there had been something about her that Anna had tried giving a name to. An attention to care, maybe something even better: Margherita withstood the conflicts of others. Married life had made her into a woman capable of accepting inconsistencies, almost defending them, like letting a mother stay in the lounge with a cumbersome makeshift bed and then immediately accommodating her request to move back to the bedroom; like helping along a father who wants to die sooner than intended, letting herself be crossed by a supposed betrayal.

Margherita wheeled her to the centre of the bedroom, carefully turned her around so she could be next to the sewing machine, lowered the blinds a little and started carrying through the rest of her stuff from the lounge. Then they opened the wardrobe and her mother could see the clothes hanging inside.

'Thank you.' Anna looked at the shawl she wore the day of her wedding. The cellophane let through the lightness of the fabric. 'I wore it backwards,' she whispered.

'I know. A gesture of subversion in the 1950s. But I think you just made a mistake.'

Anna smiled at her, settled herself into the pillow and felt the tiredness wash over her. When she woke up, it was dark and the only light was coming in from the lounge. The nurse had moved the armchair and was watching over her while leafing through a magazine with a reading light. She felt as if she needed to cough, but held it in. Her breath had shortened and

213

she shifted to find some lung strength, the skin on her leg was cool and she wasn't afraid, because the only smell coming out of the sheets was cleanliness. She looked out of the window and noticed that the air under the street light was tangled with some sort of dust; she looked harder and saw it was the March snow.

'It came,' she hissed.

'Hi Anna, what can I get you?' asked the nurse.

'Is it snowing?'

'Very light dusting, started about an hour ago.'

She wished for the light snow to get harder, and when she saw it happen a little later, she felt like getting up and going out there: she was the girl from Via Padova who'd won the snowman contest – she'd used a courgette for the nose and black-painted newspaper balls for the eyes.

It was snowing! Andrea wanted to tell Giorgio but bit his tongue. He went to the window and hoped the white would settle on the tarmac and on the mound under the walnut tree, then he worried César might get cold: his comma of a tail, wet eyes, all that cold on his wound, on his side, his paws, his muzzle. He grabbed the window handle and felt arms holding his shoulders from behind. Giorgio hugged him and held his cheek against his neck.

Milan is never ready for the snow . . . Margherita thought it was a good sign for her husband's interview. She got excited and walked across the Concordia living room and tapped on the glass, Carlo pulled himself up from the sofa and switched off the TV, joined her; he also thought it might be a sign, for his interview and more. He held his wife. She'd had the same scent since they'd met; he wished that it were just the two of them and had the certainty that it would never be just the two of them. 'My Margherita,' he whispered to her in the silence of Concordia and his wife grabbed his arm and held it tight, then told him to wait for her in bed.

The snow was light and swirling in the wind; a bright light came into the room from outside. She walked down the corridor to Lorenzo's bedroom. He was sleeping with a foot out of the duvet, but she chose not to tuck him in and reached the desk at the entrance. It was an early-twentieth-century piece of furniture, restored by her father, and her mum had given it to her when they'd moved here: she also used the first drawer from the top. She opened it and rummaged inside, found the small antihistamine bottle. Her husband had stopped taking it with him and she had stopped reminding him about it. She took one step closer to the coat rack, plunged her hand into Carlo's coat pocket and let the bottle fall in, she plunged her nose into the collar.

In the pocket of her mother's overcoat, Sofia had found an old receipt from Lidia's, her hairdresser, in Largo Bordoni. She'd brought it home from the shop and was now looking at it under the desk lamp: cut and perm for twenty-eight euros, dated fifteen years ago, on 13 September.

She put it on the bedside table and climbed into bed. Tommaso pulled the covers over her. The mattress was small and when they were together she'd feel a little embarrassed as she had to keep turning – all those curls, the noisy breathing that interrupted her sleep. She grabbed his hand under the duvet, tangled it in hers and felt weird, what with her father probably not asleep two rooms away.

The wind outside was beating against the shutters. She switched off the lights and they watched the glow outside filtering into the room, dozed off. Tommaso woke her by stroking her hair. She liked how he touched her short hair, then he said he had to go and she didn't hold him back. She watched him as he got dressed, the large body careful in its movements. She walked him to the door, came back to her room and reached the window to fully close the blinds, found the snow. 'Oh,' she said, and was taken over by joy.

In Milan, the story goes that on the morning of Sant'Ambrogio, around ten o'clock, three keys are hung on a pine tree across the Parco Sempione Arena. The tree is the furthest out at the beginning of Viale Malta. The legend tells us that the three keys lead to a flat beyond the Arco della Pace, in Via Eupili number 6A: it's a stuccoed building and the first key opens its gate, the second the wooden front door, and the third the flat on the top floor. The place is well kept, with a small lounge holding a table and a velvet sofa, well-stocked bookshelves. A bathroom with a tub and scented salts, a small kitchen with good food. There's also a bedroom with a comfy mattress, clean sheets and three blankets. Whoever gets the keys down from the tree can stay in the flat until the following morning, abiding by three rules: keep to the time limits, don't go looking for the owner, only one person can enter.

When Carlo had asked Franco to look into the legend it had been Sant'Ambrogio in 2005 and they were queuing outside Cova for the chocolate and raspberry cake. Franco had pretended not to hear him, kept queuing, and Carlo had said it was still five past ten, they still had time.

'It's late.'

'Franco, come on.'

Margherita's father hadn't moved.

'Hey, Franco.'

'What?'

'You told me the story.'

'It's just a story.'

'Who told it to you?'

'All of Milan knows it.'

'Have you ever gone to the tree?'

The man had shaken his head and slipped his wallet back into his jacket. He was a big man and had looked at him, furrowing his Schnauzer-like eyebrows. 'The women are waiting for us for the cake.'

'How long can it possibly take? We look for the pine tree and come back.'

Franco had pinched the bridge of his nose with his fingers – he always did when he was concentrating. He'd checked his watch, put his hat back on: ''Ndem.'

They'd used the Toyota Corolla and it had taken them twenty minutes to reach Parco Sempione, where they hadn't found anywhere to park. Franco had said, 'You go.'

'A son-in-law doesn't leave his father-in-law.'

'You and Margherita aren't married yet.'

'But I'm going to.'

'I giürament d'amur düren un dí.'

'I mean it, Franco: one day, we'll get married.'

Carlo had got out of the car, Franco had put the emergency lights on, and they'd snuck into the park in a semicircle across the Viale Malta gravel. The tree was the first one there and could easily be seen from the path. Their breath was visible in the cold; they'd reached the tree, they'd stopped.

Franco had taken off his hat.

Carlo had moved closer to the bark: they were hanging on a nail at the base of the highest branch. Three keys. The best way to reach them would be for one to help the other up.

Franco had joined him.

Carlo had looked at him. 'Come on, help me take them down.'

'Don't tell the women anything.' He'd rubbed his hands as if from the cold.

'Let's take them.'

Franco had lowered his head. '*Mí sun cuntèent inscí.*'

'And I want to go to Via Eupili.'

'*Mí sun cuntèent inscí,*' and he'd pinched his nose, turning back.

Carlo pinched his nose when they called him into the interview room. It had become his lucky tic – Margherita didn't know, Anna didn't know – and every time he did so he summoned Franco's shocked expression under the pine tree.

They invited him to sit in a room with a wooden table and you could see the Piazza della Repubblica junction covered in snow from the window. He recognised a Depero poster, with a man wearing a trilby raising a tankard in cheers. Carlo removed his coat and placed his rucksack on the floor, sat down, stood up again when they walked in and shook their hands. They made some small talk about the weather, then they told him he'd receive a series of questions and the second part of the interview would be conducted in English; was he ready to begin?

Carlo nodded.

'Mr Pentecoste, are you aware of the fact that your CV is, how can we put it, *all over the place*?'

'Meaning a variety of experiences?'

'A degree in literature, a job as a copywriter, strategic planner, part-time lecturer for an MA course on Narrative Techniques, editor for a travel book publishing company.'

'It comes down to what fitted best at the time.'

'What fitted . . . I see. Might you call it indecision?'

'I'd call it flexibility.'

'Applying for a job in marketing for the beverage industry is quite a leap.'

'Well, marketing combines a lot of my interests.'

'How so?'

'Thinking about a story, being able to tell it.'

'Might you call it manipulation?'

He thought about it. 'Seduction.'

'Even when it comes to beer?'

'What matters is the effect.'

'What do you mean by effect?'

'The passion you can elicit.'

'You're telling me that teaching students or writing a catalogue about the Maldives or talking about a double malt all draw from the same reservoir of passion?'

'The result, in all those cases, has to be emotional impact.'

'Are you aware of the fact that, since 2010, consumers have progressively lost what we call "purchase happiness"? They currently show only about a third of their usual willingness to engage emotively with a product. How would you work around this problem?'

'By convincing them to talk about it over a beer?'

They smiled.

'So would you describe yourself as someone good at convincing others?'

'Good at sharing knowledge.'

'Are you referring to your teaching experience?'

'Also, yes.'

'I see that your experience in the field has come to a halt.'

'They weren't paying enough.'

'So would you say that the financial motivation is more important than, say, the emotional one?'

'They both matter. As does arousal.'

'Arousal.'

'Lust for life.'

'Meaning . . .?'

'Self-discovery.'

'Very well. I'll suggest a number of scenarios to which you must, on a scale of one to ten, quantify their emotional impact, or if you prefer, their "arousal". Lack of emotion or arousal is zero. Total engagement or full arousal is ten.'

'Please, I'm ready.'

'Teaching a lesson about Shakespeare to fifteen students.'

'I don't know Shakespeare well enough.'

'Quantify, please.'

'Seven.'

'Compiling an instruction manual for the latest iPhone model.'

'One.'

'The same manual, but with suggestions on how the iPhone can simplify everyday life.'

'Five.'

'Giving a tour of an art exhibition.'

'What kind of exhibition?'

'Quantify.'

'Give me an artist.'

'Picasso.'

'Five.'

'An exhibition on the Coca-Cola bottle designs.'

'Eight.'

'Giving a public talk about a new vacuum cleaner patent.'

'Four.'

'Giving a talk on the psychological convenience of travelling first class, despite the increased cost.'

'Eight.'

'On a non-toxic weedkilling product.'

'Seven.'

'Seven?'

'It's something new, right?'

'On a traditional weedkiller then.'

'Zero.'

'On a strawberry-flavoured drink that promotes weight loss.'

'Three.'

'Managing a Facebook page for an emerging pop band.'

'Six.'

'Give me an example of what you consider a ten.'

'A ten?'

'Yes.'

'Getting up every morning to go to work with people I like, working eight hours a day on something that doesn't taint me, getting paid regularly and fairly on the effort–satisfaction scale, having time for my family.'

'What do you mean by effort–satisfaction?'

'Not being exploited.'

'Are you aware of the fact that you're applying for a senior position?'

'Of course.'

'So you're also aware of the fact that you'll have two supervisors and two other people above you.'

'Of course.'

'Who may be younger than you.'

'No problem.'

'Who may be single.'

'What do you mean by that?'

'That they don't value time the same way as you. Some might work on Saturdays too.'

'No problem.'

Lorenzo.

'Are you aware of the fact that during ad campaigns our offices stay open beyond usual business hours?'

'I've been told.'

'I see that your English level is Pre-Intermediate.'

'Correct.'

'And French is Intermediate.'

'I've practised it for longer.'

'I'll now suggest some spare-time activities, and I'd like you to keep quantifying on the same scale. Reading.'

'Eight.'

'Gardening.'

'I have no idea. Four?'

'Travelling.'

'Ten.'

'Dinner with friends.'

'Seven.'

'Cheese-tasting.'

'Seven.'

'Wine-tasting course.'

'Two.'

'Social media.'

'Six.'

'We've noticed that you don't use it that often.'

'I'd rather not.'

'Rather not?'

'They might take me in.'

'They might take you in – and wouldn't that be arousing?'

'It depends.'

'I understand.'

'Do you?'

'Another five questions before moving to the English part of the interview. How flexible would you call yourself concerning positive changes?'

He was done after seventy minutes. He took a few steps along the station road and the smell of snow pierced his nostrils. He slowed his breathing and snuck into a café, asked for a macchiato. He undid the buttons on his coat and took out his phone, called Margherita and said, 'It went well.'

'What are they like? The place, I mean.'

'Good, human, I like it.'

'What did they ask you?'

'How's Anna?'

'She's fine.'

'It was a good chat.'

'My love, I'm happy.'

'You're happy?'

'I am.'

'This'll work, you'll see.'

He held his phone tighter. 'This morning Lorenzo told me Dad can do it.'

Margherita said, 'Dad can do it.'

When he left the café his legs were tired and his head awake; he covered his eyes and opened them again, slowly. He headed to Milano Centrale station, bought a ticket for the 10.35 fast train and he felt as if something was missing, and a wanting, and a need: getting on a train in secret, sitting for three hours next to a window looking out on the fields of Lombardy and Emilia and Romagna. He opened up his rucksack and took out his notepad, as if the risk he was about to take could bring him inspiration to write something. He just needed a single good sentence to be surprised, a single sentence to believe he'd get the beer-marketing job. He'd put out a book, he'd no longer linger on a time when he'd crack for a twenty-two-year-old. The train left and he looked out. Not long after, the Piacenza countryside appeared to him, soft. The snow dulled the sharp edges of the earth with its fruit trees surprised by the ice, chimneys blowing out dark smoke. He'd been to Rimini as a teenager and, with Bucchi and the others, had gone dancing at Baia Imperiale. They'd stayed overnight in a hostel in Rivabella, of which he remembered nothing except an ochre sign and the sofas and the ashtrays. What would he tell Margherita? He called his mother and asked her to look after Lorenzo after school, he'd come and pick him up after dinner. What would he tell Sofia?

He checked his return options and calculated he had just about three hours. He put away his phone and settled into the seat: how reckless was he, from one to ten? He smiled. In his mind was the face of the man who'd grilled him at the interview, his bald dome of a head and acetate glasses, the bow tie on his prominent Adam's apple. He imagined him walking a dog in winter, maybe a Wiener dog. He'd liked him, maybe from how he tried holding back his reactions, his nervous leg under the table, the sip of water at the end, when he'd launched into a *We'll be in touch, Carlo*.

We'll be in touch, Anna's femur, Lorenzo doing the breast-stroke like the previous summer in Elba – the thoughts of a forty-four-year-old heading for where, where? The only thought: Sofia in the back of the hardware shop and him behind her finishing what he had never finished, while she grabs his arm like she did when she said goodbye in her flat in Isola.

He looked out of the window, the snow in Parma was lighter and the black soil was surfacing. At Bologna he had the urge to get off and get onto a train for Milan. He bunched up his scarf against the glass and used it as a pillow, and the train manager woke him up at Cesena. Carlo showed them his ticket, then put his coat and scarf back on, moved to a space between the carriages, and only then noticed the presence of something in his pocket. He checked with two fingers and found the antihistamine bottle. He took it out, turning it in his hands as the train came to a stop, held it tight. The doors opened and he was in Rimini.

He buried himself into his coat. He remembered the square in front of the station. Twenty-five years earlier he and his friends had arrived on a regional train amidst the summer crowd selling tickets for the Bandiera Gialla and Lady Godiva clubs, the shouting and the lights of the promenade; now it was shrouded in a light mist. He found himself on a road that became pedestrians only. On his left he spotted the Duomo; the ivory of the front blended into the frost and he felt sleepy. He walked past a row of shops; the square was a little further ahead and the people of Rimini were huddled under the porticos. He halted over a star shape on the cobblestones, checked the map on his phone and found that its name was Piazza Tre Martiri. Largo Bordoni was two kilometres in the same direction, the Adriatic Sea was in the opposite – he would've liked to see it – and now he was also hungry. He inhaled, could smell the sea and the end of a storm.

'Now go,' he told himself, and followed music coming from small speakers along the side of the road. He stayed close to a bicycle, moving slowly because of pedestrians; a man with a moustache was riding it.

'Sauro!' someone greeted the bicycle man from a newsagent's. Sauro responded and Carlo tried keeping up. The bike stopped in front of an *enoteca* called Morri, he thought about stopping for a glass of wine – but no, the centre of Rimini was behind him and he knew what he was doing: the university bathroom, her waist pressing against him, the smell of ammonia, her lips and porous tongue, her sighing, 'We can't . . .', 'How Things Are', desire – it all came from these streets and trees and people. He was sure he had experienced all of it and he was sure he'd seen nothing. How does memory settle? He crossed a busy road, the early outskirts, so reassuring compared to Milan, the tidy houses and the bikes left next to the doors. He continued down a road with trees on either side, Via Dario Campana. He checked the map: it suggested a twelve-minute

226

walk. He came across a grassy roundabout with a ruby-red hut, and two hundred metres away was Largo Bordoni.

He felt like he did when he was about to enter room 67 or a stranger's bed – a sense of anticipation. A little further on came the council estates, with their meek elegance and geometry. He checked his watch: it was two twenty, the shops should've been opening soon or maybe the hardware shop already had. He walked by the houses' railings; there was a small supermarket and a fishmonger, someone was crossing the road with heavy bags, said hello, stopped for a chat then set off again. Sofia had written in her story that she lived in one of these big buildings; he remembered a first or second floor – the day of the accident the Fiat Punto was parked in front of it and she and her mother had got in and turned on the radio.

He reached his destination: Largo Bordoni was an opening in the road. On the pedestrian side there was a portico with a dairy, a café, a newsagent's, a launderette, and a wide terrace ran before the shops, with a number of windows opening onto it. He passed the shops. On the opposite side of the road a florist was opening up; he spotted a green patch with two benches and a handful of chairs after the fork in the road, and finally saw it: Ferramenta e Casalinghi Casadei. The lights were off and there was a display with watering cans outside. He moved closer and noticed that in one of the windows there was an intermittent light, red, a Christmas decoration that ran along the products on show. He peered in. The cold had fogged up the glass and it was dark inside; he could see the counter with its plastic cap box, the snap hooks and the key rings. The back was a wall of drawers with writing he couldn't read. He pressed a hand against the glass, marking a line across the condensation. Someone brushed past him on the street and he spun around, then he spotted a movement at the back of the shop. A shadow was moving between the shelves: a man, who gestured him to wait, turned the keys in the door and opened.

'If you need anything, we're here.'

'I was just looking, thanks.'

'We're rearranging some shelves; if I keep the lights on people keep coming in but we'll be open in a few minutes.' The man was thin; he spoke softly and his eyelids closed when he did. 'You sure you don't need anything?'

'Yes, thank you. Sorry for bothering you.'

'Not at all! Have a good day.'

He could've been her father. He regretted not having shaken his hand, the man from Sofia's story who couldn't make decisions but could take care of others; too quiet, too kind, decisive only with his customers. Carlo looked at him one more time and took a few steps back, spinning around again, as if he knew: he saw her. Sofia was on the other side of Largo Bordoni. He couldn't focus on her but he knew, waited to be sure of it, then he moved from the window and hid behind the corner.

The man came to open the door, said something to her. Sofia took off her coat and bag, hung them up, put on a blue overall, stretched her arms. She was beautiful, she was herself. A little tauter in her face, the short hair . . . her neck looked long and sinuous. She rustled around the counter, the lights turned on and she touched her ear.

Time had made her cheeks less childish. He recognised the dimples from when she'd try concentrating in class; it was a bout of nostalgia and he knew that nostalgia carries tenderness with it. He would've loved to have had tenderness sooner, him only a teacher and her only a student; he would've loved not having had any other women, to have let their bodies wash over him and count them among his painful regrets. He was cold but didn't tighten his scarf. He pulled up his rucksack and leaned against the wall, he kept looking through the window, trying not to be obvious. He saw Sofia roll up her sleeves. She was wearing bracelets and now he felt sorry and relieved at the lack of arousal: it hadn't been put to sleep, only tamed. The girl among a hardware shop's shelves, whose features and movements and possible indecencies he recognised, had taken on a specific form in a specific frame, soft and dull. She was the beauty of time gone by. He felt the desire to wave at her, he kept watching as she talked to the man and rummaged around in a drawer behind her.

Sofia moved up two steps on the ladder, her strong legs peeking out of the overall, then came back down and told her father, 'Go eat something.'

'*A'no fema.*'

She still handed him the plastic container, she'd made some couscous with vegetables. 'Take two spoonfuls.'

Her father pointed to one of the windows. 'Christmas has been over for two months now.' He headed to the spot and clambered over the products on display, grabbed the red-lit snake and started pulling it gently, undid it and rolled it around his arm and shoulder. 'Unplug it for me, Sofia.'

But she burst out laughing at her Christmas tree of a dad, a really skinny man lit up by fairy lights. 'Hang on.' She took out her phone and took a photo.

'My daughter's the worst.'

'Come on, strike a pose.'

'*Va' là!*'

'Come on, Dad!'

He unravelled the red snake and went to switch it off. 'Don't put me on the internet.'

'Can I?'

'No.'

'Why not? You look great, come see.'

Her father put the lights to one side and looked for the orders book as Sofia showed him her phone: he'd got so old; at least those lights added some joyfulness to him. 'I don't care.'

'I'm posting it, then.' She edited the shadows a little so her father's face was a little less visible, captioned it *Father Christmas keeps insisting, will spring ever come?*, added seven hashtags and the location, shared it on Instagram.

Margherita saw the post forty-two minutes later as she was waiting for an answer about an upscale three-roomer in the Moscova area. The fun, sweet photo, the father's half-amused face – she thought they must be good people. She had the temptation to call her husband; she didn't. She made do with having heard Carlo satisfied after the interview, knew she just had to let the day end. She settled back in her chair. She could see Corso Garibaldi from her position, loved watching young couples stopping to read the listings and then come in. She always insisted on greeting them herself, had learned to be direct, slyly warning them if there were any issues, pipes to fix, noisy neighbours, revisiting of building association fees. It was part of her making amends for Concordia, but also because of a new awareness she'd reached: her work was almost an annoyance; a little, not too much, but to be in the room with seven other colleagues on the prowl, invoicing for an American company, having a desk complete with a stationery kit . . . well, at the end of the day she wanted to have given a sense to it all. She'd wring her hands any time she walked past her old agency: lately she'd be doing so on purpose – it had been turned into a café, but the wooden floors were the same, as were the finishes on the wall. She'd go in and order something and stare at the familiar space around her, telling herself that those times would come round again.

She stood up without waiting for the email confirming the upscale three-roomer in Moscova. She told her colleague she had to rush to her mother – nothing serious, she'd follow the deal on the phone. She left and walked up to Monte Napoleone, went into Cova and asked for a selection of *mignons*, making sure to include the *diplomatici*, and imagined her mother at the counter between the fur-coated ladies – the seamstress of Via delle Leghe, so small, in her customers' citadel; the shy mothers in the patisseries of the wealthy and the kind fathers with Christmas lights around them.

When she got home she found Anna half asleep. 'Look at what I got,' she told her, and watched her open her eyes like a newborn. She placed the tray of small baked goods on her bed.

'The *diplomatici?*'

Margherita nodded and pointed at them. 'Let's eat them with the boys tonight, darling, they love these.'

Sofia's father piled up two boxes on his arms and loaded them into the Renault Scénic in front of the shop. Carlo stepped further away from the window, and further, his last image of her on the ladder, on the tip of her plimsolls, her legs strong and light and elegant.

'Bye Sofia,' he whispered as he left the portico in Largo Bordoni, walking with his hands in his coat pockets, without slowing down, holding on to the image of the man wrapped in the fairy lights and his daughter, and when he reached the ruby-red hut he felt that he could finally let go of the last of his youth.

And now he wanted to see the sea, and the entire time it took him to reach it he felt as if Rimini knew that it was a farewell; all those people and the bicycles and the roads that criss-crossed to let him through, pointing him in the right direction, from the early outskirts to the Ponte di Tiberio and from there to the fishermen's village. He crossed the historic city centre and into the station underpass, reached a fountain with four stone horses that poured water out of their nostrils. The Grand Hotel overlooked it and he headed for it with the fog starting to thicken again. He crossed the promenade and took the walkway to one of the concessions. The paint was faded and the number 4 was on the side; he walked past it and over a low dune. The Adriatic was calm and small waves curled up onto the shore, his breath steamed up and he looked for a boat but saw none; the fog swallowed him.

One evening, the phone had rung in Via delle Leghe; Anna was having dinner with Franco and Margherita. They'd been alarmed as no one ever called at that hour. Anna had rushed to the phone, had answered holding her breath, had listened to the voice of a woman from the fashion house she worked for every now and then: she wanted to talk to the person in charge of mending clothes. Anna had said it was her and had then carefully listened to the request, had replied that she'd do her best. She'd hung up and come back to the table, telling her family that some people were coming over for an urgent job.

'Right now?' Franco had said, starting to clear the table.

Anna had nodded, and Margherita had fed her doll Marisa with a piece of bread, then climbed off the chair and gone to sit on the sofa.

The people had arrived half an hour later, two women in long coats and a man who'd stayed outside on the landing. The women had come in with a clothes carrier bag and Anna had welcomed them into the lounge. Franco and Margherita had locked themselves in the bedroom.

They'd opened the carrier together and had pulled out a cocktail dress: Yves Saint Laurent. Anna had worked with couture before and knew the Saint Laurent cuts; the issue was the sizing. She'd arranged a cotton sheet on the table and had laid out the dress, looked at it as if at a piece of art: the dark skirt, the precious materials, all of those designs on the fabric.

'It's Matisse-inspired,' one of the two women had said. She had precious-looking earrings and was wearing another cocktail dress under her coat. 'I wore a backup one in case we can't make it.'

'That one's also stunning.'

'But they sent me this one. And it felt, I don't know . . .'

Anna nodded. 'When is your party?'

'An hour and a half, at the most.'

There was a robin's-egg-blue bow on the stomach, the bodice was slightly low cut with long black sleeves, and she'd noticed patterns in the satin. The rip was on one side and was biting into the skirt's hem too. 'I'll do my best, but you need to wear it to help me out.'

'You're so kind. At the designer's they told me you were the only one here in Milan.'

'The only one at this time, maybe.'

They'd smiled. Anna had offered them a coffee which they'd kindly refused, and sat down at the table. She'd started working and hadn't looked at them again. The rip had to be hidden by a symmetrical double fold; it had taken her forty-five minutes and she lost concentration when the bedroom door had opened and Margherita had come out; she'd heard her go to the bathroom and had felt ashamed of the sound of the flush and for Franco telling her in dialect to be quick.

'How old is your girl?' the woman had asked.

'She's four.'

'I have a boy and a girl.'

Anna had looked at the dress more closely; the Matisse leaf designs were red and green and ochre and she had brushed them with her fingertips. She always got excited when she could see the wrist of the designer as they sketched, the frame of their glasses and the hair to one side. He was almost the same age as Anna, and she found traces of her own discernment in his

233

work. She'd taken a couple more minutes to admire the work, bent over the dress, then she'd pulled herself up and asked the woman to try it on.

She'd asked Anna to help her remove the other one and ended up almost naked on one side of the lounge – Anna had been able to see how beautiful she was: the photos in the tabloids didn't do her justice. Then Anna had gone to fetch the mirror she kept between the bookshelves – the handful of books only took up one shelf, the rest was trinkets and knick-knacks.

'It's better than ever,' the woman had said.

Anna had lightly touched the mended material. 'Be careful when you twist around.'

'It got stuck on a hanger, today.'

'It happens.' Anna had finished smoothing it out, tweaked the bow on her stomach – she was thin – adjusted her necklace. 'There you are.'

The woman had looked one last time, had turned towards Anna, had reached out a hand and stroked her shoulder. 'You're an artist.'

'I'm a seamstress, madam.'

The woman had gestured to the other to deal with the payment – it was in a rice-paper envelope.

Anna had held the envelope to her stomach and had thanked them both; she'd helped her guests back into their coats with the other hand and had walked them to the door. 'Goodbye.'

The woman had lingered on the landing. 'My husband is here, in the car.'

'Oh,' Anna had said, and looked away. 'Please tell him that Milan is lucky to have a mayor like him.'

'I'll tell him Milan is lucky to have a seamstress like you.' She'd smiled at her and headed out, a flash of red leaf peeking out of the coat, Yves walking down the stairs of Via delle Leghe. The red leaf of the Saint Laurent and the thin stomach of the woman, that's the image she had when Margherita, Carlo and Lorenzo came into the bedroom to offer her some cake again.

'Would you like a *diplomatico*?'

Anna barely looked at them. She was trying to remember Franchin's expression after she'd given him the envelope and he'd opened it and couldn't believe his eyes, all those notes.

'No *diplomatico*?'

'Can you bring me the note from the mayor's wife, please?'

'The mayor's wife?' Margherita furrowed her brow. 'The mayor's wife's note, yes,' and she handed the plate with the *mignon* to Carlo. Lorenzo was eating his marzipan, staring at his grandmother. Anna turned towards him. 'Your grandma's going to show you a secret.'

Margherita came back and handed her a white note. Anna held it with the fingers peeking out of her cast; the handwriting was tidy but she could no longer read it.

Carlo took it from her and softly read out, 'For your kindness and your art, thank you. On behalf of Saint Laurent, too.'

Lorenzo bit into his marzipan and Anna smiled at him: 'Your grandma's stroke of luck.'

'You know, I can't remember anything about that night.' Margherita lowered the upper half of her mother's mattress.

'You were very young, darling.'

'Dad used to say that you had to disconnect the phone after that night.'

'We got a lot of customers, but we never disconnected anything.'

'Franco used to say that the mayor himself started coming in for his own clothes.' Carlo rested his chin on his son's head.

'Franco had a very fervid imagination.' She'd let herself be taken over by nostalgia ever since she'd started lying about her leg getting better. In fact, she had a dull pain throughout her body, all the way to her head; her temples throbbed and she felt a rock on her chest. She hated complaining; she'd lied to the night-shift nurse and the day-shift nurse, she'd lied to Andrea that afternoon. She looked out of the window, looking for the snow on the roofs but it had melted. Then she felt like sleeping. She prayed to the Virgin Mary before sleep every once in a while – it'd take her a moment to find her confidence, this was girls' talk. She'd ask her some favours for others, only asked for no pain for herself. It was her earworm, the limbs in pain and not being able to do anything about it, being bedridden and weighing down on her family – she would've loved to take an evening walk down Via Monte Napoleone, taking her time to look at the lit-up shop windows. She gestured to Carlo. He just needed the gesture; she saw him put Lorenzo down and tell him to go help his mum in the kitchen. When they were alone she grabbed his wrist. 'You need to do like we did with Franco if you have to.'

'Anna.'

'Please.'

'We don't have to.'

'Don't you allow me to—'

He stroked her fingers. 'What's going on, Anna?'

'I . . .' She held his hands tight. 'I'm scared.'

Carlo stayed until Anna fell asleep. Then he turned off the main light, left on the small lamp next to the sewing machine, slipped the note from the mayor's wife out of her hand and put it on the table. He went into the kitchen. Margherita was doing the washing up and humming a song. She pressed her back against him and took her hands from the tap but he told her, 'Carry on.'

Margherita rinsed the sponge and Carlo stood there with his chin on her shoulder, told her they should spend the night there. She grabbed another plate and rinsed it, asked him if that was her mother's request and he insisted, 'We're sleeping here.'

She nodded and he took her hand, dripping onto the floor. She turned to face him, noticed that outside the French window it had started snowing again. 'I was afraid you wouldn't come home today . . .'

Andrea removed the hood from his head and let the cold bite him, locked the car and crossed the road, reached the building and looked for Milan once more in this March winter, before stepping in.

He shook his shoes on the entrance mat – he really wanted to be back home and he realised it as he climbed the stairs, two at a time. Since he'd stopped living alone he often took the steps two at a time and every now and then he'd stop on the landing and notice some sort of relief. He turned the key in the lock and almost automatically announced himself. The house was half dark but he didn't turn on the lights, frozen between the outside and the inside. He took one step forward and was sure no one else was in. Then he spotted Giorgio on the sofa in the lounge, sleeping, his shape was elongated and curved and blue in the dim light.

He gently closed the door again. He would've woken him, he would've let him rest . . . He stopped and almost smiled, a voice seemed to come up from the street, from the snow.

'Franchin, I am a turquoise fish, Franchin I am . . .'

The voice echoed from outside and it took Carlo a minute to realise it was actually Anna. He shot up from the armchair and went into the bedroom. The glare of the snow-capped roofs lit up the night and he could see her as she slept. He waited in the doorway to listen to her breathing; it was a quiet hissing. Then he walked past Margherita and Lorenzo's closed door, went back to the lounge. He went to the record player. Lucio Dalla was still on the turntable. He lowered the light of the lamp and took one step closer to the bookshelves to brush his fingers across the spines; they were all lined up and some had a plastic dust-cover – on each, Anna had written the month and year of when she'd read them. He stepped away from the shelves. He was calmer; he sat in the armchair of the man who'd shown him this life, the pine tree and the three keys, *Mí sun cuntèent inscí*. I am happy right here. A type of fidelity.

He stretched his legs out on the coffee table, sank into the cushions and made the leather covers creak. He dozed off, the light of the lamp filtering through his eyelids. He didn't switch it off – as a child he'd always slept with a light on at the end of the bed. Then Anna's voice sounded again and this time it was definitely her. He rushed to the bedroom. She was in the same position, her head slightly tilted onto her right shoulder, a line of drool on her chin. He moved closer. Anna's eyes were open, looking at the wardrobe, she wasn't breathing.

The wary turquoise fish watched over her.

They set off from the hardware shop and Sofia saw the Ina Casa with the jasmine flowers on its balconies. Her father drove carefully and when they reached the ruby-red hut she asked him if she could take the wheel. He put his indicator on to pull over, even though there wasn't much road left to the wholesale warehouse, and they switched places and fastened their seatbelts again, driving in silence as far as the northern walls. Then Sofia turned on the radio and drove along the historic centre, ending up where the small boats were docked – the wholesale store was just before the military docks and she swerved in the opposite direction. Her father pointed out she had to turn back but she kept driving towards Rivabella. He asked her where she was going, she said, 'To see Mum.'

So her father fell quiet and never let his back touch the seat until the hairpin turns to the graveyard, where they took the narrow road and drove around the wall. They parked on the grass and she left the car first. Her father was slower and as he got out he lit himself a cigarette. His forehead was wrinkled and his mouth smiled with uncertainty – she understood she'd be going alone and headed in.

She walked past the flower stand and through the entrance. She spotted the boat-shaped mausoleum of the Rex, the tomb of Fellini and Masina and their child; the bronze was reflecting the sun. She turned left and it took her a couple of steps to remember the right path. The lights of the dead followed her to her mother's grave.

The headstone was the third one from the right; her father's roses were still fresh and she pulled her hands out of her pockets to straighten them out. She looked at her, her wavy hair to her shoulder, the shy look in her eyes, she was always shy in photos but liked the attention nonetheless.

'I'm here, Mum.'

Margherita stepped into the bedroom, the medical bed was still in there, as was the sewing machine. 'I'm here.' She opened the wardrobe, one door then the other. Those clothes, all those clothes! She touched the patterned shirt that her mother would wear as temperatures got warmer and that marked the beginning of the nice weather for all of them.

How long would it take her to empty the wardrobe, to carefully sort out the tailleurs and trousers and shoes, to put them away somewhere, keeping something for herself? She wanted to tell Anna that Carlo had managed to get a trial period at the marketing job and that Lorenzo was sure that Grandma Anna was swimming in the sea; she wanted to tell her that whenever she stepped into the house she'd see her on her stool, at the record player, feet on the table. Sometimes she spoke to her. 'Hello,' she'd whisper, and hesitate between the living room and the corridor; she'd look at the gauzes and the washing materials in the bathroom, she'd look at her hands that had washed her. She could've done it better, been more gentle with her. She could've been less inhibited, not coughed to hide the gagging, keeping her company when she wasn't expecting her. She'd never taken her anywhere, never once to her St Petersburg.

She removed the patterned shirt from its hanger and laid it

out on the bed, did the same with the rest of the clothes, piling them up carefully, came to the wedding shawl in its cellophane wrapper. She took it out, removed the wrapper, went to the window and saw that the fabric had kept well, then flipped it backwards and threw it over her shoulders: 'A free married woman of the 1950s, I'm here.'

About the Author

Marco Missiroli was born in Rimini and lives in Milan. His first novel, *Senza Coda* (2005), won the Campiello Opera Prima, the Italian equivalent of the Costa First Novel award. His novel *Atti Osceni In Luogo Privato* (2015) became a runaway bestseller in Italy, selling over 150,000 copies. *Fidelity* was a number-one bestseller in Italy and is currently being made into a Netflix limited series.

About the Translator

Alex Valente (he/him) is a half-Tuscan, half-Yorkshire white European currently living on xʷməθkʷəy̓əm, Sḵwx̱wú7mesh and səlilwətaɫ land. He is an award-winning literary translator from Italian into English, though he also dabbles with French and regularly struggles with Mandarin Chinese, Japanese and Dutch. His work has recently been published in the *New York Times Magazine*, the *Massachusetts Review* and the Short Story Project, and he has two novels due in 2021.

Translator's acknowledgments
To E, for the other words from the other room.

Help us make the next generation of readers

We – both author and publisher – hope you enjoyed this book. We believe that you can become a reader at any time in your life, but we'd love your help to give the next generation a head start.

Did you know that 9 per cent of children don't have a book of their own in their home, rising to 13 per cent in disadvantaged families*? We'd like to try to change that by asking you to consider the role you could play in helping to build readers of the future.

We'd love you to think of sharing, borrowing, reading, buying or talking about a book with a child in your life and spreading the love of reading. We want to make sure the next generation continue to have access to books, wherever they come from.

And if you would like to consider donating to charities that help fund literacy projects, find out more at **www.literacytrust.org.uk** and **www.booktrust.org.uk**.

THANK YOU

*As reported by the National Literacy Trust